FUSED IN FIRE

Also by K.F. Breene

FIRE AND ICE TRILOGY
Born in Fire
Raised in Fire
Fused in Fire

FINDING PARADISE SERIES
Fate of Perfection
Fate of Devotion

WARRIOR CHRONICLES
Chosen, Book 1
Hunted, Book 2
Shadow Lands, Book 3
Invasion, Book 4
Siege, Book 5
Overtaken, Book 6

DARKNESS SERIES
Into the Darkness, Novella 1
Braving the Elements, Novella 2
On a Razor's Edge, Novella 3
Demons, Novella 4
The Council, Novella 5
Shadow Watcher, Novella 6
Jonas, Novella 7
Charles, Novella 8
Jameson, Novella 9
Darkness Series Boxed Set, Books 1-4

FUSED IN FIRE

BY K.F. BREENE

Contact info:
www.kfbreene.com
Facebook: www.facebook.com/authorKF
Twitter: @KFBreene

CHAPTER 1

F IFTY YARDS. THAT was all that separated me from the lethal, pasty-white monster intent on slicing me in half. Long, gnarled fingers ending in wicked claws dangled at the sides of stringy, bowed legs. Sharp fangs descended from black gums, and swampy-looking skin sank between sharp ribs.

The thing was hideous. I would never get used to the vampire monster form, a vampire's stronger, faster form that allowed it to inflict incredible damage. This monster in particular, an elder, could boggle the mind with his power and viciousness.

Knees bent, mind focused, I waited with my hands slightly in front of me. As soon as he made a move, the time allotted me to plan or strategize—hell, even to yell *oh shit!*—would be minimal. I would only be able to react and hope my weapons landed before his did.

The vampire twitched. I flinched.

Fooled me.

Stillness resumed, drowning the area in silence. A battle was about to kick off, like it had every couple days for the last month and a half since Darius had given me this large warehouse.

I yanked out ole trusty, my sword, while desperately trying to access the ice magic that allowed me to fling things telekinetically. It was a super-cool power in theory, but each time I used it, the cold energy expanded to fill my entire body, freezing my humanity, stealing my breath and my emotions.

Using the ice power reminded me of my heritage. Reminded me that, technically, I was demon royalty—and if I wasn't careful, I'd become just like the horrible, disgusting demon that had awakened this ability in me. I'd defeated Agnon in Seattle, but I'd never forget how it had used its power to turn humans into violent, vengeful horror shows.

I feared I would lose myself every time the cold power consumed my body, and that very fear was blocking my ability. I knew that, but I couldn't seem to get around it.

"Waiting for this to start is easily the worst thing about training," I said. Rocks of all sizes and other debris littered the ground near the walls. "Darius's monster form is a close second."

Callie huffed from her position way off to the right. Her husband Dizzy tsked, away to the left and (hopefully) out of the danger zone. The four of us made a big diamond.

"Reagan, that isn't very nice," Dizzy said. He adjusted the football helmet covering his head. "He can't help what his fighting form looks like. I bet you never make fun of shifters after they change."

"They turn into furry, pettable creatures." I rolled my shoulders.

"She makes fun of shifters *before* they change," Callie said with a grin. She palmed her helmet, which was a size too big. "Why are we wearing these things, Dizzy? It flops down and then I can barely see. That's got to be more dangerous than not wearing one."

"Remember the last time?" he asked, his voice rising. "Reagan exploded our spell and blasted us."

"I fell on my butt that time. Not my head." Callie adjusted the satchel draped around her shoulder and across her chest. "Give me a butt guard if you're so concerned."

"You need a mouth guard," he muttered, bending back the flap on his own satchel so ingredients and spells were easily reached.

I shook my head to wipe away the smile. I loved when the dual mages ragged on each other, but now wasn't the time. I had to focus. I had to pretend they'd actually kill me if given the chance, which was hard when I knew the worst I was likely to be subjected to was some deep gashes—something that was, annoyingly enough, not enough to jump-start my ice magic.

Sometimes I really hated my fast-and-loose approach to danger.

I cleared my mind and saw my surroundings with fresh eyes.

Two high-powered mages waited to the sides of the cavernous space, facing me, pulling ingredients out of their bags in preparation to take me down. In front of me, a mere fifty yards away, waited an incredibly fast monster, his arms slightly out to the sides and claws splayed. He surveyed me as prey. As something he would capture, consume, and toss aside.

The vampire launched forward. Faster than thought. Headed in a straight line right for me, his claws out, his fangs dripping saliva.

"Oh sh—" I threw up a sheet of flame, forcing him to run through it. His black, stringy hair caught fire. He kept coming, ignoring the pain I knew my fire must have caused him.

A jet of red streaked toward me from the right. I ripped the fire from its current location, shifting it into the path of the hex. I unraveled the spell easily as green shot toward me from the other side.

Then Darius was right in front of me, slashing. His claws raked my leg before I could block. Searing pain bit into my flesh. I grimaced as I slashed with my sword, cutting his side. He dodged back, but I didn't have the chance to advance on him. A tornado had filled the warehouse, the turbulent air whipping at my hair, my clothes, and even my sword. I sent a stream of fire to disintegrate it as Darius slashed again. The triumph of dodging him was short-lived. He bodily picked me up and threw me.

"Use your power!" Callie yelled at me. I could barely hear her over the roar of a magical beast somewhere in the vicinity. That had to be one of Dizzy's spells. He loved making larger-than-life creatures that were all bark and very little bite.

I ignored it as I hit the ground and rolled. Claws came at my face.

I flinched and rolled again, jumping up and catching the arm already coming at me. Before I could throw him over my shoulder, a spell splatted my ankle. Instant agony throbbed up my leg.

Darius spun, whipping me around. I flew again, right toward a massive tiger with glowing red eyes and too-large teeth. It opened its mouth as I neared, unable to stop myself or alter course, before chomping down on my middle.

Another flare of intense pain joined that of my ankle. I hollered but retained the presence of mind to cut down with my sword, stabbing the animal's amazingly real-looking shoulder. Glowing red seeped through the honey of its magical fur before the spell burst, spraying out magical knives.

Heat coursed through me. I made fire coat my body, fizzling the magical projectiles as they hit and neutralizing the spell that had attached itself to my ankle. My power now raging within me, I turned up the heat intensity but reduced the size of the flame, making a sort of head-to-toe body armor.

Darius grabbed my arm, probably intending to throw me again. Instead, he flinched almost immediately. His hand sizzled.

"Ouch, huh?" I said, blasting him in the face with more flame. "There go your eyebrows. It's the worst, I know."

He reeled backward. I landed two quick punches into his middle and swiped my foot toward his legs. He jumped over it and shoved me, sending me rolling across the floor like a tumbleweed. A green spell hit my fire armor and exploded, knocking me backward for another ride across the floor.

My head thunked against the concrete floor. I made sheets of fire drape down around me on all sides, closing me in and hopefully giving me a moment to recover.

A ghastly face pushed through the layers of flame, followed by that swampy body. He struck, those three-inch claws aimed center mass. Fear shot through me, tied to my survival instinct. Cold surged up, out of nowhere, hampering my fire. The heat around us dwindled and the ice throbbed in my middle. Strange thoughts crowded my head before I realized they weren't mine.

She is not making enough progress, I heard from Darius.

Darius is improving beyond measure, Dizzy thought.

That vampire better not hurt her, or I will make it wish it wasn't turned, came from Callie.

My breath dried up and I reacted without thinking. Air condensed in front of me. Sparks flew as Darius's claws cut through my invisible shield. I pushed outward. An explosion of magic picked the vampire up off his feet and hurtled him across the room.

Rage rose inside me. Vengeance. Every dark emotion I'd ever had, intensified.

I am solely yours, mon ange, *for all eternity,* echoed from Darius's mind as he skidded across the ground. I loved when he called me his angel, a sentiment that was hard to hang on to just now. *You are my sanctuary. My soul.*

Your mother would be proud, echoed from Callie. *She loved you so much.*

Is this the part where I'm supposed to think things to help her? Dizzy asked himself.

The cold throbbed within me, radiating out from my middle and through my limbs. Rocks and boulders rose into the sky from near the walls, hovering. Darius stopped rolling and jumped to his feet, facing me again. His body flexed, ready to attack, but this time, I wasn't nervous. This time, I wanted to pull his arms out of the sockets and toss them away. I wanted to punch into his chest and yank out his blackened, still-beating heart.

Two streams of magic came at me from either direction. My fire licked at the ice magic, begging to be used, but most of its potency was blocked.

That didn't matter.

I flicked my hand, lazily tossing up an invisible wall. I didn't know how my magic could manipulate the very air, but it did, and in some situations it worked even better than the fire.

The spells hit it and melted, sending steam curling upward. A laugh left my mouth, inhuman and raspy. A demonic sound.

I saw Callie and Dizzy retreating, heading for the door. It had just gotten too dangerous for them. *I* was too dangerous for them. But I couldn't come back. I'd forgotten how to turn away from the aching need to tear apart the world and every living thing within it.

Rage beat in time to my heart, begging me to *kill*.

No, to permanently maim.

No, to use a living being like a puppet. To turn the human race into my slaves.

But first, I would make this vampire beg to serve me. I would devour him.

He ran at me, his movements graceful, his speed slower than it had been. No, I realized, he was moving just as quickly—my reactions had sped up to match his. When he reached me, I dodged his strike and countered. His rib cracked.

Something deep inside of me quailed. My fire fluttered to life, but the cold quickly doused it again.

I picked up the vampire and threw him, slamming him against the far wall. The sweet agony of wrath pounded through me, harnessing the rage, the hate, the glory of destruction, and turning it into a vicious soup.

I rose into the sky—five feet, then ten—and hovered there. The rocks sailed toward me, and I made them circle my person as I drifted toward the faltering vampire. Shields of air filled the spaces between the rocks. If a spell or attack came, I would be completely covered.

Pull back, my beloved. Focus on me. Stay with me. Darius rose to his knees with obvious effort.

Somewhere in the back of my mind, I realized how much pain that meant he was in.

My fire fluttered up again, but I couldn't latch on to it. The cold surged up in greater power, sucking me under. Wiping out my ability to feel anything but hate. Making it impossible to want anything but destruction.

"Will you not fight, vampire?" My voice clawed out of my throat, sickly and cracking. "Are you content to remain on your knees before me, like a coward?"

"I will always remain on my knees before you, my love. I will fight for that right. I am yours." The pasty monster turned back into a man. Deep burns covered parts of his skin. Rips and scrapes marred his chest and arms. A bump in his ribs suggested a bad break. "Find yourself, Reagan," he said softly. "Come back to me."

Rushing filled my ears. The need to kill flashed through me, impossible to deny. I flung a boulder at Darius, intending to crush him.

Eyes solemn, he didn't move. He'd lived through some of the bleakest times in human history, not to mention other magical creatures' attempts to wipe out his kind, only to wait on his knees for an out-of-control demon-woman to end his life. A thousand years for this...

It is always a woman. His thought echoed, something he'd said before our first intimate encounter in Seattle.

His undoing was always related to a woman.

The rock veered at the last moment, punching through the wall to his right.

I screamed in frustrated rage, warring with myself. More rocks flung themselves at the walls all around him. They crashed against the ground. Ricocheted off the ceiling. The door ripped off its hinges. The larger loading bay doors flew outward, twisted and bent. Glass shattered, littering the warehouse floor.

Still I hovered, in turmoil. Freezing. Trying to fight my way back, but not sure how.

"Remember your mother," Darius said softly. I somehow heard him over all the noise of my destruction. "She, too, kneeled before you. Remember the stories you've told me in the quiet hours we've spent together. She would've given her life for you, as I will. Remember her."

Memories crowded in, of my mother on the bright green grass in front of me, her head bowed, telling me to either end her life or fight for my own. Her again, this time decked out in leather and sweating as the forest around us roared with flame. More images, of a similar battle I had fought with myself, trying not to lose myself to the lure of my power. To the feel of my magic.

That had been with the fire.

Now I battled with the ice.

"It is within you, Reagan. Your strength far surpasses your power. Come back to me."

Emotion welled up. Using it, I internally grabbed at the fire magic and yanked it up from my depths. Like ink in water, the two halves of my magic feathered around each other, but they would not merge.

Balls of flame sprang to life throughout the warehouse. I dropped a few feet in the air. Any rocks I hadn't yet thrown dropped with me, becoming ten times heavier. The rage receded and the agony of heat rose until the two were nearly the same potency.

I inhaled a lungful of sweet air, sighing it out in relief a moment later. Both halves of my magic throbbed, equally functional but not very strong. It was all I could manage.

"Can you rise higher?" Darius asked me, standing in jerky movements. He clearly hurt something awful.

A pang of guilt hit me. The rocks around me plunked down onto the concrete, becoming too heavy for me to keep afloat. The fire kept on, though, moving lazily through the air.

Wanting to make his sacrifice worth something, I focused on the dull ache of cold and tried to push myself higher. Instead, exhaustion came over me and I sank. An echo of his thoughts twirled, just outside of my grasp.

"That's it, I think." I let the fire wink out. "That's all I've got." I shook my head, the guilt intensifying. I half wished I couldn't remember the things I did under the influence of the cold power. "I'm sorry about...you know."

A furrow creased his brow as he stiffly walked toward me. "You have learned to cap your fire magic."

I frowned as he stopped in front of me and feathered a thumb across one of my eyebrows. I may not have gotten enough of a hold on the ice magic to stay sane, but at least I could use it to prevent the fire from making me look weird. You had to look at the silver lining.

"A cap?" I asked, surprised. I'd thought he was going to comment on my apology. He usually told me not to be absurd.

"You hold back. You don't give yourself to it. Just now, you pulled back the ice magic until it was manageable, like your fire magic. When it is manageable, it is also greatly diminished. You are trying to find a happy, safe medium with the ice as you did with the fire. It lessens your power."

"Ah. Well, I'm not sure if you noticed, but I nearly killed you just now. With the fire, I burned half of a forest once. A *forest*. I'm not safe. I have to find the happy medium, as you said, so the power won't destroy me or those around me."

He shook his head. His thumb was now tracing the edge of my bottom lip. "I don't think that's it. I think you need to find another way to deal with the power." He dropped his hand to my shoulder. "I need to get dressed. I want to talk to the dual mages."

"To get healed faster?" I asked, limping after him. Now that I was back to normal, each injury was trying to pull the diva act so I'd notice it.

Callie's head, still covered in the helmet, poked in

through the doorway. When she saw us walking toward her, the rest of her body made an appearance, decked out in another classic sweat suit. If "classic" meant fluorescent green velvet and obscene messages scrawled across the chest.

"Is it over—" Her eyes widened as she looked past us. "Holy bluebells, Reagan." Her gaze traveled to the ceiling, then the row of open loading docks. "You've never destroyed the place like this. And here Darius worried you weren't improving."

"She isn't," Darius said. He was great for honest answers, though I rarely wanted to hear them. "She needs near death to enact the other half of her magic, and then she loses herself in the power. Callie—"

"Good God, Reagan, look at this." Dizzy stepped into the doorway, staring like Callie was. "We heard the commotion, but I didn't realize all this was going on."

"Didn't you see the rocks going through the walls?" I asked.

"Going through the walls, no. I saw the thing with the door and figured it was time to hide behind a tree. I'm glad we did." He looked in through the door. "This is something."

"Callie, did you ever meet Lucifer?" Darius asked.

CHAPTER 2

S HIVERS SLID DOWN my arms as I followed Darius out of the gaping doorway. The way he said my dad's name was so blasé. Like it wasn't a big deal that my father was the lord of the underworld, something magical people called the Dark Kingdom.

"I met him, yes." Callie turned and followed us, leaving Dizzy inside. "Why? And I hope you're putting on clothes now that the training is over. There is only so much skin a person needs to see."

"Did you ever see him use his power?" Darius asked, ignoring her comment.

"He unraveled a couple of my better spells. At the time, I thought he was using a counter spell to do it. I assumed he was a mage, one of the more powerful ones I'd ever met, much like Reagan's mom, Amorette. Other than that, he seemed like a completely normal man. It wasn't until we tracked Amorette down after she tried to disappear that we learned the truth."

Darius paused beside his extremely expensive sports car, staring at a dent in the passenger door. His gaze slid mournfully to the rock lying in the dirt below it, then to the hole in the warehouse that the rock had flown through.

"Sorry," I said quickly.

His lips tightened as he gave me a flat stare. He might not care about any harm done to his person, but I happened to know that he *did* care about his cars. He took great pride in some of them.

Without a word, he crossed to the other side and took out his clothing. "Did Amorette ever describe how Lucifer acted after he used his power?" he asked.

"Let's not throw his name around willy-nilly." I glanced at the wide-open space around the warehouse. Two spots of light traveled along the highway in the distance, a car passing by. "Vampires have those cloaks that make them nearly invisible."

"We are alone," Darius said as he stepped into boxer briefs. "No one knows where I am. I was not followed here."

"You might have a tracker on your car or something. Vlad is wily. You can't trust him."

"A great many vampires are wily," Callie said. "And no, you can't trust any of them."

I heard her emphasis on *any*. That was why she'd never know I was dating Darius. The end result would probably be a dead vampire and a cover-up story.

"Yes. Exactly. His is not a name to throw around." I

pulled out the band holding my hair up so I could redo it. I probably looked like I'd been traveling through the briars.

"Using his name is no different than speaking of Eustace, the elf queen. The two are supreme to their kingdoms and hold both magical and species power, but they are not gods." Darius grimaced as he lifted his right arm to thread it through the armhole of his button-down shirt.

My gaze shifted from Callie, tapping her finger against her chin, to Dizzy's head, which had just appeared in one of the holes in the warehouse. "She didn't describe him so much as marvel at what he could do," Callie said. "I do remember her saying that every-thing was done with absolute ease. All the power at his disposal, and he didn't exert much effort to wield it."

"Would you view Reagan's power similarly?" Darius moved to put on his blazer, but hesitated and then put it back in the car.

Callie surveyed me for a second. "When she is in the throes of it, her power is awesome, but her use of it is obvious. She fights it."

Darius braced his hands on his hips and looked out into the nothingness beside the warehouse, land he'd bought to ensure I could practice without anyone witnessing it. "This form of training is doing more damage than good."

"And how would you know that?" Callie countered. "Her mother thought it was the right way, and it seemed to work. Her mother would know over anyone. She saw *his* power in action."

Darius's honeyed gaze fell on Callie, and while his peepers were very pretty, the power and confidence in that hostile stare was not. "She saw it, yes, but she couldn't be expected to know how it worked. How best to train a pupil. She was a mage—she thought like a mage—something Reagan could never be. If Reagan tried to create a spell, her magic would unravel its properties before the spell was realized. Because her father's magic is ten times stronger than that of her mother's. Than yours. No, this is wrong. This is embedding the fear deeper into her, I saw it in there. I could see her misery when she tried to kill me, and I see her guilt every time she thinks of it."

Callie blinked for a moment in surprise at the "killing" bit before she charged back into the argument. "That's just the thing. Despite the magic issue, she is half human. She isn't okay with killing a…friend."

"Lucifer is always described as a sound and just leader. His punishments are harsh, but his rewards plentiful." Darius glanced to the warehouse as Dizzy shuffled out, his expression pensive. "He has an open invitation to the Realm, which includes the Golden Hall in the elves' mansion. A rage-drowned killer would not be viewed in a positive light. Therefore, he can't be consumed with that byproduct of his magic. Furthermore—"

"What is this, a verbal essay?" Callie crossed her arms over the *HOT* stenciled across her chest. I swore she ordered those sweats specially.

"—if Reagan's mom, whom I can only assume was a strong woman, since Reagan is her daughter, saw Lucifer wield his power and stayed with him, he must be as charming as the rumors say."

"Let's not forget, he is the ruler of demons," Callie said. Dizzy nodded, clearly on her side. "They aren't a nice bunch. Or did you forget about the one in Seattle?"

"That is just one type of demon," Darius said. "There are also demons who lust. Even some who love."

"Okay, so what are you saying? How do we train her?" Callie asked.

"We could summon a demon," Dizzy suggested.

"Um…" I raised my hand. "I realize I'm not integral to this conversation, despite it being about me and all, but I think we've seen what all can go wrong with calling demons. A lot, basically, not the least of which is that the shifters would reattach themselves to my ass and watch my every move. It's rather nice being left alone. I'd like to stick with that."

"Just having a demon in her proximity seems to bolster her magic," Darius said thoughtfully, still looking at

Dizzy. "From there, maybe she'll push through the consuming need to wreak havoc and see what's on the other side. I am confident she can come back from the brink of destruction."

I waved them away. "Thanks for your help, everyone, but *nope*. Not going to happen. Time to head home. I have dinner to eat."

Dizzy crossed his arms and looked down at his feet with a wrinkle between his brow. It was his problem-solving look. "My circles can easily hold a level-four demon. That should be enough to get her on the right track."

"You can banish it with the command to remain silent about what it learned while on the surface?" Darius asked. "That is the most important piece."

"Seriously, hello?" I rapped on Darius's car. He flinched as though I'd stuck a sword through his gut. "This isn't going to happen. Let's go."

"What do you take me for, a greenie?" Dizzy scoffed, ignoring me. "I know my way around a circle, thank you very much."

"I will be there to double-check his efforts," Callie said, eyes narrowed in thought.

"Callie, you too?" I ran my hand over my face. "Look, you guys, here's the long and short of it. The only way I would show up to a demon-calling party was if the world was literally about to end and Superman was otherwise engaged. That, or if my dad sent me a letter telling me to prepare the guest room because he's coming for a visit. That's it. Okay? So let's drop it. I'm hungry."

"You're always hungry," Callie said before pulling her lip through her teeth. It was another indication she was mulling something over.

"No, Callie. Stop it. Darius, congratulations, you are driving me home. Get in the car before I dent it somewhere else."

"But wait, what about the warehouse?" Dizzy asked, surveying the nearest hole. "The damage is extensive."

"I'll take care of it." Darius opened the driver's-side door and looked at me across the roof of the car. "Come. Get in."

"Not only are you *not* planning to open the door for me, you're being pushy as well? Good grief. Pain doesn't suit you at all." I grinned in jest (and also apology) before pulling open my door.

"Reagan, I *am* holding the door for you. The car is ruined. You can drive it home if you'd like."

Joy surged through me. I had gotten a car after our trip to Seattle, but it was more or less a beater that didn't go very fast. My version of fast, anyway. While Darius had access to the equivalent of fighter jets on wheels, he wouldn't let me drive them for fear I'd scratch, dent, or otherwise tarnish them.

He refused to believe me, but the one time I'd run a guy over, it had been on purpose. Mikey, my neighbor, had asked for a favor. A guy had been selling drugs to the kids in our neighborhood. The thug had needed a good scare, and everyone knew I was better than Mikey at acting crazy. Had I been behind the wheel of a very pretty Ferrari in pristine condition, I would've taken the extra effort to get out of the car to give him a lesson. That was just common sense. I'd taken the lazy route and stayed behind the wheel.

I'd only hit him hard enough to give him a limp, and the ding in my hood from the altercation was very small. Hardly noticeable. If anything, the whole thing showed what a great driver I was. Hitting a guy with hardly any damage to show for it? Just call me Ace.

Darius had not agreed.

I paused with my hand on the door. "Not to talk you out of it or anything, but the dent is relegated to the door. You can get a new door, and everything would be fine…"

He sniffed in a condescending way and continued to wait patiently.

Sold!

"Are you sure you don't want to ride with us?" Callie asked as I limp-skipped around the car.

Even though she still ardently mistrusted vampires (like all self-respecting people), she'd lightened up a lot when it came to Darius. Everything he'd done for me—buying me the warehouse, getting me a new identity, hiding my parentage from everyone (including his maker), and, most importantly, putting his life on the line so I could practice my magic without holding back—had softened her up just enough that she didn't complain too loudly when I spent time alone with him.

That didn't mean she'd be okay with me dating him, of course. Neither would Dizzy. Vampires as old as Darius usually didn't have much humanity left. They thought in terms of logic and strategy, creating intricate webs with their plans, often at the expense of everyone but themselves, including other vampires. Emotions were not their strong suit.

Something had happened with Darius, though. Ever since my near-death experience on our foray into the Island of Eternal Light, where the unicorns lived, his humanity had been creeping back. He claimed he was falling in love with me. It shouldn't have been possible, and maybe he was lying, but based on his actions and the changes I'd seen in him, the evidence was hard to deny.

Which put me in a bit of a predicament, I had to admit. I couldn't deny that I also had feelings for him. I didn't want to attach any L-words to it or anything, but falling for a vampire was as crazy as it was stupid. His species was known for entrapping prey with their sensuality. For using it to take control. If Darius was playing me for a fool, acting like he was invested in our budding relationship and coaxing me to fall for him, he'd be in a unique position to accomplish his ultimate end game: to bond me, emotionally linking us in such a way that severing the connection would cause great pain.

So while it seemed like he was really into what we had going, and that he was genuine in the sweet nothings he said to me in the quiet hours we spent wrapped in each other's arms, there was a very real possibility that he'd figured out how to manipulate me into getting exactly what he wanted.

A smart girl would've run away screaming. A sane girl would've kept her distance. Clearly I was neither of those, because I just couldn't get enough. The man in him was like a disease without a cure—he ate away at me until I had no option but to submit. He was a sickness I loved to hate.

Even the vampire side of him had me on board. Dizzy was right: our practices had improved his already impressive abilities. He'd gotten faster. Stronger. More skilled. If he wasn't better than Vlad at this point, he was as good, taking away Vlad's upper hand physically. I doubted there was anyone in the world that could fight alongside me, complementing my abilities with his own, as well as Darius could. And if the two halves of my magic warred with each other, leaving me defenseless, I also doubted there was anyone who would protect me as viciously and ardently as he would. The girl side of me was totally into that. It was very hot.

"I'm good," I said to Callie as I slid into the driver's seat. The leather bucket seat welcomed me like a long-lost friend.

I wonder if he'll let me keep it…

The door shut with a soft *plunk.*

I pushed the ignition button, then smiled in glee when the engine purred to life. My soft pump of the gas pedal made the beast rev in a refined sort of way.

"What a beauty," I said in a terrible Australian accent.

Darius sat into the passenger seat a moment later. The dual mages got into their car as well.

"Do you know how to drive it?" Darius asked as he closed the door.

His asking meant I probably didn't.

He proceeded to explain the paddle shift gearbox and give me some tips on how to keep from losing control. "Most importantly, Reagan," he said seriously, "don't kill us."

"Do not kill us…" I put it in gear. "Got it."

I stomped on the gas. The tires spun, kicking up dust and slapping the warehouse walls with dirt and rocks. That poor warehouse really had a hard life now that it belonged to me.

The car shot forward.

It would take a lot to kill Darius or me. Game on.

CHAPTER 3

"THAT WAS SENSATIONAL," I said as I neared my house twenty minutes later. I would've made even better time if Darius hadn't insisted I obey the stop lights.

Party pooper.

"Yes. You have a knack for reckless behavior," he said.

"I feel like that shouldn't be a surprise for you. I've never tried to hide that flaw in my personality."

His lips tweaked upward into a half-smile. When I'd put it in park, he took my hand, turned it over, and kissed me lightly on the inside of my wrist. "Will you allow me to feed from you tonight?"

Butterflies filled my stomach. I tried not to smile like the idiot I was. "Not if you use the word *feed*, I won't. We've talked about that."

"Will you allow me to make love to you in the way I do best?"

The heat rushed to my face, and I shut off the car with a small shrug.

When I got out of the car, I was immediately greeted with "What the hell?" Mince, a resident in the neighborhood and an ex-boxer with the nose to show for it, came along the sidewalk in front of my house. He stopped beside the car and shot me an accusing stare. "What did you do, Reagan? *What did you do?* And, more importantly, what is he going to do to you for doing what you did?"

"Words, Mince. Use your words. Preferably ones that make a little sense." I walked around the car as Darius got out, managing to look like a million dollars despite being hurt and missing most of his hair. It wasn't fair.

Mince shoved his finger toward the dent. Every line of his body screamed indignation. "Are you serious?" He turned to Darius, his expression now pleading. "Dude, for the love of all that is holy, do not let her drive your car. Because she did this, right? She's responsible for the dent? You don't have to answer. I already know." He bent over his phone, his fingers tapping the screen. "We're going to have to get someone to look after it, or it'll be stolen before you close your door."

"Smokey will watch it." I made my way up the stairs. "He'll let me know if anyone goes after it."

"That creepy guy is in the hospital. He ain't watching nothin' but the drip of the painkillers in his IV." Mince shook his head at the dent again.

Shock ran through me. Smokey was definitely creepy, always loitering around the neighborhood and watching what went on, but he was harmless and really excited about the supernatural, something humans shouldn't know about. Humans also shouldn't get chased down by an *aswang,* an evil, soul-sucking being, because they knew me. I tended to let the weird factor slide with him. "Smokey is in the hospital? What happened?"

"Just kidney stones. Happens to the best of us. He's got medical, though, so he's fine."

I took a deep breath. Mince was terrible at realizing what was newsworthy and what wasn't. "You know, in the future, maybe you should lead with news about any attacks, B&Es, or *people in the hospital* before lamenting a small issue with the door of an inanimate object. It would really help me out."

Mince looked at Darius in bewilderment. He hooked a thumb my way. "Is she for real? *Small issue*?" He shook his head and chuckled, focusing on Darius. "You got problems, son. I do not know what you are doing with her."

I leveled him with a look. "Just remember—if I'm fine with denting a million-dollar car, I am more than fine denting your head with said million-dollar car."

He took a hop-step toward the cemetery on the other side of the street, one of the more interesting views I could think of for a homeowner in New Orleans. His hands rose into the air. "Don't get excited. We understand each other."

I turned and let myself into my house.

"You have colorful neighbors," Darius said, following me.

"You've said that before."

"And I am surprised anew each time I'm confronted with them."

"Cognac?" I grabbed a bottle of wine for myself. He nodded and went to my pantry, no doubt remembering my declaration of hunger. Darius cooking for me had turned into one of my favorite things.

Before I sat down at the kitchen table, a knock sounded at my door.

I frowned as Darius paused in his efforts. A moment later, his large frame was in the archway of the kitchen. "Are you expecting someone?"

"No. What's with the rigidity? Are you expecting an attack or something?" I hopped up and ripped out my sword, uncertainty seeping through me. I didn't think he still kept things from me that might put me in danger, but I hadn't threaten-questioned him lately. It was anyone's guess.

Without a word, he zipped to the front door, claws elongating from his left hand. Nothing else on his body changed, a sign of his excellent control, something that came with age for a vampire.

I took his place in the archway. "Use the peephole—" I cut off as the handle turned and the door cracked open.

Darius stepped to the side and flattened against the wall, clearly intending to use surprise to his advantage.

"She likes us to knock!" Dizzy sounded harried. "How many times does she have to tell us that?"

The breath I hadn't realized I'd been holding left my lungs in a gush.

"No, she likes strangers to knock. She doesn't care if we just come in," came Callie's reply as the door swung open.

Dizzy filled the doorway, looking back at his wife. "What is your head made out of, wood? Darius's people breaking in makes her jumpy. She wants us to knock!"

Shaking his head, Dizzy turned and took two steps into the entryway. Before I could ask what they were doing following me home—even though I had a sinking suspicion I knew—he glanced over and noticed the large shape with claws.

Dizzy had jumped, reached into his satchel, and thrown a spell before my brain could shift from *Why are you here?* to finding an appropriate four-letter word to yell.

Darius flinched and tried to dodge, but he was too late. The spell puffed like baby's breath before sparkling blue and green. It was very pretty, which meant it was also potent and probably dangerous. Dizzy liked to build a false sense of security into his spells, usually by way of lovely colors or smells. The spell that shot magical acid strong enough to rot flesh looked like a fuzzy puppy before it exploded.

I was so glad he was on my side.

Darius convulsed and his fingers bent backward, cracking.

"Oh no!" Dizzy said, finally realizing who it was. "Oh no. He's trapped in the spell. Callie, hurry!"

"What's happen—Oh! I need to find—"

I didn't wait for Callie to dig into her satchel.

Fire shot out from my fingers and covered the spell, but it had a volatile heat that immediately went to war with my fire magic. It would take finesse to keep it from exploding as it unraveled. Darius's limbs clearly didn't have that kind of time.

Another crack filled the air, making my teeth grind, and I opened up and let the cold surge through me. I didn't try for it, or work at it…I just surrendered to the moment. My fear for Darius ate through the rage that pulsed up with the power.

A solid wall of air wedged between Darius, and Dizzy and Callie, my subconscious clearly wanting the threat kept at bay even though logic said the dual mages weren't an enemy. Back in control, I draped the spell that was torturing Darius with my colder magic, the effect manifesting as crystals of ice, frosting over the spell and wiping out the lovely sparkly affect. Another crack sounded from Darius. Fear pumped up my adrenaline.

My fire magic swirled beneath the ice, power pumping higher than I could comfortably control in normal situations. This time I didn't balk. I used the fire to drill down into the spell as the ice slowly ate away at it from the outside. The intricate hex unraveled, fiber by fiber, getting angry as it did so.

I pulled out the fire and pushed the ice down into the frayed spell, the effect like water freezing within the cracks. The swell of magical violence stopped immediately. When I cracked the crystals of ice encrusting the spell, the whole shebang shattered like glass, falling to the floor before melting into nothingness.

I rushed forward. "Oh my God, are you okay?"

Darius's tightened eyes connected to mine like a lifeline. A vein in his jaw pulsed. That was the only indication of his intense pain.

"You are not having a very good day," I said, ready to grab his fingers and bend them straight. Though gross and stomach-churning, that would make it easier for him to heal.

"I can fix that," Callie said, knocking at the solid air in front of her. It didn't make a sound. "Reagan, let me in and I can heal him. Mostly. I think. Worst case, I can dull the pain while you straighten his fingers."

"Clothes," Darius said with a heavy voice. Those last two breaks were arms. That must've hurt something awful. He was clearly ready to escape into his monster form to heal more quickly.

"Yeah, sure. Callie, close the door," I said, hurrying to undo the buttons on Darius's shirt. "Can I just rip this, or…"

"I'd prefer you didn't."

"Only you would rather endure horrible pain than see harm come to your designer clothes," I mumbled.

I pushed the fabric off his shoulders and carefully down his arms. At least they were in reasonably straight lines. I quickly undid his belt and pants before pushing the fabric down his legs. Without hesitation, I hooked my thumbs into the elastic of his boxer briefs and pushed them down as well.

"Crisis aside, I do not like how comfortable you are with taking off his clothing, Reagan," Callie said.

"Not his specifically," I answered quickly. "Just guys in general. I study the arts of removing men's underwear."

"This is no time to joke, Reagan," Dizzy said, picking at his nail. "That was a truly nasty spell. Penny worked with us on the power for that one. Normal men would've passed out from pain. Lesser vampires would've slipped into a rage and killed us all upon being freed. We shouldn't have created it. We shouldn't do something just because we can. But…in our defense, it was only because we were nervous about the Mages' Guild coming for us. We—"

Clothes removed, Darius wasted no time turning into his monster form. Claws from his feet clicking on the hardwood floor, he made his way back to my room.

I grimaced on his behalf. "That guy deals with an awful lot where it concerns me. He and the warehouse are going to turn on me one of these days." I sighed, because even if I told him to get lost (and I had), he'd stick around. And he'd keep on sticking around, I had no doubt, regardless of what came.

The surge of power within me drained away, my fire back to normal, and my ice disappearing altogether. I'd need to think on how I'd managed to summon and use the ice so readily. Although, admitting to the *why* of that situation would be dicey. That might call up the dreaded L-word.

I grimaced. I was in pretty deep where it concerned that vampire.

The invisible partition I'd put up had dissipated with the ice magic. I started into the kitchen, thankful that Callie and Dizzy followed me in.

"Does Penny have one of those spells?" I asked as I took down a bottle of whiskey. I hesitated. "Would you rather have wine than the whiskey?" I asked them.

"Whiskey. Two fingers. No ice." Dizzy ran his hand over his glistening forehead. "Maybe three fingers."

"A glass of wine for me," Callie said.

"Penny has a few different spells that are just as powerful," Dizzy said as he sat at the small round table in the corner of the kitchen. "Any spell she helps us with, or makes on her own, will be potent. But I trained her on the importance of safety when carrying around spells of that magnitude."

I couldn't help but laugh. "You taught her the importance of safety, did you? The same guy who just blasted an ally?"

"Let's hope the pupil surpasses the teacher," Callie huffed, and shook her head. I could always count on her to see the humor in dire situations.

"I didn't expect him to be there!" Dizzy yelled. I couldn't as easily count on his levelheadedness. "I was worried about barging into Reagan's home, since she can be unhinged when people just waltz in. Then a larger-than-most vampire was hulking by the door, claws out and war on his face—what did you expect? You've dragged me along to all these battles lately. I'm jumpy."

"Darius is jumpy, too. He was not happy about someone showing up at my door unexpected," I said softly, feeling the uncertainty rise again. It annoyed me.

I wanted to stab something because of it, but it was all my stuff. I'd have to replace it or fix it, and that was too much effort. "Do you think he knows something I don't?"

"Reagan, how many times do you need to hear this?" Callie accepted her glass of wine with a thanks. "He will *always* know something you don't. A great many things, probably. Most won't concern you, sure. But some probably will, and you are only in the loop when he needs you for something."

I shook my head and looked away. That wasn't how our relationship worked anymore. We'd advanced to another level.

At least, we'd better have.

I really should've threaten-questioned him more recently...

Dizzy gulped down his whiskey before handing it back. "Another. With a cube of ice. I'll sip the second one."

"I'm driving, then?" Callie asked.

"Yes. That spell was nasty. I feel terrible. I should've known there wouldn't be danger in Reagan's house. With her in it, I mean. Poor Darius." Dizzy shook his head.

I furnished him with the bottle.

We stopped and started a dozen trivial conversations, each of them interrupted with Dizzy asking,

"Should you go check on him? You never did bend back his fingers."

"If he needed help, he'd ask me," I would say.

"Vampires don't ask for help."

"This one does. From me, at least. Trust me, Dizzy, he'll let me know when he needs something." I just hoped he waited to ask for that something until the dual mages were gone, because I knew it would be blood he needed.

A half-hour later, a hard rap sounded at the door. I paused with my glass of wine halfway to my mouth. Callie's eyebrow quirked.

"I'm not usually this popular." I frowned. Was this what Darius had been worried about?

I stood slowly and tapped the gun wrapped in a holster around my thigh.

"I admit it, you were right," Callie murmured to Dizzy. "From now on, we'll knock out a code and wait for her to answer the door. She's too keyed up for a normal house call."

"All my friends are within these walls," I said. "And it's too late for a door-to-door salesman, assuming any are brave enough to come around here. I can't see this being a normal house call."

"Then what is it?" Callie asked as she stood and opened her satchel for easy access.

Dizzy stood, too, but the quick motion caused him

to sway. He braced a hand on the table. "Let's hope it's the salesman, because I'm not so steady."

"I got it," I said, stalking out of the kitchen and toward the front door. Callie followed but stopped in the archway of the kitchen.

The hard rap came again.

"A polite person would've rung the doorbell, not practically busted down the door with their knocking," Callie said softly.

I had to agree. But at least they were knocking.

I pulled open the door in a fast, smooth movement, ready to draw and fire without hesitation. Shock bled through me as my fingers curled around the grip of my gun.

"What are you doing here?" I blurted.

CHAPTER 4

ROGER, THE ALPHA of the Northwest Region of shifters, stood on my porch with his empty hands loose at his sides. He stood a little taller than me at about five ten or so, but his bearing, and his frame stacked with muscle, made him seem so much bigger.

His piercing gaze—one blue eye, one green—trained on me. "I have some information you may want."

"That *I* may want?" I asked, dumbfounded.

As a rule, when I needed information, I badgered (usually with violence) Red, one of the lower-status shifters. Their species never came to me. That Roger, one of the most important shifters in the entire world, would impart knowledge was...odd. That he would come to my house to do so was...worrying.

I glanced behind him, noticing a racy muscle car parked on the other side of the street. No one sat in it or stood beside it.

"Are you alone?" I asked. I needed to establish the parameters for this crazy situation. At the moment, my gut was automatically screaming, *It's a trap, kill every-one!*

"Yes. Can I come in?"

I blinked rapidly. "In…my house?"

He didn't nod, just stared at me. Apparently that was *yes*. Or maybe, *yes, you moron, do you not understand English?*

"O-kay." I took a hesitant step back. "I should probably warn you that—"

Before I could finish, Roger's dual-colored eyes darted past me. His expression, naturally hard, as befit someone who had fought for his position and therefore couldn't show weakness, morphed into a terrifying mask of rage.

I glanced over my shoulder to find Darius wearing a ladies' silk bathrobe—mine—and standing in a balanced sort of way that screamed *enemy—kill!* His condescending smile didn't reach his hard eyes. He didn't flex his straight fingers. They probably still hurt.

"Mr. Nevin," Darius said. He sauntered closer. "To what do we owe the pleasure?"

"Why is he wearing your bathrobe?" Roger asked. A shimmer of green outlined his body, his shifter magic threatening to change into his wolf form. He was clearly also thinking *enemy—kill!*

"He likes women's clothing. He's eccentric in that way." I winked at Roger. "Anyway, do you still want to come in, or would you rather fill me in on the porch?"

Roger studied me for a moment. "I'm not here for trouble. In the house is fine."

"I should probably warn you that I have two mages in the house," I said, stepping to the side. "If you try to call in some reinforcements to attack Darius, it won't go well for you."

He hesitated and his eyes narrowed. "You have two mages and an elder vampire in your home in the middle of the night?"

"I'm popular."

He paused before starting forward. "Like I said, I'm not here for any trouble."

"Wow. A guy like Roger Nevin coming for tea is something you don't see every day." Callie's eyes widened.

"The same could be said of Darius," Dizzy called from the kitchen.

"Do you want something to drink, Roger?" I asked.

"No thanks, I'm fine." Roger slowly passed through the archway into the kitchen. His gaze swept the area. "You haven't been by to bother Red in a while."

"I'm not doing any bounty hunting." I took up my wine and settled into a chair. "I haven't needed information. I figured he'd want to be left alone."

"I'm sure he thanks you for that. As do I." Roger leaned against the counter.

Darius, who'd disappeared for no more than thirty seconds, reappeared in the archway opposite the shifter, fully dressed, though his clothes were slightly wrinkled. He leaned against the frame gracefully. The two men stared at each other. Heavy silence filled the room.

"Well, this is cozy." I took a sip of my wine.

"It isn't helping my buzz any," Dizzy muttered, looking back and forth between Roger and Darius.

Roger shifted and crossed his arms over his chest. He finally tore his eyes away from Darius and refocused on me. "As you know, I view what you did in Seattle as a selfless act. You were in danger, both from that demon and the Mages' Guild, and even though it wasn't your town to save, you didn't back down until the mages were stopped and the demon was banished. I commend you for that."

"My people made the first step at beating back the guild in that town, but I don't recall receiving a formal thanks from your office." Darius lifted an eyebrow.

"You did what now?" Callie asked.

Roger's head turned slowly toward Darius, and the shimmer of green surrounded him again. "With vampires, it is never a selfless act. Let's make one thing clear—you will never rule the supernatural in that town."

"The guild took over Seattle and you did nothing. But now that they are losing ground you intend to fight?" Darius tsked. "How much money does the guild pay you to stand on the sidelines and look the other way?"

Every muscle on Roger's body tightened. "We don't have the resources to beat them back. Not with the magic and power they have at their disposal. Had I found a couple of wild naturals to work with us, like you did, we would be—"

"Naturals? Wait." Callie held up her hand as suspicion crossed her face. "Are you talking about Penny?"

"We're off track," Darius said in a way that cut through the room. He offered me a slight bow. "I apologize."

Roger's eyes widened.

"I agree," I said. "Callie, you can yell at Darius later. Roger, you were saying?"

"One good turn deserves another," he said. "I have it from a reputable source that the demon you banished didn't die."

"Not on the surface, no, but there wasn't much left of it when it got its ticket back to the underworld," I replied. "You don't have to worry about it coming back."

Roger shifted his weight. "What I mean to say is, it did not die after banishment. The rumor is that it is joining with others of its kind and forming a sort of army."

My jaw clenched shut as a cold shock of fear washed through me. I'd spent my whole life trying to avoid this. Trying to keep the knowledge of what I was from people who could take it to my dad. And now a high-powered demon, who had *seen* me in action, was alive and below, holding the key to my entrapment.

The desire to run pumped through me, so acute it was hard to breathe. Not fight, *run*. I was no match for my father, and I knew it. If he wanted to show up, grab me, and haul me back down to the Dark Kingdom, he would. The people who stood in his way would die, especially if he brought a host of high-powered demons to help him.

Dizzy's warm hand covered mine.

Roger nodded solemnly, clearly reading my face. "I had heard that you went to great pains to kill it. I thought you'd want to know."

"How did you come by this news?" Darius asked with a firm expression.

"We've gathered the information piecemeal from a few sources before assembling it, as we often do," Roger answered. "I could be wrong, but I didn't get to where I am by waiting for trouble to find me. If a demon army is coming to the surface for vengeance, I have to prepare for them."

"You did nothing to help her kill the demon in Seattle. Why are you suddenly making this your task?"

Darius asked, not hiding his suspicion. At least not from me.

Roger squared his body to Darius and uncrossed his arms. It was rare for an alpha to reveal so much agitation in his movements, which meant Darius was tap-dancing on Roger's *I want to kill you!* nerves. "The real problem in Seattle was mages killing people. Our hands were tied until the demon went rogue, and as soon as it did, Reagan was on it. She extinguished the problem without calling for—or needing—our aid. But the situations are vastly different. That was one demon, and we need to prepare for an *army*. As the elves' right hand in the Brink, sanctioned to protect humans, or at the very least keep them in the dark about magical people, this is my duty. If what is rumored comes to pass, I'll need all the help I can get."

He had missed an important bit of information in those rumors. It wouldn't be him that needed the help—it would be *me*. Because kidnapping me was clearly their purpose.

He was right on one thing—we'd both need all the help we could get.

I bowed over my hands as irrational emotion surged. Fear-induced tears were trying to get out, of all things. Since when was I a crier in the face of extreme danger?

"Who originated these rumors?" Darius asked.

"I don't reveal my sources," Roger replied.

"Then how can we substantiate these claims?"

Dizzy cleared his throat. "We can—"

Callie elbowed Dizzy. He grunted. "Ask some of our friends what they've heard." She shrugged. Being that she normally wasn't a shrugger about matters of importance, she had to be hiding something. I had a feeling I knew which "friends" she meant.

A crease formed between Roger's brows and his eyes narrowed. He might not know about the shrugging, but he certainly knew what it meant when someone elbowed someone else in order to shut them up.

The dual mages weren't very subtle.

"Any additional information would be welcomed," Roger said slowly.

"The night is getting old." Darius turned, showing his profile to Roger. It was his polite way of saying *get out*.

Roger caught the meaning. He pushed off the counter after shooting one last look at the dual mages.

"Thanks for letting me know," I said, standing.

"Then I can count on you?" Roger asked.

"If I can count on you." Lord knew I would need the shifters' help if a bunch of demons came calling.

He stuck out his hand and I shook it. A deal made. I was aligning myself with the shifters. I had already aligned myself with the vampires—a connection that had been doubled down by my discovery of their biggest secret, their alliance with the unicorns. So basically, I was the squishy part between the rock and the hard place. Super.

It belatedly occurred to me that I hadn't introduced Roger to anyone. I was the world's worst host. Someone should really get me a trophy for it.

Before I could fix that issue, Roger was striding away. "I'll be in touch."

"Right. Okay." I followed behind him, waving at his back while he headed down my front steps, waving at the side of his head when he turned to get in his car, and finally gave up waving as he closed his door.

"Well, that is shitty news," I said as I closed the door.

"That information came from Vlad," Darius said, still in the archway. He was studying me. "I'd bet my life on it."

"How do you know?" I headed back into the kitchen.

"First, who else would know? He watches the underworld closely. No one else has all but taken up residence there. Second, when he wants to influence matters with an unseen hand, he spreads clues for his marks, leaving it to them to piece it together. That makes them feel privileged to the information. They are more inclined to believe it. I've known him a long time. I know how he works."

"You had me at *who else would know*." I sagged into my seat. "But still, we don't know if it's true, or just his way of screwing with the shifters."

"True. If Vlad is planning something and wants to keep the shifters' focus directed elsewhere, it would be an easy thing to create rumors, then let a couple demons loose for them to deal with."

"We can find out," Callie said.

I shook my head, because I knew *how* she could find out. Why they were so hellbent on calling demons after all we'd been through, I didn't know, but it was really annoying.

"A simple circle to call a weak demon should suffice," Dizzy said, confirming my suspicion. "The demon might not know the answer when we call it, but we can send it back to find out. It's pretty simple."

I dropped my head to the table. "If what Roger said is true, Agnon is running around the underworld telling all its friends about me. They are probably on their way to tell my dad now." A weight lodged deep in my gut.

"What are the odds we can summon that particular demon?" Darius asked.

Callie chewed her lip. "We know its name, and its…essence, I would call it, so that would help, but if it crossed the river into the Dark Kingdom, it would require a *lot* of power for us to summon it. It's too high level, even in its weakened state, and it's harder to call a specific demon. Plus, if it is traveling with its sect, they can block our summons."

"In other words, our odds of summoning Agnon are next to nil," I muttered into the table.

"*If* it crossed the river." Callie drummed the table.

"Worst-case scenario: what if we find out that the demon has crossed the river, is with its friends, and is on the way to tell my dad?" I asked, trying to push through the fog. "What are my options?"

"We hide you," Dizzy said.

"If Lucifer is looking for her, Vlad will volunteer his services," Darius said. "He's been seeking a relationship with the demons, and this would be a perfect way to make the connection." He crossed to the counter to pour himself a snifter of cognac. "Hiding her from the two of them would be…challenging. In the short term, I can manage it. But eventually they would find her."

"Is the short term enough time for her to learn the extent of her powers?" Dizzy asked.

Darius nodded thoughtfully. "Perhaps."

I wasn't so sure.

I sat back in my chair. "Just spitballing here, but can we command a demon to be a hit man?"

Dizzy frowned and scratched his nose. "I have no idea. I can research and find out."

"What about burying you behind a wall of all the shifters, vampires, and mages we can get on our side?" Callie asked. "If they come, we'll tear them down."

"Few vampires would stand against Vlad," Darius said. "Shifters and mages would keep the lesser demons at bay, though it would be a stretch if they're faced with a large host of the higher levels. But Lucifer?" Darius shook his head. "There are very few creatures on this earth that can kill an elder vampire one on one in hand-to-hand combat, and when Reagan is operating at the higher levels of her power, she is one of them. Lucifer would be mightier still. No, standing against him would not be an option. Another worry would be, if a large host of demons come to the surface, and the shifters—which represent the elves' presence in the Brink—have to stand in their way, what will that mean in the grand scheme of things? Will it be the conflict that starts an incipient war between the magical species? A conflict that Vlad has been attempting to orchestrate."

"Whoa. Can we just back up a second?" I held up my hands. "If Vlad is the one spreading the rumors, and the rumors are true, he must also know how detrimental this situation is to me. He'll know why."

"Yes. We have to assume he is privy to at least part of what you are." Darius took a sip of his drink. "He has been unusually quiet of late, and it being so soon after Seattle, where he made known his interest in Reagan, only backing off after I'd told him I'd submitted the bonding paperwork—"

"You *what*?" Callie jumped in.

"He didn't." I dramatically shook my head. "He just said he did to get Vlad off my back. He really didn't." I sure hoped he hadn't, at any rate. Because that was *not* going to happen.

"I've suspected he has secrets he is trying to keep from me," Darius continued as though we hadn't interrupted. "So the question is, what are his goals? He would've taken this to Lucifer himself if he had simply wanted the connection with your father."

"Maybe he doesn't know what to do, which is why he's lobbing it at us?" I asked.

Silence filled the room, no answers to be had.

"Well, first things first—we need to make sure the rumors are true." Dizzy knocked on the table. "Let's get that warehouse fixed up, because we're going to call a demon."

CHAPTER 5

TWO DAYS LATER, enough time for the dual mages to research the right circle to use and, presumably, for the warehouse to be patched up, I parked in front of the warehouse next to Dizzy's beater. Clearly the dual mages worried about my propensity to damage property when using my magic. Darius's sleek sports car was parked half a mile away. If he'd just lower himself to driving the town car, something he never did when he didn't bring a driver, he wouldn't have to worry about damage.

I turned off the car and hung out for a second, weighed down by the rock I'd had in my gut the last two days. Something inside of me said this was legit. That Vlad wasn't just blowing smoke to freak out the shifters. He'd witnessed some of the chaos in Seattle. It wasn't out of the realm of possibility that he'd followed me once or twice without us knowing. There had been plenty of opportunities for a savvy onlooker to get a glimpse of my special abilities. Being that he had a presence in the underworld, he'd have more pieces to the puzzle than anyone else. That was all someone like Vlad needed.

The question was, why was he indirectly warning me? Was it because he knew that the only way to keep this from escalating was to cut it out at the root, Agnon, and I was the only one who could get past the river to do it? Maybe he didn't want Darius to know that he knew what I was for some reason.

When had my life gotten so complicated?

As soon as I'd hooked up with elders, that was when. They were so high maintenance.

I blew out a breath and leaned my head against the steering wheel. Cutting out the root was a tall order. While bounty hunting was sort of my thing, or at least it had been, normally I had breadcrumbs to help me find a mark.

Normally I knew my surroundings.

If I attempted this, I would be going into the underworld as probably the only thing resembling a human, full of latent magic (which could as easily turn me into a monster as save me), and with absolutely no clue as to where I was going. I might as well paint myself in neon and strut around with jazz hands. *Hey, y'all, look at me!*

This would be an extremely well-paying job, being that I'd get to keep my freedom, but some jobs were just too great. Too complex. I didn't have the chops to complete it.

Realistically, though, what was the alternative? Let Darius hide me, like the mages had said? Try to learn my magic in time to combat my father and/or a host of extremely powerful demons?

I laughed sardonically, the sound jarring in the quiet car.

I'd been trying to master my fire magic most of my life, and I was still basically a novice. I couldn't even access half of it. Using my powers together? Yeah, right.

Learning my magic, even with a teacher, would take years. *Years!* I probably didn't even have months. The demons would come, regardless of whether my father knew about me or not, and Roger had already made it clear the shifters intended to amass in front of them. Dizzy and Callie would wade into the fray, trying to protect me, dragging a bunch of wide-eyed, blackmailed mages with them.

For what?

I was the heir. The only one in history who could survive the Dark Kingdom for eternity. The thing my father had been trying for since the beginning of time, or so rumor had it. I was a prize the demons would stop at nothing to obtain. They'd come in waves, first one sect, and then others. We might be able to fight off one wave, maybe a couple, but for something as valuable as me, they'd eventually overcome us. And they'd kill in large numbers to do it.

I'd be condemning the few friends I had, and a whole lot of innocent supernatural people with them.

To end up being taken anyway.

My laugh was louder this time. A few tears squeezed out.

"If I'm forced to meet my father, I will greet him by giving him a black eye. I absolutely will." I yanked my keys out of the ignition, jerked at the handle, and kicked open my door. It moaned woefully.

Screw tears. That wasn't my speed. Giving people hell, now *that* was my speed. If I had to go into the underworld, and things went sour, I'd give them Reagan Somerset's famous how-de-doo!

But Dizzy was right: first things first. I needed to find out for sure if the rumors were even true.

I marched toward the closed warehouse door, newly attached. The other fixes weren't so polished. Clunky, ill-fitting boards covered the holes in the walls. It looked like a drunk with a hammer had gone at it. It would work, though. For now, anyway.

The metal of the handle was cool on my palm as I cranked it and ripped it open. No, this wasn't a battle, but it sure felt like it. That meant being prepared for anything.

In the middle of the spacious warehouse, the dual mages hunched over a chalk circle. Dizzy pointed at something, drawing Callie's eyes.

A flicker of movement shifted my attention to the far wall. Darius waited, unmoving except for the swivel of his head. He stared at me, showing no expression.

Nearing the center, I let my gaze drift over one of the most elaborate summoning circles I'd ever seen. There were three rings in all, the smallest in the center of the design, the largest enclosing most of it. Figures and characters were drawn in the middle, between the rings, and outside, their placement seemingly haphazard. No blood traveled the chalk outline; the dual mages had not (thankfully) sacrificed anything for the necessary power.

"You're planning to—"

"Ah!" Callie jumped and clutched at her satchel. Dizzy flinched, staring up at me with wide eyes.

"Jiminy Cricket, Reagan, you scared the life out of me." Callie sagged, now clutching at her chest.

"She popped up like a poltergeist." Dizzy looked back down at the circle. "Very quiet."

"Like I was saying, you're planning to call a lesser-powered demon, right?"

"We're aiming for a higher level four." Callie straightened up.

"With just two mages and no sacrifice?" I frowned. "Can you pull that off and keep it in the circle?"

"We're not worried about keeping it in the circle."

Dizzy put a piece of chalk in his pocket and dusted off his pants. He needn't have bothered, given the collection of stains and holes already there. "If it gets out, you can control it or kill it. That, or Darius can kill it. We have insurance not many mages in our position do." Dizzy puffed up with pride.

Callie stared at Dizzy for a beat that clearly implied, *You are missing the important issue here.* "We'll call it by offering the blood of the damned."

I looked up at Darius. "I bet you didn't realize they'd planned to sacrifice you, huh?"

"Not his, sweetie. Yours." Callie moved around the circle, looking closely at each character.

I took a step back. "Doesn't that defeat the purpose of this adventure?"

"We just need a little, Reagan," Dizzy said in a soothing tone. "Just a scrape, a dozen or so drops around the circle, and you'll go back to being a spectator. Your blood is the most powerful in the room for these purposes. It will call to the demons."

Would anyone notice if I took off running?

"Okay. We're ready. Now." Callie speared me with her bulldog look. "We are pulling a demon from the heart of the underworld. A strong demon, at that. But don't you worry—we have triple-checked everything, and are experienced with circles. We aren't putting you in any more jeopardy than you're already in."

"What she means is that this demon won't go back down and tell everyone about you," Dizzy clarified. "We will send it back to check on the rumor, and if it can't do that for some reason, we'll kill it. We've worked that into the circle. It's kind of like a…self-destruct feature."

"I didn't realize you could do that," I said. "Why doesn't everyone?"

"Well…" Dizzy's hand moved back and forth in a so-so gesture. "It's experimental. Maybe I shouldn't have mentioned it in case it doesn't work."

"Get moving," Darius said without moving forward. "Reagan is losing her nerve."

"I'm fine," I lied, narrowing my eyes at Darius. Because yes, all my bravado from a moment ago was seeping out of me. I needed another door-kicking pep talk. It was a little irritating that he noticed, but more so that he had told on me.

"Of course. Yes." Dizzy walked quickly to a box against the wall that I hadn't noticed. He withdrew a wicked-looking dagger and made his way back to me. "Now, we just need some blood…"

One painful slice of the hand later, the dual mages were pushing me around the circle while shaking said hand, dotting the concrete floor in crimson.

"You can head over to Darius, Reagan," Dizzy said, taking herbs out of his satchel. "You aren't needed anymore."

Sweeter words had never been said. I held my throbbing hand as I complied.

"How are you doing?" Darius asked me quietly when I leaned against the wall next to him.

"Hanging in there. Any idea why Vlad is taking the back seat on this one?"

He watched the mages for a silent beat. "I can't be sure. I would assume he wants you for himself, but for that to be correct, there must be another piece to his plan. Another way he's working toward his ends, one that perhaps requires him to take a more active role. I haven't been able to find out what that might be."

"Any other ideas?"

He shook his head slowly. "Not that fit half as well."

"Super," I said sarcastically.

"I will be by your side every step of the way, Reagan."

I blew out a breath as the dual mages lifted their hands above their heads and sprinkled a green plant down. They began chanting quietly.

"Thanks," I said, because the sentiment was sweet, and I thoroughly believed he meant it, but if the rumors were true, either he would be volunteering to die for me in battle, or to watch me disappear, alone, into the underworld, since vampires could only get into the edges. One of those I wouldn't allow to happen, and the other was not within my power to change.

Amazingly, for the first time, I didn't want to work alone. I didn't want to take this on by myself. Fat lot of good it did me.

"Just FYI, in case you need a barometer reading on the day's suckery, it is high. Very high. There is a shitstorm warning in effect." I leaned my head against the wall.

A *crack* drew my focus to the circle, where a shimmering blue blob now floated in the center. Purple light sparkled within it, followed by pink. Dizzy threw something at the ground, and a flash of light gave off another *crack*.

The blue orb took shape. Darius shifted beside me, uncomfortable.

"Not a big fan of calling demons?" I asked.

"I am not looking forward to the affirmation that the rumors are true. We will have some hard decisions to make."

I bit my lip, because it wasn't necessarily the decision that would be hard, but the follow-through.

A horned, knobby thing solidified in the circle, complete with scaly gray skin and a forked tongue. Could they not have tried for a nicer looking one?

For a moment, the demon looked back and forth between Callie and Dizzy, who were still chanting and working with their herbs, then it looked at the ground. It stepped forward, and a silent blast of light flared where it had touched the circle, forcing it back.

At least the circle worked.

The demon returned to looking between the dual mages, clearly trying to work out which of them was the high-powered, and therefore higher-ranked, summoner. They were dual mages, though. Yin and yang. They were both equally in charge. It must've confused the poor demon, since it was rare two mages of high power could stomach sharing the spotlight.

Callie lowered her hands and blinked, her eyes focusing on the demon in the circle. Dizzy did so next, then beamed. "Well look at you. Wow. You're powerful, aren't you? I knew this configuration would work with just two mages and the blood. I bet we could get a five in there if we worked it at a full moon."

"Why do you call me?" the demon hissed, a sound like snakes sliding over brittle bones.

"Here, hon." Dizzy pulled a piece of paper out of his satchel and handed it to Callie, not tearing his eyes away from the demon. A small smile still graced his lips. "It's like college all over again."

Callie muttered something I couldn't hear while shaking her head. She took the paper.

The demon switched his gaze from Dizzy to Callie before looking at the ground again. It turned in a circle, its gaze roving.

"We command you..." Callie began before spouting

off a list of instructions that essentially would have the demon hunting for our answers. It didn't seem to be listening. It had bent closer to one of the splashes of blood, as close as it could get without touching the invisible barrier in the air.

"Is it sniffing?" I asked Darius quietly.

"It seems so, yes."

The demon straightened up slowly, and this time it looked beyond Callie and Dizzy.

"It senses something of higher power than the dual mages," Darius murmured. "It is searching for its true master. That will always be you, Reagan. Even with a level five, it will always be you. *That* is why Vlad would move heaven and earth to get you for himself."

CHAPTER 6

"T HIS WOULD BE a strange way to accomplish that," I said.

"That is why there must be another piece. He has kept it well hidden," Darius said.

I stayed perfectly still, but it didn't matter. In a matter of moments, the demon's gaze fell on me.

It stared for a while, ignoring Callie's command to give its name. It then ignored Callie's command to repeat back its orders.

"You will have to give the instructions," Darius said, a master at stating the obvious.

I sighed and stepped forward, feeling the throb of fire within me—like recognizing like. "Did you mean to call a demon with the fire magic?" I asked Callie and Dizzy.

"Yes. Did we get it right?" Dizzy was much too upbeat. "That was also an experiment. As far as we know, no one else has figured out how to call one specific type of magic over another. Although it probably doesn't matter for normal purposes—"

"The faster you make it obey, the sooner we can send it back," Callie interrupted, handing me the paper.

"And I have to say these words exactly?" I asked, reading through it. My ice magic sparked, though I had no idea why.

"I do not believe my great luck," the demon said, bending to one knee. "I feel both powers in you, do I not? That can only mean one thing. The legend in the flesh. But will you survive the Dark Kingdom? The Great Master pines for an heir. None has yet survived. Each failure is a blow to him."

Ignoring the ugly thing, because I'd heard all of that before, I cleared my throat, ready to read the paper. Sweet heat rolled over me, comfortable and right, reaching through the circle to grab the life force of the demon. "Others may know about me," I said, falling into the exquisite pain of my magic. Below it, deep in my gut, minimal but there, was the ice, throbbing in time to my heart. "I need to know for certain, and if they do, I will need to silence them. You must find the answers I seek, and if knowledge of my existence is known in the Dark Kingdom, you must bring me a way to destroy it."

"Why would you want to destroy—"

"Silence!" I commanded. "You will do as I bid, or I will tear your being apart bit by bit." It was scary how easily that command rolled off my tongue. My power surged on its own, and I knew I was forcing the demon to obey. I just didn't know exactly how. Story of my life, lately.

"Yes, heir. I live to serve you."

"If only you were a hot cabana boy, this might actually be cool," I muttered. Something occurred to me. "And in your quest to find answers, you will learn of the vampire Vlad's influence in the Dark Kingdom."

"I have heard his name. He and his followers prowl the edges," the demon said, anger ringing in its voice.

"Good. Find out more. Who he talks to, his plans, whatever you can. Do not dally. I need this information as quickly as possible."

"Yes, heir. As you command, so will I obey."

I crinkled the paper, scanning it again. "Did I miss anything?"

"Well, most of the actual commands, if I'm being honest, but it doesn't look like you need them, so…" Dizzy shrugged. "I guess that's it."

"Do I need to command it not to spread news of this meeting?" I asked, lowering the paper.

"Oh no, the circle will bind it." Dizzy bent to get a closer look. "Yes, that is taken care of. We drew the characters correctly, I am sure of it."

"Your command overrides this paltry circle," the demon spat out. "Mages cannot hold a candle to your greatness."

"No one likes a brown noser, just so you know." I fell into the power of my fire for another command. "Knowledge of my existence will die with you. You will be bound as the circle prompts you. Or commands you." I grimaced. This was getting away from me. "You will adhere to the circle's binding."

"I think you've got it now, Reagan," Callie said.

I nodded with authority. "Now begone. Do as I bid."

"Yes, heir." The demon struggled against something invisible. A howl of rage and pain filled the warehouse.

"We should help it." Dizzy grabbed a stick of cinnamon. "It's struggling to break through the other end of the circle."

The drops of my blood glowed before spouting flame.

I took a step back, startled. "I didn't do that. I don't think."

"It is using your blood and commands to override the magic of the circle," Callie said, pulling out a little baggie.

Before they could chant, the demon disappeared, leaving behind smoke pulsing in various colors. The fire from my blood died away, not having changed the appearance of the red on the concrete.

I sucked in air to calm my rapidly beating heart. "That was a trip."

"The demon was right. Your power over it trumps

ours." Dizzy braced a hand to his hip. "How can we combine all of ours, I wonder? Because that would be unbreakable."

"Curse breaker," Callie said softly. "She can eat through any mage's magic with her own. Clearly she can enable demons to do it, too."

"Curses imply a certain type of magic. There is bound to be a spell my magic can't unravel." I waved the possibility away and headed for the door. "How long should we give that thing?"

"Two days should be enough, I think," Dizzy said, crouching over the circle. "Oh. Why did you ask about Vlad? How will that help?"

"Me? It won't." I thought about kicking the door open, but decided against it. The poor warehouse had been through enough. "But it'll help Darius."

Before I got into my car, Darius was at my side, his large hand wrapping around the top of my door. "Will you come to my house, Reagan?" he asked quietly.

"No. I'm headed to the bars. I think I need to drink and fight and torment some shifters for sport. I don't want to be rational tonight."

Darius took his hand away, watching as I got into the driver's seat and threaded the key into the ignition. "Thank you," he finally said, "for asking about Vlad. It will help greatly."

"Helping you helps me. It was the least I could do."

I pulled the door closed and stomped on the gas. I needed a big dose of forgetful juice.

THE NEXT DAY I nursed my hangover with more alcohol and ignored texts and calls from the dual mages. I even ran around the graveyard, popping out from behind large gravestones and scaring tourists. Boy did they get a fright. One couple took off running without getting a solid idea of what they were running from.

When night came, I got lucky and caught some wannabe witches trying to call a demon.

"Oh no, a demon!" I staggered out from behind a gravestone. Their supplies randomly combusted, spraying fire in all directions. That was my doing, of course, but it looked totally legit.

"The devil!" a woman shouted.

"Different guy, actually." I waved that thought away. The fire roared higher. "Oops." I went with it. "You're right! The devil!"

The woman hitched up her black skirt and ran away like an Olympic sprinter being chased by a tiger. The rest weren't far behind, screaming and yelling.

"*Shhhh,*" I called after them. "People live around here!" I stared after them for a moment before shrugging, then bent at the waist, swaying, to look at the satchel they'd left behind. "What are these, weeds?"

"Since when are you so animated when you scare

away the tourists?"

Startled, I jumped and spun. The clump of weeds went flying.

My neighbor No Good Mikey leaned against a gravestone down the way.

"Either you are very quiet, or the rushing in my ears is very loud." I picked up a small pot they'd also left, and sniffed the contents. "Smells lovely. Can't be effective. And to answer your question, they weren't tourists."

"That wasn't my question."

"Oh no?" I could've sworn it had been. Then again, whatever he'd said had already sunk into the black hole of my memory.

I staggered out from the rubble, pausing as something crunched under my boot, before grabbing my bottle of Jack from behind a gravestone. I held it out for No Good Mikey, but he shook his head. His loss.

"Question." I pointed at him, just in case he wasn't clear on who I was talking to. "What would you do if a bunch of demons had knowledge about you that they couldn't have? Would you, *A*, hide for as long as possible, work at getting better with your…weapons, and fight when they finally found you? Or *B*, take the fight to them so they couldn't tell anyone. Now, before you answer…" I burped and held my finger in the air. I wasn't sure why. "If you hide, then when they show up to take you, they'll probably kill a lot of people. So your blood would be on their hands. Wait. Their blood. Your hands." I paused to regroup. I'd confused myself. "But if you go to the demons, they might've already gotten to your father, so really, it would be a suicide mission. Except only you would be screwed, instead of a bunch of innocent people with deaths…on hands."

I leaned forward, blearily staring at him with one eye closed so I could focus. His face was still too blurry for me to read his expression.

"Well?" I prompted.

"You're drunk as shit."

"Yes. It has been an incredible bender, I must say. I bet Roger is pissed. A were-badger doesn't run as fast as the wolves, did you know that? Not fast at all. I nearly had him. If I could've gone in a straight line, I would've. But…" Up went the finger. It was like it was operating on its own. "You did not answer my question. I'm not so drunk that I did not notice that."

"Are you in trouble or something?"

"Wow. You're great at sussing out the big picture. Bloody good show," I said in a British accent. "Yes, I am, in case the sarcasm wasn't clear. British accents do always sound jolly, so the mistake is…"

I didn't know how to end that sentence, so I just let it hang. I hadn't had a proper conversation in hours. This was why.

He took a deep breath and shifted. "You're talking crazy, so I'll just say this. Even if you were the type of gal to sacrifice people for her own benefit, you're not the type to wait around and get snatched."

"That is true. I usually do the snatching, after all. It's what I live for. To help unfortunate mer-folk like yourself. Poor souls..." I held up a hand and shook my head. "My bad. Sometimes *Little Mermaid* songs come out instead of words. Sorry. Unless you want to have a sing-along. Then I'm so in."

"Are we done here?" Mikey asked. I couldn't be sure, but his voice might've sounded pained.

"So you'd chose *B*. Take the fight to them." I nodded. "Yeah. But I really don't want to."

He motioned me toward him. When I got there, I realized it was so he could take my arm and walk me home, like I was an old woman. I couldn't tell if he was doing it to help me, or the neighborhood.

"I still don't know what you're talking about, but if you need help, ask." He stopped in front of my porch.

"Well, I could really use a karaoke partner who can sing. I got booed earlier. Besides that, you can watch my house, and if I don't come back, take whatever you want."

He nodded slowly. "Let me know when you're going...wherever you're going."

"Underworld."

"I can watch your stuff. But you'll come back...from wherever you're going—"

"Underworld," I repeated. It didn't seem like he could hear me.

"—because a chick like you, as mean as an alley cat and as crazy as they come—you'll come back. Ain't no one able to keep you down." He spat off to the side. "I'll watch your stuff."

"Aw. That's nice. I should probably mention, though, just off the cuff." Where was my finger going now? "This is all up in the air. I don't even know if the rumors are true. This could be all for nothing. The booze, the worry, the chasing of the shifters...all for nothing."

Mikey stared at me for a moment before shaking his head and stepping away. He muttered something that sounded like the Lord's name in vain. "You need to go to sleep."

I held up the nearly empty bottle. "Almost there. Then tomorrow, after a miserable hangover, I'll get an answer, good or bad." I sighed and wobbled. "It's going to be bad. I know it'll be bad. Ain't that a bitch?"

"Sounds like it."

"Yes it does. It does sound like it. Oh, how's Smokey?"

"He's fine. Home. Not up to prowling the neighborhood yet, but it's just kidney stones. Not like he got stabbed."

"Remind me not to ask you for sympathy." I tripped on the first step and splayed across the rest. My bottle of Jack bounced before rolling, spraying liquid as it did so.

Mikey didn't bend to help, or even laugh. He grunted, turned, and headed off down the street.

"No, no, I got it," I called. "I don't need any help."

"Amateur," he yelled back.

If only he knew how much I'd drunk, he'd be saluting me.

I grabbed the bottle, groaned at the realization there was only a drop left, and made my way inside. In twenty-four hours the wait would be over, and the most dangerous journey of my life would surely begin.

CHAPTER 7

"REAGAN, YOU LOOK terrible," Dizzy said as I made my way to the circle in the middle of the warehouse. Darius stood where he had a couple days before, watching me without comment or expression.

"I wrestled a couple bottles of whiskey and didn't fare so well. I got through it." I halfheartedly raised my hand. "Yay."

"Let's get this over with," Callie said, compassion on her face. "Then we'll plan what's next. You're not alone in this, Reagan. You've got us, and we know people. Even if they don't want to help, we'll make them. I have dirt on at least a dozen powerful mages."

"Oh yes, my wife keeps track of those sorts of things. She can really call the troops when she needs to." Dizzy patted me on the shoulder.

I held out my hand. "Do you need blood?"

Out came the wicked-looking dagger. Why they couldn't use something normal, like a Swiss Army knife, I didn't know. That thing looked cumbersome. If they slipped and sliced a hand off, then where would I be?

We went through the same steps as last time: pain, stooping while walking around the circle and shaking my bleeding hand. Not long after that, they chanted the demon into the circle. It was the same one, which Dizzy and Callie expected, and I was impressed by. They did know what they were doing.

"Heir," the demon said, wasting no time in looking past the dual mages. It held a scroll.

"You guys have paper down there?" I asked, amazed.

"Of course, heir. How else would we write things down?" It unfurled the scroll. "I have some of the answers you seek."

"Tell me," I commanded.

I listened quietly as the demon told a story of a badly wounded demon that was treated in the edges and then moved across the river by one of the powerful sects. None of those who'd treated the demon had been left alive.

"What was the sect that took the wounded demon?" Darius asked from the wall. I wasn't sure why he didn't want to come closer.

The demon barely spared him a glance. "The Noctis sect. They are one of the more ambitious sects in the Dark Kingdom."

"Are they traveling to Lucifer?" I asked.

"No. They brought the demon to their territory.

There is no notice of their sect requesting an audience with the Great Master."

"Is there any speculation about what they wanted with the wounded demon?" I paced beside the circle as anxiety ate away at my stomach.

"No one seems to know, but there is a rumor of many dead in the wake of the sect moving through. They are trying to keep something silent."

"Me. They are trying to keep Agnon's knowledge of me a secret."

The demon bowed. "If that is the case, they have a mighty prize. I can feel great power within you, heir. The Incendium magic rages, begging you to flare it higher. I feel it calling me. But a dark pit within you prevents it. That is the Glaciem magic, if I am not mistaken, correct?"

"Yup. You nailed it. I'm ripe for the training. Agnon made that clear when I spoke with it." I ground my teeth. "I am going to yank its knobby little head off."

"Why wouldn't they take that to Lucifer?" Callie asked me.

"They want to grab me, train me, and present me to my father. They hope to gain favor by doing all of that, and probably make me an ally. Joke's on them, of course. I'll make them all very sorry they got mixed up in my business."

The desire to cry had dried up with the challenge

fully presented to me. Now I wanted to storm the gates of hell and blot out the threat. Which was good, because that was exactly what I'd have to do. I knew that as surely as I knew I could control the demon in front of me.

"Fine. The rumor was right. How do I cut them down?" I asked the demon.

It unraveled the scroll, then focused on a spot of nothingness in front of it. "I have maps. Routes. I can guide you. It would be my honor, heir. But you must find your way to me. I cannot cross certain areas. I don't have enough power." It focused harder on the spot of nothingness. "You have to burn away the circle so I can pass over the scroll."

"Routes into the underworld? Now that's just asinine. Right, Reagan?" Callie demanded. "Tell it it's talking nonsense."

"Don't burn away the circle, Reagan," Dizzy said in warning. "Those things are tricky. It's up to no good."

I ignored them both, because while I wasn't crazy enough to trust a demon asking me to deliver myself to it, I was crazy enough to give it an opening in a controlled situation so that I could get that scroll. A risk, but not a huge risk.

Fire crawled up the circular wall in front of me, burning away the invisible barrier. I felt the demon's magic pulsing within my own, then saw it create a sort of bridge between the newly created edges, keeping the rest of it intact. I latched on to its efforts, realizing that it was helping me. Showing me how to work my magic with greater intricacy. His mastery of weaving the magic together was awe-inspiring.

"Why are you helping me keep you trapped?" I asked as it reached the scroll forward. It did not make a move to cross the divide, though it could have tried.

"When you assume your intended throne, remember your allies. Remember those who helped you ascend."

"It knows you could easily kill it if it tried to run," Callie said dryly. "And you'd still get the scroll."

I knew that, but I'd wanted to hear its response.

I wrapped my fingers around the scroll and then held it out to the side. Darius was there in an instant, taking it from my hand. "You have a better memory. Read it now in case it's written in invisible ink or something. Demons are tricky. I'm not taking any chances."

"I speak for my sect when I say that we are here to serve, heir. We will join you. Will fight those who might oppose you, and help you ascend to—"

"I got it, thanks," I said as I concentrated on weaving the fire magic to stitch the circle back together. Wherever I grabbed the spell, though, it unraveled, leaving a larger hole that my fire magic had to bridge. I tsked. "Tricky, tricky, tricky. The circle only appears complete. It isn't structurally sound. The demon would be able to escape." I huffed out a laugh. "I may not know the extent of my power, but I'm not a complete idiot."

"Yes, heir. I knew you'd discover that, heir."

Of course it did, I thought sarcastically.

I tried to work at the ice magic, see if that would create a patch for this particular demon. It wouldn't rise, though. It stayed lodged deep in my gut, pulsing in time to my heart. Taunting me.

Frustrated, I scoffed. "Darius, how is that scroll looking?"

"I will remember everything on it. The maps are detailed. Vlad's connections are not."

"Do you want more on that?"

"If it is possible, yes. If not, I can work with what is here."

I threw out more commands to the demon, eager to get out of there and think on my next moves. When I was done, Callie stepped forward. "Do you want us to send it back?"

"Yes, thanks."

"I will be ready for your next summons, heir," the demon said even as the dual mages started their incantations to send it back to the underworld. I put my hand out for the scroll. Darius passed it over without hesitation, and I unfurled it as the demon disappeared.

"Ink is still there. No trickery yet."

"I must speak with you, Reagan," Darius said softly. "In private."

"Do you have somewhere in mind where the dual mages won't know to follow me? Because there's going to be a fight, and they won't want to let me out of their sight afterward."

"Reagan Somerset," came Callie's low voice filled with warning. "You had better not be thinking what I think you're thinking. That is the very opposite of why your mother spent all those years hiding you. The very opposite. She would be turning over in her grave if she could read your mind right now."

"Told you," I muttered to Darius.

"Reagan, you aren't honestly considering going into the underworld, are you?" Dizzy asked hopefully. "That is a horribly bad idea."

"Horribly bad," Callie said.

"No one could go with you. You'd be on your own. That is quite possibly the most dangerous plan that you could come up with."

"Horribly bad," Callie said again.

I walked from the warehouse to my car, knowing they would follow me. When they did, I paused by my door. "I can't hide anymore. It was fine when everyone thought I was just weird, but now Vlad is interested, not to mention really powerful demons. How much longer do you think I possibly have to live in relative freedom?"

"We just need to get you trained up. Then not even Vlad would be a threat," Callie said stubbornly.

"That level four just taught me how to work my magic more intricately than I have ever done. Level four. And that is with the type of magic I thought I knew. I can't even call the ice magic on command. I don't have time for the training that would help me escape this. You must know that."

"So your plan is to go into the underworld without any knowledge at all?" Callie jammed her fists onto her hips. "At least in the Brink, you have other magical people who can help you. Shelter you."

"And die for that privilege." I laughed sardonically and shook my head. "No. I'm not going to ask people to do that, and I'm not going to hide. It's time to face my fate. I'll sneak in there, find the sect with dirt on me, and kill whoever knows. Then I'll sneak back out. In all honesty, I've had worse plans in my life."

"You've never had a plan worse than that, no." Dizzy picked at his satchel. "In fact, I don't think I've ever heard a worse plan, and I've heard some really bad plans in my day."

"What do you have to say about this, vampire?" Callie demanded, turning to a silent Darius, who was standing to the side.

"I think she will go regardless of your bullying," he said softly, his eyes delving into mine. "And I will go with her."

"You can get through the gates, but you won't be able to go much farther," Callie said. Her expression was imploring me now. "Let's give this a few weeks and think about it, Reagan. Weigh all the options and figure out what we can do."

I sighed and felt a weight settle on my heart. I knew what I had to do. I hated that it would hurt those I loved in the process.

But at least they would live, even if I did not.

"Okay." I sank into the driver's seat of my car. "Two weeks. But I need a few days on my own to let this settle before you start trying to convince me I'm ridiculous."

"Come over to our house when you're ready, Reagan," Dizzy said. "I'll cook you dinner and we can chat. We'll figure this out, just you wait. Callie and I can be pretty resourceful when backed into a corner."

"Okay," I said.

Callie sagged in relief, and I felt more guilt in that moment than I had in years. The dual mages hurried to their car, thinking they had a promise from me.

I hoped I was around to beg forgiveness after this was all through.

CHAPTER 8

"T HAT WAS NECESSARY," Darius said as the dual mages drove away.

"Oh good. I'm taking ethics advice from someone who hoodwinks humans so he can feed off them." I started my car and went to pull my door shut.

Darius was there before I could, catching it. "I would like to speak with you. My residence in the French Quarter?"

"That depends. What do you have to eat?" Since I knew Darius didn't plan to stop me, I figured I might as well let him help where he could. Lord knew I needed someone smarter and savvier than me to help plan this trek into the belly of the beast.

"Anything you want. Shall I surprise you, like usual?"

When it came to food, I'd never received a bad surprise from him. "See you there in a while."

He hesitated. "Do you plan to go straight there?"

"Wow. I didn't peg you for the insecure type." When he didn't move, I grinned. "Yes, darling, I will go straight there. I promise I won't heed the call of the bar and the challenge of catching that danged were-badger."

"You were thinking about it," he said, flashing me a smile.

I laughed and shut my door, because there was no denying it. I needed to take my mind off this awful situation for a while, regardless of whether that was a good idea. Food had a stronger pull, of course, and Darius put on the best spread in town.

"ALL THIS IN under an hour, huh?" I stood in the doorway to his dining room, a large space with a huge table laden with a feast. All the chairs except for two had been removed from the room. This was due to the fact that I had once mentioned the twenty or so empty chairs weirded me out, and could I please eat in the kitchen? That had been just one of the many reasons I'd begged to eat in the kitchen, but it was the only one he'd latched on to. He didn't seem to get that it was the unreal finery of the room that put me off.

"I knew I would be speaking with you tonight," Darius said, holding out his hand to insinuate I should have a seat. "I also knew you would be hungry. I had this prepared in anticipation."

"But how did you know I would come here?" I took off my dirty boots and left them on the rubber mat set out just for me. I slipped into the cozy slippers next to it, also there for me. I'd eaten at Darius's a time or eight since I'd met him. He knew I was afraid to get the cream-colored…everything dirty.

"I didn't. My staff was standing by, waiting for my order. I would've had the meal taken to wherever you were comfortable."

"Crazy," I said, sitting in my chair.

"Crazy amazing, I think you would say." He grinned, and I blinked at him for a few seconds, because when we both let our guards down, I couldn't shrug off how G-D handsome the guy was. A real panty melter.

I blew out a breath and stood with my plate. My lady bits were growling as loudly as my stomach. Waiting around for one of Darius's staff to serve me was not in the cards.

"I will allow you to have your way, this time, as relates to the server." Darius rose and moved to the door. It closed with a soft click.

"Aw, whadda guy." I perused the options.

"But I will not allow you to fill your plate like a peasant." He took the fine china from my hand. "Go sit down and be attended to like a lady should."

"Ladies don't do what they're told. Callie says so. Of course, ladies aren't fools, either." I laughed and did as he said, because why not? If he wanted to wait on me, so be it.

He finished loading my plate with a bit of everything, obviously knowing I wasn't picky when food was handed to me. He placed it in front of me with a small bow.

"Thank you," I said.

He sat gracefully. "May I speak to you regarding our present situation while you eat, or would you rather wait until after?"

I glanced at my empty crystal wine glass. Then looked around for the wine bottle I hoped loitered just out of sight.

"Forgive me." Darius stood smoothly and disappeared from the room. My mouth was full of mashed potatoes when he returned with a bottle of red. "Here you are."

"No cognac for you?" I asked as he finished pouring my wine and sat.

His gaze was deep and open. "Not just now." He paused for a moment, and a surprise wash of tingles raced across my skin. "You didn't answer me earlier. Would you be open to speaking about our situation?"

"Sure." It was hard to swallow. Something in that look, in his open regard and the depth of his gaze, made me want to run. It also made me want to melt into him while he carried me away.

"Yesterday I spent time with one of the oldest vampires I could easily track down." He leaned back, his eyes taking on a keen edge. "She resides in the Realm like a hermit, mostly removed from the rest of my species, and only visits one or two other magical people when she needs to feed—which is not often, given her age."

"Is she much older than you?"

"Yes. A great deal, from what I have heard."

Darius was nearly a grand, a term I used because a thousand years old sounded too ancient to comprehend. So she must've been crazy old. Crazy, silly old. Too old to put numbers to, surely, which was why I didn't ask for specifics.

"Why is she a hermit?" I speared a carrot.

"I did not ask."

Not inquisitive, this vampire. "So what *did* you ask her?"

"How a vampire could travel into the heart of the Dark Kingdom."

I slowed my chewing. He stared at me silently. Clearly he needed prodding to continue. "And did she have an answer? Inquiring minds, and all that."

"Yes. As far as she was concerned, it was simple. Bond a demon."

"Ew. I hope there are some nicer-looking ones than I've seen. Although, if you go after it in monster form, it will be tough to say who is grosser."

"When we bond with another being, we impart some of our vampire traits and strengths to that being, like seeing in the dark, increased speed, things like that. From those we bond, we often get an increased sense of emotion and empathy. If we bond with a stronger species, it has been said that we can last in the sunlight a hair longer. Certainly we can withstand the glow a bit better. Higher-powered demons certainly count as a strong species, and therefore, we are apparently imparted some of their gifts, one of which is the ability to travel across the river."

"If that were true, Vlad would be shacking up with a demon already. Or can he already travel those lands?"

Darius shook his head, watching me closely. "He cannot. While it is not written in our laws, it is socially forbidden to bond a demon. Taboo. This I heard from Ja—"

"Ja?"

"That is the vampire's name." He waited for me to nod before continuing. "I did not even know it could be done. It has been out of favor for so long, I bet only a very few know it is a possibility."

"Why wouldn't that occur to you? Or are there other magical creatures you can't bond?"

He rose and reached for my plate. I scooped up the last morsel of sauce-soaked potato before letting him get me seconds. "I'm sure there are, though I don't know which. I don't know why it didn't occur to me. With such a social stigma, one would think a rebellious sort of vampire would question. But then again, the demons are mostly confined to their world, whether because they want to be, because they are forced to be, or because Lucifer has made it so following an agreement with the elves. Out of sight, out of mind."

"Maybe the idea will cross Vlad's mind eventually," I said, sitting back and rubbing my belly. I was almost full, but I would do my best to have more. Darius really did put on the best dinners in town. And in New Orleans, that was saying something.

"Perhaps. Regardless, the ability to enter the Dark Kingdom is within my grasp. Ja has been there."

I grimaced on his behalf. "Easy-peasy lemon squeezy, except for the fact that you'd have to call a level-five demon, somehow convince it to swap blood, actually swap blood with a gross creature, because it wouldn't be able to stay in human form when giving a lot of blood, and then be bonded to—"

The words died on my lips. A moment later, the moisture dried up in my mouth and reappeared on my forehead…and between my thighs. My heart started to hammer and the fight-or-flight reflex kicked into high gear.

"Stupid me," I whispered, realizing what he meant.

"Yes, Reagan." He set my plate down in front of me, his gaze probing mine. He lingered for just a moment, and I breathed in his spicy, masculine scent tinged with divine cologne. "You were being incredibly dull-witted just now."

I let out a quivering breath as the implications dawned on me. My arousal rose, matching the potency of my need to run really fast out of the room. Then the house. Then the whole dang town.

I had sworn I would never go down this road. Sworn it. Feeling things for a vampire was one thing. Dating him, sharing his bed, spending large quantities of time with him—all of those things were temporary. They ended when I wanted them to. I was in control.

Bonding took the control away. Burned up the temporary status. All the fail safes.

Bonding was forever.

I shook my head, everything in me wanting to back away (except for the distinctly feminine parts, which I worked hard to ignore).

"No," I blurted. "I can't."

"Regardless of the fact that you don't yet know how to use all of your power..." He sat down slowly, his eyes hungry yet soft. Sparkling with lust and emotion. "You are an extremely powerful creature. If you don't rival the elves now, you will when you grow into your birthright. You will impart to me more than the level-five demon that bonded Ja. You can get me into the Dark Kingdom."

"But...I can't."

He entwined his fingers and pushed his chair back so he could cross an ankle over his knee. "I know this frightens you. I also know that if I had a group of mages summon a level-five demon so I could bond with it, you would convince yourself my going with you would be blood on your hands." My eye twitched with the ease of him getting that saying correct. "You would wish to protect me. You'd be long gone by the time I bonded with the creature, and sick with jealousy if—*when* you got back."

I narrowed my eyes at the jealousy comment. I continued to ignore the distinctly feminine parts of me begging for his everlasting kiss, and now the emotional parts that wanted to knife a bitch if she/he/it touched my man.

"Look." I ran my fingers through my hair. "I know you think this is a perfect solution. That you'd gladly go with me in spite of the danger. I know that. But I just can't give myself to you in that way, Darius. While I would gratefully accept your help, I can't in good conscience do it. I'm sorry."

He held up a hand to stop me. I didn't like his calm assurance, like he'd already mapped out this game of chess, and he was waiting for me to make the necessary moves to assure his win.

"Can I present to you my thoughts?" he asked eloquently.

I clenched my jaw. Oh yeah, he had the game mapped, all right.

He ignored my shaking head. "Without me, you will go alone into an extremely dangerous situation that you aren't prepared for."

"I've been alone for a great many dangerous situations," I shot back lamely. We both knew this was vastly different. I wondered if he knew how afraid I was. I hadn't even totally admitted it to myself, besides the fear that my ice magic would take over and eat away my humanity.

His voice softened, as if he *did* know. As if he could read me better than I could read myself. Which was annoying just now. "I realize that you would rather work alone. But we have learned to work together well, have we not? It was a boon to us in Seattle. I have learned when to back off, like with your decision to go into the Dark Kingdom, and when to push, which I won't give you an example of or I will have to develop another tactic."

I quirked my eyebrow at him and earned a gorgeous smile. My expression turned into a glower. Now wasn't the time to flash his handsome at me. Or his charm. When it came to bonding, he was the enemy.

"Your next concern is that the connection will trap you to vampires," he went on. "But you are already trapped. You can't know about the unicorns and expect to go on your merry way. You will be watched for the rest of your life. It is not in my power to release you of that. I know what you'll say." He held up his hand to forestall the argument. "That connection isn't personal. It's business. It's not a bond, but a liability." I nodded, because yes, that was true. Very, very true. "Which is correct," he went on. "However, you and I have already established a deep personal connection."

I tightened my lips, because I was damned if I would admit that.

His teasing smile earned another glower. "Will you not agree?" He paused, saw I would not, and continued. "*Love*, Reagan."

My stomach fluttered and my chest tightened. Warmth overflowed from my heart and burned down to my feet. I could scarcely breathe around the depth of what I felt, triggered by that one word and the emotion soaking through his gaze. By his desire to risk death to follow me into the Dark Kingdom, not wanting to leave my side in my greatest hour of need.

"What I had hoped for has come to pass," he said softly. "For the first time in all of history, I am in love, Reagan. With you."

CHAPTER 9

SPARKLERS WENT OFF in my stomach, and the pull of emotion sucked me under, drowning me. I wiped my forehead of moisture and took a gulp of wine, not sure what to think, not wanting to admit how deeply this was affecting me, let alone the fact that I was undeniably in the same boat.

"You feel it, too," he murmured, "but you do not need to admit it. I mention it merely to prove a point. Right now we wish to be near each other at all times, and when we aren't, we long for our missing halves. We are not whole without each other. If we bond, only our physical selves will be separated when we part. Our hearts and souls will forever be one."

Warmth filled me to the brim, surging through my heart.

"There is no downside to bonding," he said.

There were downsides. I knew there were. I just couldn't think of them right then.

He watched me patiently and finally I came up with a new argument. "But if you die, I'll go crazy, right?

Isn't that what happens?"

It wasn't a great argument, I grant you.

"You'll feel pain, but you would anyway if I were to die. Nothing will change that for you. Nor for me if something were to happen to you. We are currently bonded with love, a more powerful connection than a mere blood bond. For you and me, bonding will make what we already have much sweeter."

A tear overflowed from my eye. I blinked the others away.

"I told myself I absolutely would not do this," I reminded myself. The last holdout before letting this surging emotion consume me. "I would not."

"And if it weren't to help you in the most dangerous endeavor of your life, I would not push as I am now. This past month I have been content to keep things as they were. As you wanted them. Love is extremely powerful. I had no idea. It is unlike anything I have ever felt. I would bend the worlds to make you happy, *mon ange,* and my not mentioning my desire to take our connection one step farther was a small price to pay for your smiles.

"But things have changed. You cannot go into the Dark Kingdom alone, Reagan. You will be putting yourself into the hands of those who wish to use you. And if by some miracle you happen upon a sect of demons that only wishes to turn you over to Lucifer, you will still be trapped down there for as long as your father chooses. You need help, and though I will not be nearly enough, I am the only one in a position to provide it."

I cleared my throat and wiped away another tear. The man was smooth, sexy, and deep. I'd never stood a chance where it concerned him. I doubted there was anyone who could resist him. "I can't believe I am actually asking this, but what is involved in bonding?"

"It takes six days. Five days of feeding from each other, and the last for the connection to finish taking root."

Damn the tears! Why wouldn't they stop? And why did I have a sudden, devastating need for my mother to know this man, followed by the soul-crushing realization that she never would...

"That's it?" I asked weakly. "Feeding from each other?"

His eyes stayed rooted to mine. It was the most intimate moment I'd ever experienced. "Each night, I will deplete you nearly to your threshold, past your tolerance."

I struggled to get myself under control. "What do you mean, my tolerance?"

"When a vampire takes enough blood to deplete a person to the brink of death, what we call the threshold, the person will do one of two things. They will either succumb and die, or—if their survival instinct is at all reasonable—they will try to fight off the predator. This is why vampires have heightened strength. If our prey fights, we can easily overpower them. You, however, are not prey. And you are extremely dangerous, even to me. When your survival instinct kicks in, you will want to kill me. And you will most likely be able to."

"And yet you still want to bond me," I whispered.

"With great risk comes great reward." He threw me that mouthwatering smile. Foul play. "You have nearly killed me before, most recently in the warehouse the other day, and yet you always pull back at the last moment. Your compassion will overcome your rage."

"You've admitting to taking too much of my blood a couple of times," I said. "But I didn't flip out. Or even notice."

"Even at those times, and there were three, I was nowhere near your threshold. And no, before you ask, I don't know what your threshold is. I don't know when the pleasure will cease and the fear turned aggression will start. We'll find that out together."

I traced the base of my wine glass, breaking eye contact. "After I am nearly drained dry, and obviously weak, then what?"

"You feed from me to revive yourself. After that, we make love or sleep, depending on how we feel, and wake up to do it all over again."

"That's it? Swap blood, sex, sleep, and lie in bed? Do people bring cards or something? Surely that has to get boring after a while."

He gave me a small smile, but didn't comment.

I shook my head and had a sudden urge to shove my plate away. Maybe even surge to my feet, knocking over my chair. Turn over the table. Kick down the door. Stain the cream rug.

"I can't." I was back to that again. That was all I had. My very last holdout, other than hiding in a closet under a blanket while rocking back and forth. "I can't. My mother would be so disappointed in me."

"I imagine she would rather you bond me and have someone to protect you in the underworld than for you to go down there alone."

"She would rather I didn't go at all."

"Precisely, but you will go anyway."

Yes, I would.

The need for my mom to know Darius surged again, drowning me. It wasn't the reaction I'd expected to have when faced with this situation.

"Okay," I said, turning my face away. I couldn't believe I was agreeing to it, and knew absolutely it wasn't because of the desire for someone to go with me. It was because of him. "Okay. Please don't make me regret it."

"I would never. You are the most precious thing in the world to me. I would never tarnish that. Not for anything."

We would see, but the decision was made.

I was a fool.

"When?" I asked so quietly that the word barely left my mouth.

"Tonight. Now. We have little time to lose. I suspect only this sect's commanders or leaders know the sensitive information about you, but as they develop plans to go to the surface and capture you, they will need to share the information. We need to get in there before that happens. You should know that I also spoke with Ja at length about the nature of the underworld. And while many things could have changed, the magic probably won't have. I am as prepared as I can be."

I nodded with my heart in my throat. That would be very comforting information later, I was sure, but right now, I couldn't think about anything other than what I was about to do. It had happened so suddenly. Given how opposed I'd been to the very notion, I'd agreed so easily.

Are you sure, Reagan?

I wanted to say no to myself. To change my mind. But I knew the answer was *yes*. I wanted him every bit as much as he wanted me. I felt as deeply as he did.

He stood, extending his hand. "Come."

"I'd be careful with the commands, if I were you. I'm not one of those docile bond-mates you've probably heard about."

His laugh eased my nerves. "I am well aware. I would not be pleased if you were."

"What about formal approval?" I asked as he led me to the door. "Don't you have to get a green light from someone?"

"The paperwork has been submitted, but there is no time to wait for a decision. Besides, you will easily be approved. It is just a formality at this point."

He opened the door and stepped out. "Mr. LaRay," he called.

"Yes, sir," came Moss's voice.

"Is the country estate ready?"

"Of course, sir."

"Good. We will head there now."

"Which car would you like?"

"The Hennessey."

"Yes, sir."

"And Mr. LaRay?" Darius said.

"Yes, sir?"

"I do not want us disturbed. Post sentries. No one goes into that house while we are there."

"You will remain in the Brink for this, sir?" Moss asked in a low tone.

"Yes. There is nowhere else. We cannot go to the lair and risk someone finding out."

"That doesn't sound like *just a formality* to me," I

mumbled.

"I will see it done. Good luck, sir," Moss said, his voice moving away.

"Neither does that…" I frowned hard at Darius when he turned toward me. "It sounds an awful lot like you are going rogue, Darius."

"It does, doesn't it? Have no fear. This is all just a precaution." He held out his hand to me. "Let's get moving. We are running out of night."

I found myself jogging toward him, the worry at what I was walking into overshadowed by his anxiety to get moving. He was acting like we were criminals with cops on our heels.

The car out front took my breath away. Sleek, gray, and squashed like a giant had stepped on a normal car, flattening it. The thing screamed *fast*.

"Wow," I said, pausing on the sidewalk. "Can I drive?"

"Not on your life. Please hurry, my love."

The urgency in Darius's voice started me forward. Moss climbed out of the driver's side and left the door open.

"Oh, but he gets to drive it, does he?" I couldn't help sounding like a petulant child.

Moss must've sensed the extent of my pining, because he smirked at me, the jerk. Darius had already opened the passenger door for me.

"What about all my stuff? Will we pick that up later?" I asked, sitting on the passenger seat. He'd used his vampire speed to get situated on the driver's side. "And I need to leave an apology note for Callie and Dizzy."

Darius threw it in gear, and the tires chirped as we launched forward.

"I've made preparations. The supplies will be brought to us. We'll have to travel light." Of course he had. Stupid question. "As far as the note, you can write it at the estate and have Moss deliver it. I have also arranged for unicorn blood. You can only take it a certain number of times before it will negatively affect you..."

His words drifted away as a need to have unicorn blood *right then* rose in me, the effect of taking it only once. I pushed it down, realizing he'd stopped talking. "I'm not sure that's a good idea. I'll grow dependent on it, won't I?" It was the most potent of drugs, capable of boosting energy and magical ability. It was also incredibly addictive for everyone other than vampires. The vampires protected the unicorns, whose blood they used in the serum to make new vampires—it was a symbiotic relationship.

"Not after you bond me. My blood will prevent the physical craving. You will be responsible for the mental craving, however. That will be mind over matter, as they say. I will work to take your mind off it."

My body and face lit up with heat. I breathed out slowly, not trusting my voice.

A THRILLING HOUR of very fast driving later, we turned into a small driveway and crept toward a massive plantation house with a walkway leading through huge oak trees weeping moss. We drove around the side to a much newer structure that had been built some ways from the main house.

"Is that a five-car garage?" I asked. "Why do you need all these cars, anyway? You're driven around by Moss eight or nine times out of ten."

"When I purchase collectible cars, I need somewhere outside of the city to store them until I can arrange for shipment to a milder location, weather-wise."

"You have a lot of collectible cars, then?"

"Yes. I have a lot of collectible everything. Every one item that holds its value far outweighs the three or four that don't."

"That's where your fortune comes from, then?" I waited until he parked in the empty garage before climbing out. He must've recently sent out a shipment.

"One of the many places. I have my hands in many pots, which ensures I will monetarily survive things like stock market crashes and great depressions. I also take care to establish the brightest of my children, setting them up for long-term success."

"How does that help you?"

Darius guided me out of the garage by the small of my back before closing the door. The trees swayed in the gentle breeze as we made our way to the gorgeous three-story house. Butterflies surged in my stomach. I was actually doing this. I was tying myself to a vampire—*this* vampire—forever.

Shouldn't I be scared or horrified instead of nervous?

"I get a percentage of my children's earnings," he said, rubbing my back. He probably noticed my stiff walking and constant fidgeting.

"Like a mob boss?"

He frowned at me. "I couldn't say. I have not looked at a mob boss's books."

"So you get a percentage of that nice hotel in Seattle?"

"Yes. The idea is that we will put greater care and attention into training our children and helping them flourish if there is a financial benefit. This helps our whole faction."

"And those who aren't bright?"

"Survival of the fittest doesn't just apply to humans. Dimwitted vampires rarely make it out of adolescence."

"Ah." I stepped onto the wide wraparound porch that looked perfectly restored.

He waved his hand to unlock the door, a vampire's most useful party trick, before pushing it open and stepping back so I could enter. I breathed deeply, trying to still the tremors of my body as desire unfurled within my middle.

"When did you purchase this?" I asked, needing sound. Needing trivial conversation. Suddenly Madonna's "Like a Virgin" had a whole different vibe.

"Some five years ago now." He led me to the right, into a decent-sized sitting room—well, decent compared to his French Quarter house, huge compared to anywhere else. "This was the women's drawing room after they'd eaten." Back across the entryway we landed into another sitting room of a similar size. "The men's, where they smoked and drank. Would you like to sit for a moment? Have a glass of wine?"

His hand curled around my side before applying pressure, pulling me nearer. I leaned against his hard body, soaking in his heat.

"If you'd like," I said in a breathy whisper.

"Which room would you prefer?" He bent to me, running his lips across mine.

Electricity ran between us, spicy and hot. I opened my mouth to him. He teased my tongue with his and his taste exploded in my senses. The smell and feel of him sent shock waves of pleasure through my body. I moaned, clutching tightly.

He swooped me up into his arms before leaving the room, signaling the end of the tour. No more relaxing or getting used to the idea. It was happening, *right now,* and suddenly I couldn't wait.

CHAPTER 10

H E CARRIED ME into a large room at the top of the stairs and put me down next to the bed. A beautiful silk chemise lay across the duvet. It tumbled to the ground in a shower of silk and lace when he pulled back the covers. No sooner had my feet hit the ground than my fingers were at his buttons. His hands tangled in my hair, stripped off my clothes. Urgency overcame me, dissipating my ability to feel nervous. I was nowhere near scared.

He threw me up onto the bed before crawling between my legs. "I love how you lose yourself to me, Reagan," he murmured. I sighed in delight as his body entered mine. "But when the fear of death is upon you, remember that I would never hurt you. Remember to trust me."

He began moving, slow and sensual, hitting all the glorious places within. His lips slid across mine, making my eyes flutter closed and my body coil with need. Together we moved, the sensations overwhelming.

"Here we go, my dearest. I love you."

His bite made me suck air through my teeth. "Holy sh—" I arched back, lost to the feeling. No matter how many times I had felt this sensation, which was a great many at that point, it was always so fantastically overwhelming that I couldn't think.

The draw on my neck had me wrapping my arms more tightly around his muscular shoulders. I squeezed his hips with my thighs, pulling to get him closer. Deeper. The bed thumped against the wall to his rhythm, fast now, my body so tight I couldn't stand it.

A wave of pleasure washed over me, making me shake beneath him. He shuddered a moment later, but his mouth didn't come away from my neck. Instead, he continued to suck, taking more.

Immediately, I began to build again, this situation having happened in the past. Those other times—three, he had said—he'd tried to pull back. Forced himself to slow. This time, though, his suction increased, if anything. Pulling with everything he had.

Another orgasm washed over me, dragging me under. I focused on that pull, on his hot mouth taking more from me. On his body still going, his shudder of release not stopping him. Another climax. Then another. They were coming right on top of each other now. I was probably screaming, or moaning like a banshee, but I couldn't be bothered to care. Wave after glorious wave of pleasure pounded into me even as he did, each movement better than anything in the world. Vibrating through the fibers of my being.

Like a crack of lightning, a shock of fear hit me, so strong I stopped breathing. My ice magic flooded me, overriding the fog of pleasure and restoring my thoughts to crystal clarity. My fire swirled around it a moment later, the ink-in-water situation, mixed but not fused.

Air condensed around Darius, pulling him off my body. Fire swirled between us. Floated around the room. Frost coated the windows.

"We have found your threshold, my love," he said softly, hovering above me. A smile spread across his face. "Look at how powerful you are. I doubt anyone has ever bonded someone such as you. I am the luckiest man alive." A crimson drop fell from his full bottom lip and onto my skin. For some reason, it calmed me.

I cut out the fire and gently lowered him back to my body. Back between my legs. "Oops, my bad."

"I think, for you, that feeling will get worse." He kissed me softly. "I had hoped to power through it, but I see now that that will be impossible. You'd throw me out the window without meaning to."

"Why are you taking such joy in my crazy?"

"Because I know that you will allow me to do this based on your regard for me. No one else would be able to. You'd kill them long before they could complete the first draining."

"Why you, Darius?" I asked. "Why us? You've said it a million times—this shouldn't be possible. You shouldn't be able to love anyone, let alone a prickly girl scared of loving you back. And, as said prickly girl, I should die alone with ten cats. I've tried everything not to feel this way about you." I still stopped short of using the L-word. "To ignore the effect you have on me, which is more than just fantastic bed mambo and pretty awesome vampire serum. It's you, the man at the root of the vampire. I shouldn't even be able to find him."

"I don't know," he said, staring into my eyes, "but I'm past asking for reasons. I am now allowing the feeling to seep into every part of my soul—and accepting it for the gift it truly is. So many vampires would kill to feel like I do. To reconnect with their humanity. I get that ability, and I will not shy away from it. Not anymore."

I just sighed and hugged him close, because *I* wasn't beyond asking for reasons. Everything in my person, in my past, said not to trust vampires, especially elder vampires. Yet here I was, doing just that. It had to be a recipe for disaster. *Had* to be. I wasn't lucky enough to find love, let alone get to keep it. My life wouldn't allow it.

"Go slow and I'll run interference with my magic." I slid my thighs up his hips.

"Here we go again." He slowly thrust forward. My eyes fluttered closed.

The pull on my neck wasn't as glorious as normal.

"Can you boost the effect of the serum?" I asked.

"It is as potent as I can make it." He pulled again, greedy.

My fingers tightened on his shoulders and I struggled for clarity.

He wasn't being greedy; he was actually being gentler than normal.

Another pull and I tore my hands away from his body and gripped the bed, clenching it to prevent from doing something crazy. It felt like he was killing me. Murdering me.

The suck felt sickly now, dangerous. "Pull out, Darius," I commanded as I turned my face away and put my energy into lifting the bed off the ground. It wasn't nearly as hard as it should be. "Pull out of me. This has taken a turn for the worse."

He did so without hesitation, but kept sucking, draining my life away. The bed wobbled with each pull, my energy sapping.

I squeezed my eyes shut and flexed each muscle, feeling his hardness against me and wanting it in me— and also wanting to rip it off and beat him to death with it.

"Definitely taken a turn for the worse. How much

longer?" I panted like a dog in the sun.

His answer was to keep sucking, unmoving while he did so. He must've known I was on the edge.

I hummed a little tune as more power flooded me, coming from who knew where. It filled each crevice, eating away the haze from blood loss. Eating away my worry and guilt. All the tense lines of my life smoothed. I was confident I wouldn't die. Without blood, air, food, water—everything—I still wouldn't die.

Superman complex, had to be.

I love you, mon ange, he thought.

The ice magic had kicked in enough that I was reading thoughts. This was usually where the uncontrollable rage roared to life, but I didn't feel it. Instead, I felt a deeper emotion, pulsing way down, in a place I'd sealed up after my mom had died. A place no man had ever occupied before. A squishy, emotional place that filled my body with warmth and light.

Love.

Just like that, I turned a corner. I wasn't a girl who did things by halves. Dying or not, I was going to run at this like I ran at danger. With a snarl turned smile and the refusal to be bested.

I pulled us off the bed and repositioned us so he was sitting in midair and I was straddling him. As soon as he was once again inside me, I threw my arms around him, laid my head on his shoulder, and went for it. He answered by squeezing me tightly and thrusting harder. Faster. Almost immediately, the orgasms resumed, smashing into and through me one after the other, not human and almost unbearable. I held on for dear life, not even having to focus on keeping us in the air. Power pumped into me, like I'd opened a floodgate. He shuddered as much as I did.

My fingers started to tingle. So did my toes. No haze overcame me, though. No lightheadedness or dizziness from blood loss. When Darius pulled his head away with a gasp of air and a flash of bloodstained fangs, I lifted my head to look him directly in the eyes.

A crease formed between his brows. He didn't say anything. But then, he didn't have to.

What is happening? he thought. *Does she not need blood to survive?*

"Remember that I can hear you. As far as what's happening...I probably do need blood, but I think my demonic side is overriding my human side right now. I'd probably die before I admitted I was dying, because I'm pretty sure demons need blood, too."

His eyes dipped to my lips. He kissed me passionately. "You are like a puzzle. What fun I will have figuring you out."

"Right. I'll just put us down now, and we can move on to what's next."

The bed bumped off the floor right before we

bumped onto the bed. I was pretty impressed with my own soft landing.

Is your magic receding?

"Not yet. You can use words, though, so I don't feel like I'm intruding."

You are not intruding. If I don't wish you to hear my thoughts, I simply won't think them. How fortunate for me not to have to waste energy moving my lips.

That was one way of looking at things. I doubted Callie and Dizzy would agree. That was, if they ever forgave me and deigned to speak to me again.

Assuming I made it out of the underworld at all.

"I still need to send Callie and Dizzy a note," I said, feeling the pang of guilt.

We will arrange it when we wake up.

"Talk normally, please. As a favor. Hearing you without actually hearing you is weird."

"If you wish." He ran his thumb along my chin. "Now you must take my blood. Normally, I would advise you to take as much as you wanted, but...I worry that might be foolish. So I must ask you to stop taking blood when I tap you. Or resist you. Or, in dire circumstances, attack you."

"Fair enough. What's good for the goose is good for the vampire." I glanced at his neck, then his wrist, then his muscular body and erect manhood. "It amazes me that you never seem to get tired."

"It is your blood. It acts like human crack. Or speed. Honestly, I'm not sure what the difference in effect is between those drugs. I haven't bothered to research it."

"Your pillow talk is sure something." Part of me wanted to bend down to the distinctly male part of him, but I figured I should get some blood in me before I passed out. I was probably on fumes and didn't know it. "I don't want to rip into your neck like a wild animal, so can you make a cut with a claw or something?"

"Where?" A claw extended from his pointer finger. Just one.

"Impressive."

"Your blood gives me greater control. It has since I first consumed it. I wonder what bonding will bring me. And which of my strengths will come to you."

I tapped the wrist of his other hand and he made a small slice. Blood welled up out of the gash.

"Ew. I'm not really into this. Hang on while I try to push the magic away. If I'm on the verge of death, I'll probably like doing this more." I squeezed my eyes shut and focused, pushing at the power pumping through the shell of my body. It wouldn't go anywhere. Both types of magic were pumped up and didn't want to leave.

I tried again when skin bumped against my lips. Without thinking, I latched on to his wrist with my hands and mouth, sucking like my life depended on it.

Just like last time I'd taken his blood, power surged through me, adding to what was already there. His heartbeat pounded in my ears. His skin against mine felt like velvet.

I moaned, both from our friction and the taste of him. The feel of his blood as it boosted my magic. My life force sang inside me, lifting me up. My hair felt like it was standing on end, and my stomach filled with butterflies.

I felt the tap but didn't want to stop. The climaxes had started again, and I was riding them all the way to Happy Town.

A harder tap hit my thigh.

I need to stop.

But my body wouldn't listen. The taste curled my toes. The feel of him, all of him, put me into a state of euphoria that I never wanted to let go.

I was flying through the air before I knew what had happened. I had time to blink twice before I hit the wall and fell to the ground. My head bounced off the floor.

"Ouch." I lay there for a moment, because I was still shivering in climax. Still. After being thrown across the room. "That's a good time."

My legs wobbled as I picked myself up and went back to the bed. Darius pulled the blanket over him and turned onto his side, holding it up for me to slip into the hollow of his body.

"Now we sleep, then we wake up and do it again?" I asked as I crawled in next to him.

"Yes. The sensations are supposed to get more intense as the days go by, which is why the sixth day is to recover and let the bond finish taking root."

"The sensations will get stronger?" I looked at the dent in the wall. "Let's hope my urge to kill you doesn't."

CHAPTER 11

I LAY LIKE a zombie, staring up at the ceiling. Darius lay next to me, also not moving.

It was day seven and I hadn't spoken for thirty-six hours. I'd lost my voice during day five from all the screaming and had no idea if it had come back yet. Darius was in the same condition. Guy code might've said they didn't scream, but bonding code held no such reservations.

Part of me never wanted to do that again; another part wanted to do it at least once a year. I thought I'd die from pleasure if it happened more than once *per day*. Actually die. It was that intense.

We should get up, Darius thought. He hadn't spoken out loud, other than the ululations of lovemaking, since day three. My power hadn't receded, so I could hear him just fine. *It is time to get going.*

I felt his heart beating deep down, like a slow, comforting clock keeping time. I felt connected to him in a way that couldn't be explained. Like our souls were holding hands. I didn't feel his emotions, like I had thought I would, just the ease of knowing we were together. I felt responsible for him, deeply in love with him, and a pure light originating from inside because of him.

He'd been right. It had just strengthened what we already had. We might physically be apart in the future, but we would never be separated, something that would totally suck if our relationship went south.

Call me Mrs. Glass-half-empty. Or practical; take your pick.

"Yeah." My voice had returned to hoarse and scratchy, like on day three, but at least it worked. "I might walk bowlegged. Don't make fun of me. It's your fault."

I have heard that bonding is intense and enjoyable, but that seemed excessive.

I laughed and thought about rolling toward the edge of the bed.

Come, we need to go. He didn't move.

"Who are you trying to convince, me or you?"

My body does not want to obey my head's commands.

"Are you sure it's supposed to be six days instead of seven? Because it certainly doesn't feel like we should be running around at this point. I'm still exhausted."

His body wiggled a little. *I can do this.* Finally he rolled to his side before swinging his feet over the edge.

I followed suit, hating every minute of it. I wanted to lose the entire month to him, lying in bed and reveling in his perfect body. He'd ruined my sense of reason. Absolutely destroyed it. I was not thinking rationally anymore. Callie would kill me.

A shot of adrenaline had me surging to my feet. "Callie and Dizzy!" My legs gave out and I fell to the ground. "Dang it, my legs are not obeying." I crawled to the wall and climbed to my feet. A bit dramatic, but man, I was sore and tired. "Oh my God, how could I have forgotten to leave them a note? They'll think I disappeared off the face of the earth."

I pulled on my clothes and weapons and scooped my pouch off the ground. I dug out my phone. It had probably long since died, so I looked around frantically for a charger. The least I could do was text them.

"Moss will have seen to that," Darius said, coming around the bed and placing a comforting hand on my shoulder. "I gave him instructions to pick up a letter from you and deliver it to them. I had thought we'd spend some time getting you comfortable with the next steps before initiating the bonding. There were a few things I wanted to do. As usual, of course, you unraveled my plans. He will have seen to it in our absence."

"I hope he didn't try to sign my name to it, because there is no way he could mimic me. They'll know something is up."

Darius went still for a moment. "You can send another before we leave."

I took a deep breath. "Do you have a charger?"

He glanced at my phone. "For that relic? No. We'll get you a new phone."

"Just because I bonded you—" I had to stop myself for a moment. A rush of butterflies and inner girlie squealing blotted out all thought. I tried again. "Just because I—" I gritted my teeth, because this was getting ridiculous. "—doesn't mean I want you to buy me a bunch of stuff. This phone is fine. I just need a charger."

Two backpacks, a satchel, and a new, larger pouch awaited us downstairs, along with a new set of clothes and a handwritten note. Darius took up the note as I riffled through the backpacks. Each contained a scaly sort of suit made out of stressed leather and patches of hard material, rope, a Swiss Army knife, and other survival tools. Darius's pack, the one with the larger suit, contained a lighter. Mine did not.

Moss was nothing if not thorough.

Within my new pouch was a color-coded array of spells, and a piece of paper identifying what they all were.

Extremely thorough.

I dropped my hand with the paper in it so I could see how much of the information stuck. "Oh crap."

"What is it?" Darius asked, now looking through the

backpacks.

I felt my eyes widen as I lifted the paper again. "I read the paper, looked away, and I remembered every detail. Holy crap." I smiled. "That is awesome! Totally cheating at life with humans, but awesome."

"You're welcome." His lips tweaked into a grin.

"Well, you'll get to walk around the depths of hell with a bunch of horribly ugly creatures that want to do you harm. So *you're* welcome." I strapped the pouch around my waist as my stomach growled. My brow crumpled. "I haven't eaten since we started the bonding. Is that normal?"

"For humans, no. For you? Who's to say? That raises a good question, though. Do you need to eat? Demons do not, so I don't assume there will be any restaurants down there."

"If I didn't need to eat for the last week, then…"

He nodded like he thought that was the case. "It will probably be extremely uncomfortable for you for the first few days. You will probably feel hunger again now that the bonding is no longer distracting you. There will be other physical discomforts. You'll want to breathe, but there will be no air in places. Your thirst will go unquenched. To top it off, you'll miss the sun."

I huffed out a laugh. "Of all the things you listed, I can handle no sun."

"For a while, yes. But mark my words, you'll notice

its absence."

I nodded, since he would know, and thought about raiding the kitchen for one last meal. Instead, since I should probably start the torture now so I could get used to it faster, I looked around for paper and a pen.

"Moss did not sign your name to the letter," Darius said, slipping on his backpack. He nodded toward the note lying on the couch. "He kept it vague, telling them that you were sorry and making it clear that you would have written yourself if you'd had the opportunity."

"He didn't mention why I was unable, did he?"

"Just that you had to start your journey." I stopped my search for writing implements, but my relief was short-lived. "You will need to tell them eventually," he continued. "What we have will never go away, Reagan. You will be my darling for all of eternity, traveling the world by my side. We are one, you and I. They will catch on eventually."

"Let's just slow down with the dramatics, shall we? And 'darling' is something that can go, that's for sure." I pulled my hair up in a ponytail. "I think I liked you better when you thought I was a nuisance."

"That is fear talking."

"Pretty soon it will be violence talking, so you have that to look forward to."

I looked back and forth between my older pouch and the new one. There was really no need to keep the old one, as beat up as it was, but it had been with me through a lot. I was a little sentimental. Besides, if something happened to the new one…

I emptied the older pouch of used casings and the few intact spells and stuffed it into my backpack. The pinch of hunger was starting to be a problem. Already. Though after a week, it probably should've been way worse. It was probably a mental issue.

"Are we waiting for something?" I asked, hefting my backpack. "And what does the suit do?"

Darius zipped up his backpack and slung it over his shoulders. "Let's go. I'll explain the suits at another time."

"I assume you know how to get into the under-world? I also assume it is nighttime out right now?"

"There is a gate into the Realm not far from here. We will enter that and head to one of the entrances to the underworld. From there, we will hope the demon's map is correct."

"I wonder if Callie and Dizzy called that demon again." I let him direct me out of the front door. A shape moved off to the right, almost imperceptible. It took me a moment to realize two things. One was that the shape was indistinct because it had one of those camouflaged sheets over it, and I had noticed it anyway. The other was that my vision was crystal clear, better than my sight in daylight. The difference was like that between watching an HD TV versus a TV made twenty years before.

"A great memory, and better night vision. Awesome. And all you got was a key into hell." I shook my head. "Sucks to be you."

"I have received boons from you, I have no doubt. They will be revealed in time."

I grimaced. I sure hoped so, for his sake.

"Shall we?" He started to jog, not worried about the lurkers, which meant he employed them. I kept up easily. When he sped up, so did I. Even faster, and I still kept pace. It wasn't until he was at his top speed that I flagged. I was faster than before by far, but still not as fast as him.

One thing I hadn't gotten was enhanced hearing. The words coming from his moving lips were caught by the wind and thrown away.

"Huh?" I yelled.

You do not need to shout. I can hear you just fine.

"Right. Sorry."

Some of your enhanced traits might be the effect of your greater access to your power. I assume it still rages as it has been?

"Still powerful, yes. Both types, almost equally. You had the right idea in our practice sessions about getting me to the place where I thought I would die. It started when I thought you would kill me during the bonding."

And your ability to work them? Do you feel just as dexterous?

"Not really, no. When I'm not thinking, and just *wanting* something, usually it happens. When I try to consciously re-create that, I can't. None of it is complex, though. Not like that demon did."

You are an apt pupil. You simply need a worthy teacher.

It was a little late for that. I would have to just try my best and hope I didn't die. Or worse, get captured.

CHAPTER 12

T HE WHITE ZIGZAG line cut through the air above a small berm in a field. Darius stopped in front of it before shooting me a sideways glance.

"I will use words until I find it imprudent for me to do so," he said.

"Sounds good. Do you want to go first?" I gestured at the gate to the Realm, the world solely inhabited by magical people.

"There is an echo of you having just been at the plantation house."

"I don't know what that means."

"An echo from you, letting me know where you have just come from. Some level-five demons have that ability—to know where someone has been moments before. The trait has been noted in a few exorcisms. It is not a vampire trait. It must've come from you."

"It clearly didn't, because I've never heard any echoes."

"Yes. I wonder why." He tightened his backpack. "This ability might be extremely useful."

"It sure would've been when I was a bounty hunter. I wonder if you can shut it off, though. Most times it'll be an annoyance. Like, why would you want to know someone just came from the restroom?"

His glance this time showed confusion. Clearly he hadn't thought of that. Or else he was wondering why it had been my first thought.

"We can go through together." He held out his hand and I took it. "There should be no danger on the other side."

Should was the operative word.

The tear in the worlds whipped at us as we passed through it. With the amount of magic we were packing, the crossing was easy. On the other side, Darius checked his satchel. I tapped my various weapons to make sure all was ready.

I glanced up at the burnt-orange sky, then moved my hand through the air, watching the dancing filaments of gold swirl around my fingers. A bench sat off to the side for those who could barely make the crossing and had to sit down and rest afterward. Fragrant flowers of pink and yellow crowded around it, outlining a clean cobblestone walkway.

"We will walk through the Realm. I don't want to raise suspicion by hurrying. I don't want to be stopped." Darius didn't let go of my hand as he started forward.

"Who is going to stop us, number one, and two,

don't you think a vampire holding a girl's hand will raise suspicion?"

"The elves would take interest in an elder hurrying." He dropped my hand. "And yes, you are correct. It seems I have lost my wits in regards to you."

"I know how you feel." My power surged and blossomed, opening up and dancing a jig. My skin felt stretched, like it could barely contain it. "The Realm always helps my power."

"Yes. Magical people are always stronger here. If not for your unique situation, I would advise you to spend as much time in this world as possible to develop your power."

"We'll probably realize that's also true of the underworld," I said with a little shudder.

"Indeed." Darius chose the way, clearly knowing where he was going.

"You've heard what we're walking into. Is this a world Lucifer created, or just embellished, do you think?" I figured I should stop calling him Father. All I needed was for one nosy parker to overhear and spread a rumor.

"Embellished. Much like the elves are constantly doing within the Realm."

"Only the elves? No one else tries to magic up their homes?"

"Their actual residences, sure. But the elves are

similar to the Brink government—they fix the streets, the travel ways, and public places like the gates. For their trouble, they're paid taxes. Even if a being wanted to do large improvements, magical or otherwise, they would need to petition the elves to do so. When I arranged for the addition on your house, I had to get permits from the city. It is the same within the Realm."

"Huh. But the elves weren't elected to that post. Or do I have that wrong?"

"They are the ruling party, yes. Like monarchs, their power is passed down through birth. Originally, they fought for their authority; every so often there is a bloody war to usurp them. The last was about five hundred years ago. So far, no one has succeeded. They have the allegiance of the fae, and the elementals, not to mention other such magical creatures to aid their cause."

"Like the shifters?" I grinned as his lips thinned. "That's an awfully long time to go without being challenged."

"Indeed. There is no such democracy in the Realm, and the lack thereof is starting to be noticed."

"Then a war is brewing." I paused just before the magical fog.

"It seems that way, yes. And our goal is not to set it in motion." He must've caught my staring. "As we walk through, keep your focus forward and don't make eye contact with other beings."

That was easier said than done. Not having spent much time in the Realm, I often saw creatures that surprised me with their appearance or their abilities. The first time I saw a faerie, for example, I gawked something awful and followed her around, staring. She was about a quarter my height, really super pretty, flying, and so closely resembled Tinker Bell from *Peter Pan* that I figured a magical person must've created that children's story. She even shed a reddish sort of dust as she flew.

Another time, I made eye contact with a half-man, half-bull-looking dude. That pissed him off something fierce. He got the idea that we needed to fight it out. I was more than willing, of course. Because really, when didn't I want to rumble? He started his charge, but when I started forward to meet him halfway, he lost interest at the last moment, content to huff at me and wander away. I didn't know what his deal was, but it should've reminded me that it wasn't polite to stare. The lesson hadn't stuck, of course. I was the worst.

Darius likely knew that, and maybe it was a small part of his motivation for choosing a fast track, one of the magical paths in the realm that seriously shortened a person's travel time. The land beside us flashed by even though we were walking. Cute little dwellings came and went, a large community off to the right. To the left were fields growing rows of a plant I didn't recognize.

My stomach growled.

Almost there, Darius thought, picking up the pace.

"Can you feel my hunger or something?"

I heard it. Now you will dwell on it, and that will be painful.

He knew me too well.

It was night, but shadows still fell across the path, magically created, casting it into more darkness. The colorful flowers beside the path lost their vibrancy and began to wilt, and a couple of supercharged steps later there were large holes in their rows that screamed *death.* The farming community disappeared, as did the lush green fields. There was barren land on both sides, deep pockets of black pooled in hollows.

"Well, there goes the neighborhood."

As I said, we are close now.

I didn't like the look of this. It looked exactly as I had feared it would, and we weren't even there yet.

Great boulders rose on either side of the path, jagged and blackened with fire. The temperature dropped, though the Realm was known for always being the perfect temperature for everyone. The burnt orange of the night sky darkened until it was almost black. That didn't bother me, since I was used to it in the Brink, but the lack of stars was suffocating. Like a cover had been thrown over the world, snuffing out all the light.

Up ahead, over the massive rocks, rose a giant metal trellis. Words twisted through the scrollwork, but I couldn't read them. We moved another step closer, and I saw a jagged line in the air, this one black and surrounded in blood red fire.

To get through this tear in the worlds, you must have a certain type of magic, Darius thought. *Vampires have it. Trolls, gargoyles, and a handful of other creatures do, too. They are welcome in the edges, the outskirts of the Dark Kingdom.*

"Why would they want to go in there?" I whispered.

Trade. Communicating. Buying goods. Staying out of the elves' kingdom. There are a few reasons, different for each species.

"Shifters?"

Cannot go through.

"Elves?"

Of course, but they almost never do. They have their reasons, one of them being that they don't want to intrude upon Lucifer's territory. Just as they don't want him intruding upon theirs unless he is expressly invited. That is the reason Vlad is trying to recruit Lucifer—he stands equal to the elves in might and power. Lucifer would greatly increase Vlad's chances of overthrowing the elves' rule. Come, let's get ready. Our real journey is about to begin.

Darius glanced behind him while unslinging the backpack. In the distance, walking toward us, was a large creature with horns twisting up from its head.

"Is there anywhere else it could be going?" I asked as I unslung my backpack. I followed Darius's lead and took out the scaly leather suit.

You saw yourself. There is nothing much in this direction. No. It will be coming in behind us. We'd best hurry and stay ahead of it so it doesn't get a good look at us.

The leather was lined with a soft material, smooth on the skin. The outfit itself wasn't nearly as stiff as I might have expected, and judging by the material of the scales, and the hum of magical vibration I felt around me, it must've cost a pretty penny. A team of mages had probably made it, though the spells were muffled somehow. I couldn't feel what they were for, and didn't want to prod them too much in case I messed them up.

"Is the collection of spells in this suit necessary? I'm worried my magic will unravel it." I pulled a cap out of the backpack and frowned. It would go over my head and face. After realizing Darius had one too, I shrugged and put it on. It couldn't look much weirder than a human wandering around the underworld.

The silk velvet lining will protect the suit from you, as long as you don't actively try to unravel the spells. The suits are supposed to repel attention, making us invisible.

If a being forces their focus to stay on you—us—the spells woven into the suits will hopefully fool the onlooker into thinking we are demon-type creatures.

"So, they *are* necessary."

I can't say what is or is not necessary. Not without seeing for myself. They might not work down there at all. Ja said magic fluxes. I don't know what to expect.

He knew a lot better than I did. Then again, he was a planner. I usually did just fine flying by the seat of my pants.

I reattached my new pouch, feeling a small twinge of guilt for liking it just as much as—if not maybe a little more than—the older one. The older one was just so scarred and stained. Not to mention the shape was not much better than a lumpy pillow. Poor old pouch.

Are you okay? Darius faced me, his gaze delving into mine.

"Can you feel my emotions?"

Some of them, yes. If they are strong enough. You feel guilty and sad. What is the matter?

"Why can't I feel yours? I'm starting to think I got hosed. Except for the speed and visibility, that is. And the memory. Those are awesome."

His brow furrowed, his eyes and a slice of his forehead the only things visible through his mask. *You seem to be blocking the bond somewhat, as well as some of your powers.* He shook his head. *We can't dwell on that now. We must get underground.*

"Okay. Well." I strapped on my gun and sword. "Let's do it. I'm ready."

Darius nodded and took my arm, walking me forward. He glanced behind us before picking up the pace. As we reached the blood-red fire burning in the air, I felt him hesitate for a brief moment before stepping through.

Prickles of heat and stabs of cold covered my body. A tunnel opened up before us, about ten feet long and surging with fire on all sides. Pulsing through the middle, attached at the top, were icicles, the points glistening and sharp, extending and retracting.

"Don't come through here; we get it." I stuck out my hand to touch the fire. The sweet heat glanced off my skin in a familiar way. "I wouldn't touch that—"

I cut off the words as Darius ran his hand through the fire. His lips tweaked, threatening a smile. *It is painful, but pleasantly so. Is this how you feel?*

"Yep. You're welcome. Except that fire isn't overly hot. If that hurts, I wouldn't go skipping through a more intense flame. You'll burn your skin off."

This is a mighty gift. I wonder if the potency of hellfire will be diminished as well.

I just shook my head. He was punch-drunk. A quick taste of the fire I'd spoken of would be enough to dampen his excitement.

We made it to the end of the tunnel. The ground dropped away sharply, leaving us standing in the air above an enormous cavern. Giant stalactites reached down from the rocky ceiling. Turning around wasn't exactly an option, because as soon as we reached the end, the tunnel behind us disappeared, cutting out the light from the fire. Below us, small hovels dotted the way, demons or other creatures moving between and around them. A drop of water fell past my face, dripping from the rocky ceiling high above. A small stream ran through an outcropping of frozen rock to our right, the glimmer like moving diamonds.

"How do you suppose we get down?" I asked, feeling my power pulsing even stronger than in the Realm. "Should I get us down?"

No. Do not use your power if at all possible. That suit is supposed to disguise your magic, but the mages were operating under the impression of a normal magic user, which you are not. Using your power might act as a beacon for your kind.

My kind. Great. That just *had* to be said.

"Fine. Then…let's…" I took a step forward and tipped, windmilling my arms to keep from falling headfirst to my death. Darius pulled me back. My heel hit off an invisible edge.

Back under control, I dangled my foot down and met a ledge. I stepped down with a smile. "Tricky.

We're on an invisible staircase. How many people have they killed with this little ruse?"

It seems as though they want only the experienced to come through.

"Experience is something you gain right after you need it."

So it would seem.

We started down slowly, me with much windmilling and exaggerated steps, him smoothly and gracefully, as though he made a habit of walking out of the sky on invisible steps of differing sizes.

The fire and ice tunnel suddenly spilled light down onto us. That creature had to be coming through. The light shimmered off the wide staircase and highlighted the railings at the sides. Landings broke up the decline every so often, so I wouldn't have tumbled far before landing in a heap on my face.

"Tricky," I said again as my power surged. Not thinking, I let a small amount of fire run down the steps from my feet. Next I sent a pulse of frost the same way, just to see what would happen.

The stairs within the sphere of magic glittered to life, shining like marble. The railing glowed and gleamed, solid gold.

"Wow," I breathed as Darius grabbed my arm.

I said not *to use your power.*

"Sorry." I cut it off, pitching us once again into

darkness. "But wasn't that fantastic? I wish I could light the whole staircase up. I bet my dad does, just to create a scene. Why else have the ability?"

Darius glanced behind us, worried about the traveler on our heels. He—or she, it was hard to say—clicked on a light, the sound echoing down to us. The glittering stairs shone in the beam of light. Everything outside of the small beam stayed hidden.

"Ah. A secret flashlight. Clearly Ja didn't fill you in on that."

He didn't comment.

We hurried along, trusting that the invisible steps would meet our feet.

A drip *plunked* onto the center of my head. I looked up at the rocky ceiling far above, a usual reaction to something falling on me when it wasn't raining. Another drop splashed against my suit-covered cheek.

Near the bottom, we descended between jagged rocks like the ones we'd seen near the gate. These looked even more treacherous, though, replete with sharp edges and points. Falling into them would be a good way to tear yourself up.

"So far, besides the stairwell when lit, this place is not welcoming."

Not at all. It has lived up to my expectations.

"Mine, too, and that is a real bummer."

The stairwell deposited us onto a dull gray rock

path, pockmarked and uneven. It was wide enough for four people to walk abreast, or two people and Darius, with his big shoulders, so there was enough room to avoid the unwelcoming rocks lining the way. Those rocks tapered into a fine edge at the top, and while I could probably get over them without killing myself, it would hurt a lot, not to mention torment my boots.

"I don't like that they're trying to keep us on a select path. Will there be a test to see if we're worthy to be here, like with that stairwell?"

Darius shook his head, his eyes hard. That meant he was anxious. And *that* was a very bad sign.

CHAPTER 13

W E WALKED ALONG the path, the ground gradually sloping upward. Behind us, the other traveler still had their light trained on the ground, revealing the same thing I could see with my bare eyes.

The hovels and movement we had seen from the stairs were obscured by rising crags all around us. They hadn't looked so big from above, or maybe I had misjudged them. Whatever the reason, they blocked our sight now, making it impossible to see what we were walking into.

A path intersected ours, nearly identical. Darius hesitated, clearly not knowing which direction would be best.

"Left," I blurted without meaning to. Darius swung his gaze to me, his eyes assessing. "Unless this was on the map?"

He shook his head. *We did not come in the way the map suggested. I did not trust it.*

I nodded, because that was wise. We started walking to the left, slow and steady. I had a firm suspicion something would jump out at us, and that it wouldn't be long now.

"The map is in your pack, right?" It was a rhetorical question, since I remembered seeing it in there, which meant Moss hadn't trusted me to navigate. Before my memory upgrade, that would've been wise. "We should stop and have a peek when we can."

Only the edges near the entrance the demon had chosen were clearly defined. We need to find our way across the river, then we will have more information.

"We are ridiculously underprepared for this," I muttered, not seeing any approaching change in scenery.

Yes.

Sometimes I wished he wasn't so habitually truthful.

"How big is this place?" I whispered.

As large as the Realm, but finite, like the Brink.

"What does that mean?"

The size is similar to the Realm, but as we can see, there are definable edges. The Realm, on the other hand, has strange pockets and weird fluxes that seem to go on for infinity. And they might. Creatures have wandered in and never come out.

I had not known that. And now I never wanted to run around there again without knowing exactly where I was going. Knowing me, I'd probably trip into one of those pockets.

A presence ahead of us, out of sight around the rocky bend, pressed on me in a weird way, throbbing in my middle and telling me to get lost. Usually my intuition told me to get ready for a fight. Not this time. I wanted to tuck my tail between my legs and run.

"Okay." My voice was so soft, I could barely hear it. I pulled his arm back the way we'd come. "Maybe this way was…"

The thought of going back made me freeze up. It felt like a worse idea than staying.

Crap. What was happening? Was I second-guessing myself, or was this a totally screwed-up situation?

Let's hope it's just second-guessing, I thought.

"We are going to need to go slow and keep our eyes open," I whispered. "I don't have a good feeling about this."

Remember, he thought, *we have the suits.*

He even sounded confident in his thoughts. How was the guy always so sure of himself?

I felt my sword pressing against my back comfortingly. Going on a killing spree wasn't a great idea—it would be like putting up a billboard directing everyone to notice me—but if something came at me, I would take it out. No way would I allow something to kill or capture either of us.

After another ten feet, the urge to about-face and sprint away vibrated through my body. I took a deep breath, only then realizing there was still air. Not that it mattered at the moment.

I put out my hand, directing Darius to the side of the path, keeping as close to the jagged and treacherous rocks as I could. Voices floated toward us. I couldn't make out the words. I couldn't pick up on any stray thoughts, either. Scratchy and deep, the sounds were almost animalistic.

Darius put a hand on my shoulder. I paused, thinking he wanted me to stop.

You are unpredictable in tight situations, he thought. *I can better monitor you by touch.*

Ah yes. He'd told me that once before. Whatever worked.

I continued forward, feeling a warning itch at my back. Not eyes, like I was being watched, but like an army was closing in and squishing me into a less-than-optimal situation.

"We need to hurry," I whispered, feeling urgency press in on me. "We need to get out of this area. I get the feeling it's a rough sort of place."

It seemed the narrowest of the edges, and it's one of the few entrances not currently watched by Vlad's people.

"There is probably a very specific reason for that, and we're more than likely about to find out what it is." I chewed my lip as we stalked forward. My vision narrowed and my hands drifted in front of my chest, a biological response to danger.

I pulled out my sword, my personal reaction to danger.

Claws poked my shoulder. Darius's response.

The rocks on the sides smoothed out and shrank, giving us more visibility. We started around the bend. A few heads bobbed ahead of us, some with horns, some with hair, so it would seem a variety of species and beings were communicating.

That was probably good, right? Not fighting, but talking?

So why was my entire person ready for war?

The path straightened out again, and I saw the first hovel. It was much bigger than I'd expected. As tall as a one-story house and about fifteen feet wide. The side facing us was open and two beings were inside, gesturing wildly. One held a boxlike item. Both creatures were demons, one with protruding teeth and a rough hide, and the other with no nose and a large mouth filled with matchstick teeth.

A lizard-looking creature crossed our path, following an intersecting walkway. Its long tail ended in a fierce spike. That would put a nice-sized hole through its enemy.

"On second thought," I said softly, "maybe we should go back to the Brink and take our chances. Dizzy was right. This was a terrible plan."

Number one, it's too late. Second, you know you can't. It would only give them time to organize and plan your extraction. We don't have the resources to protect you for long.

"Stop talking sense. It's not welcomed here." I gripped my sword tightly, my arm shaking.

I was the chick who ran at problems. That was my shtick. So what was up with the fear?

I was overthinking things. Had to be.

After a deep breath, I sped up. My gut pinched. Our path ended and more structures dotted the way. Shacks almost. Maybe huts. Most of them were open to the elements, like the first, and many of them were occupied by creatures talking in low voices. Judging by the wild gesturing I saw in one hut, some sort of bartering was underway, and the shoppers were arguing for a lower price.

Which way? Darius thought.

Flattened against the rock, I glanced right, seeing more creatures crowding the throughway, all on foot. Or whatever served for feet. I spotted one creature that had a human-type shape, though with odd proportions and too much hair. Maybe we wouldn't look so odd if the suits didn't work.

The other way was a little sparser, and there were more loners, not many of which paused to talk to others.

I jerked my head right. "That way. Stick to the sides. Let's try to blend in."

We will soon see if the suits work, Darius thought.

Yes, we would. And if they didn't, we would also see if I could keep from freaking out and accidentally killing things.

I stuck to the side and hunched, trying not to look so utterly human. A knobby thing staggered my way, and adrenaline dumped into my body. I kept walking, braced to lop off a body part should the creature swing one of those six-inch-long claws at my person.

Something jostled the creature and it hissed, but not at me. It looked over its—dislocated?—shoulder at whatever had tripped it. I couldn't see the other creature, but it mustn't have apologized, because the knobby thing swung around and lashed out. A splash of black blood hit the rock to the side. Creatures pushed away, opening up space for the fighters. The knobby thing lashed out again, but its target, a squat type of troll, roared and struck it with a spiked club. The club battered the knobby thing in the side, smashing its other shoulder and making it holler.

I plucked at Darius's sleeve and moved into a stream of creatures edging around the disturbance. As long as we weren't the only ones heading out instead of hanging around to watch the bloody battle, it was fine to move on.

Something dull and hard poked my arm. A different bony, gross thing bumped into me. Darius's hand tightened on my shoulder and his claws dug into my suit as he pulled me away.

In front of me, a creature turned suddenly. Its half-torn wing jabbed my chest.

A blast of anger turned lightheadedness rolled through my consciousness. Fire roared in my middle, and I shoved the oddly squishy being without meaning to. My logical mind told me to stop, to make my way to the edge of the path so I could regroup, but I stalked forward like a woman turned battle-axe, forcing people out of my way.

My power pumped higher, daring any of these beings to challenge me. My power didn't seem to call to anyone. The suit was at least partially working so far.

In the back of my head, I felt the underlying fear from before, telling me to get lost. It had never been so easy to ignore something in all my life. Not with more beings jostling and bumping me. Straying in my path when I was clearly the big man on campus.

Where are these feelings coming from, Reagan? a tiny voice thought in my head.

I had no idea, but I was powerless to stop them.

The crowd that had formed around the fight thinned at the outskirts. Something howled from within the press of creatures. A spray of blood shot out over the beings. I ducked just in time. The glob hit a scaly creature next to me.

There was definitely a reason Vlad's people weren't hanging around these edges. The brutality was intense.

I hated that a part of me thrived in it. The part my father had passed down.

An opening on the left gave us an option to leave the main drag. The question was, would it take us toward the river?

I had decided to go for it when a huge shape ducked out of the nearest hovel. I swerved as best I could, but my backpack bumped into it. The impact had me careening away, staggering to get my balance. Darius was beside me in an instant, helping me straighten up.

You know what else was straightening up?

The huge freaking creature that had just come out of the hovel, that was what.

Up and up until it was a little more than double my height. Horns like a mountain goat's curled around its head and under its ears. Pointed ears stuck out of a leathery face with a hole for a nose. From huge shoulders hung monstrous arms, much too long for its body. A short waist and then thick thighs led down into weird, dinosaur-looking feet.

I dropped my sword a little, because regardless of the feeling from a moment ago, I did not want to tango with this monster.

Please work, suit, I said to myself as I turned slowly and continued on my way. *Please work. Don't let it see me. Don't let it—*

"What is this?" it said in a deep, booming voice.

Was it too much to hope that the creature was talking about some other idiot who'd bumped it with her backpack?

"Does 'ooman scum dare invade my pride?"

I didn't know what pride meant in the context of that sentence, since the thing clearly wasn't a lion, but I did know the suit wasn't keeping me invisible. The creature had a problem with me. Joy.

I also knew that it clearly knew I was part human, not a demon with a human form. So that was unfortunate.

I took a moment to try and read its thoughts, but came up blank. It was blocking me, somehow. I ripped off the mask so I could see better. If the suit wasn't hiding me from eyeballs, there was no use half blinding myself.

"You grew tired of summoning us to do your bidding, filthy 'ooman, and thought your reign would transfer down here?" It blew out fire through its nostrils, the flame washing down my face.

"Dang it! I wasn't ready. There go my freaking eyebrows again."

I turned to face the monster, much more horrible

than Darius's monster form could ever be.

"How dare you speak that filthy tongue to me, 'oo-man!" the creature roared.

Do you know what the creature said? Darius thought-asked me.

"Yeah. Don't you?"

No. It is speaking a language I have never heard.

In other words, I could randomly understand a demonic language without ever having heard it before. That was odd and terrifying, though helpful.

It seems the suit is working for me, since the creature has not noticed me, Darius thought. *We're drawing a crowd. We need to make a move.*

"Well, bully for you," I said sarcastically, sizing up the situation. I adjusted my grip on my sword. "And yes, we do, but running is not going to work. What a crappy way to start an adventure."

One word pulsed within the quickly gathering crowd, chanted out loud over and over.

"Blood! Blood! Blood!"

Can we end this peacefully? Darius thought.

The creature reached for me.

I dodged its hand and slashed down with my sword. The blade cut halfway through. "Not anymore."

CHAPTER 14

T HE BEING DIDN'T howl like I'd thought it might. It roared, shaking the ground and making the crowd shrink back in fear.

"Crap, of all the beasts I could run into, it had to be the one that all these brutal creatures are afraid of."

It stuck its arm into the air, and through a strange sort of rustling, bone and skin stitched back together before my eyes, faster than I'd ever seen something regenerate. Ever.

A swear word drifted out of Darius's thoughts, also unhelpful. I didn't hear any thoughts from the creatures.

"This is why I usually stick to pouches." I dashed forward and hacked at the creature's leg before stabbing it in the stomach. "Pouches don't trouble anyone."

The creature huffed fire at me, raking it down my front again. I capped my head in ice magic, keeping it subtle in the hopes it wouldn't be seen, to save myself from going completely bald. Call me vain, but I liked my blond locks.

Once again, the demon's wounds magically righted themselves. I needed to get serious.

"Say hello to my little friend!" I blasted it with a stream of hellfire. Since I wasn't the only creature capable of producing hellfire, I felt safe in showing that little trick.

The hellfire punched a hole in its middle.

It screamed, a horrible, high-pitched sound that shook me to the core. Panic bubbled up, wild and paralyzing, begging me to run, scream, cry, or just cower at its feet. I could barely think through the terror.

"That is a great trick," I said through clenched teeth, fighting the effects of that sound. "That's some magic that would *really* help the bounty-hunting gig."

The hole didn't stitch back together, so I hit it with another blast, square in the chest.

Realizing its magical scream hadn't produced the desired effect—on me, anyway; all the other creatures had scattered, and even Darius had jogged backward a few paces—it launched forward, swiping at me first with one hand, then the other.

"How are you still going?" I dodged, dove to the side, and rolled, barely getting out of the way. I jumped up and slashed, catching its wrist and severing its hand cleanly this time. Chancing my ice magic, since the place had cleared out and I'd already decided this demon couldn't be left to live and tell tales, I smacked its feet with hardened air, pushing them out from under it.

Shock bled through its expression. At least, it could've been shock. I only had a moment to catch it before its face smacked against the rock.

I jumped onto its back and hacked downward like a wild thing. My blade sliced through its neck, which, thank all that was holy, didn't stitch back together.

Its arms and legs flailed. I kept hacking. The thing was made of strong stuff.

Finally, I separated think tank from body. It rolled two feet away and I barely kept from gagging. Severing heads was seriously gross. I hated doing it.

Unexpectedly, the body gave a huge jolt, bucking me off.

Darius caught me midair and set me to rights before stepping back, clearly content to let me handle the situation as long as I didn't land on my head. What a gentleman.

The demon's body wiggled again, and steam rose from its collapsed form. A moment later, it half melted, or maybe decomposed, onto the ground.

Breathing heavily, I watched it for a moment to make sure it wouldn't hop back up and yell, "Psych!"

Look around you, came Darius's thought.

I turned to find a bunch of creatures creeping toward me. They formed a half-circle, their eyes going between me and my sword and the giant demon at my feet. Not one of them made a sound.

Make a statement, Darius thought.

He was right. If I shied away after taking down a mammoth like that, it wouldn't look right. I needed to give them a show—something nuts enough that it would start an urban legend, and people down the road would shrug this off as a tall tale. Stories of bullies getting beaten were always exaggerated with time.

I pumped my fist in the air and yelled barbarically, guttural and savage. I hopped from one foot to the other, raising each knee high and bending my arms, like a mountain man on too much moonshine. Then I surged forward and kicked the head. It bounced off someone and skittered away. My "Ahhh!" turned into "*Ugh…*"

That was probably enough.

I made a circle in the air with my finger, letting Darius know the bus was leaving, and stalked away, shoving with my ice magic when someone didn't move out of my way fast enough. The creature—which I couldn't identify—flew ass over end before skidding on its face.

My agreement not to use my magic wasn't going well.

"And we're hurrying," I said in an undertone as I passed Darius. "We are moving quickly, now." I put on the jets, using my new vampire-enhanced speed.

That will certainly leave a lasting impression, Darius thought as he caught up with me. Did pride color that thought? Because if he was smart, he'd be more than a little wary. I'd just lopped off a fire-breathing monster's head and kicked it at the onlookers. I wasn't the kind of girl to take home to mother.

"I have goo on my boot, and I'm too grossed out to try and scrape it off." I took a left at the next crossroads. A drop of water *plunked* off my head. "And why is the ceiling dripping? Never mind; I don't want to know."

We came to a fork in the road. A hideous creature, half spider and half typically ugly demon, sidled toward us from the right side. Its head, featuring four eyes and no visible mouth, stared at me for a beat too long.

Irrational rage surged up out of nowhere. Before I could help it, I brought fire down out of the sky, turning the demon into a ball of flame.

"Oh crap, why did I do that?" I snuffed out the fire and looked around quickly. The empty corridors greeted me. Thankfully, nothing had seen my *faux pas.*

I turned back and found a lump of char in the creature's place.

"Oops." I grimaced and turned left. "You better get your money back for this suit, Darius, because it is the pits."

No. Go right. I think that creature had recently

crossed the river.

I hesitated for a brief moment before altering course. "It would be cool to have that magic. Not that I'm bitter or anything." I breathed out slowly, checking in on the rage still simmering in my gut. "I feel like I'm losing control. I'm not in my right frame of mind. I had no idea I would blast that demon with fire until after it had happened."

You are reacting to your environment with the part of you that understands it. While I would certainly advise you to hold back whenever possible, don't keep a demon creature alive at the expense of getting found out.

"It will be impossible for me to keep a low profile. Which, of course, is the reason I didn't stay in the Brink." I shook my head, seeing a clear way ahead. For now. "What could I possibly have been thinking?"

Your choices were limited. You chose the path the enemy will least expect, and one that will keep your friends safe. In addition, you are a survivor. You adapt almost immediately to new, hard-to-navigate situations. This journey isn't ideal, but I think it was the best option available to you.

"You need to do some inspirational seminars. Maybe self-help talks. You'd rake in the dough."

Those who need inspiration and self-help talks are useless.

"'Present company excluded' might've been a nice

ending to that sentence. Just saying."

The rocks had become taller again, though every so often we could see the top of a hovel peeking out over them. We had returned to some sort of alleyway, traveling behind the huts where the demons were wheeling and dealing. It was the first stroke of luck we'd gotten.

Incoming.

I saw them as Darius's thought registered. A group of four creatures walking toward us. Probably all demons (though I was no expert), with thick cords of muscle on powerful frames. Most were shorter than me, and only one might've reached my height.

Darius drifted to the side, back to his role as the lurker, which would hopefully turn into a silent killer should I need him.

I didn't alter coarse or drift with him, choosing instead to own my space and wrap myself in confidence. I knew not all demons were brutal, but the ones in this cesspool seemed to be, and I needed to keep my brazenness front and center or risk getting pushed around.

They noticed me, and their scratching, grating voices fell silent. Their group, previously taking up three-quarters of the path, spread out to fill the whole thing. A blockade.

The rage surged up again, hot and heady.

Don't be stupid, demons, I thought desperately, staring straight ahead. *Don't pick a fight with me. I'm barely hanging on to control.*

"You are far from home," the demon walking straight at me rasped. They all slowed, ready for a confrontation.

I ground my teeth as a molten wave of wrath ate at my gut. Something else appeared on the path behind the demons.

They have all come from the river, Darius thought, slowing with me. *We are almost there.*

"That's super, but I'm about to go crazy." I rolled my head then shoulders, trying to loosen up. "And there are witnesses."

I cannot understand you.

Oh good. I was talking the demonic language that I had never learned. It was like waking up in a foreign place with no idea how you'd gotten there.

"We don't tolerate human spawn, maggot," the one in front of me, Mr. Chatty, said, clearly thinking I was the product of an incubus or something similar, a demon who seduced humans and begot a child. It spat to the side. The spit sizzled on the rock.

"Acidic spit. That must really kill your love life." Flame licked at my fingers, begging to be set free. My magic flowered. I spread my hands and grinned as my control slipped. "But, as you see, I made it through the gate. I have a right to be down here."

"You only have the rights I say you do." The demons stopped, challenging me.

I kept walking, closing the distance. "You'll want to step aside," I said in an easy-breezy tone at complete odds with the inferno raging within. "Or I'll be forced to yank off your arm and beat you with it."

Mr. Chatty laughed. The others joined in.

"Wrong answer." Aching cold slid down my arms and pounded inside me. The fire swirled around it. The desire to *maim, kill, destroy!* thudded in time to my heart. "I shouldn't have come down here," I said, breathing heavily.

"You are just now realizing that?" Mr. Chatty asked.

I stopped two feet in front of it, red tinging the edges of my vision. The desire to blow this whole place up was so strong that my limbs shook. "That thought is on a loop. I think it every few minutes. Regardless, you'll want to move. *Now.*"

Though it didn't show in my voice, I was begging it. What *did* show in my voice was that part of me—the crazy-powerful part—hoped the demon would force me to retaliate.

I didn't know much about split personalities, but I knew they weren't good. And my power was forcing me to develop one. This was the start of the breakdown, I was sure of it.

"I will move...right after I kill you," Mr. Chatty

growled.

The ice magic overcame me, and before I knew it, air had solidified in front of the demon. Barely realizing that it was me working the magic, I grabbed the demon's arm with the air, yanked it off, and slapped the creature across the face with it.

"I did promise to do that," I said with a grimace.

The others started and about-faced. They took off as one.

I sent a fireball over the first demon and rolling after the rest, ending their ability to tattle. The weave was different than the straightforward flame I usually used. I'd picked up a little something from the demon we'd summoned in the Brink.

Silence drifted down onto the newly stilled path.

"I should go home and lock myself up. This can't be good. I think I have a rage problem." I wiped my sweating forehead, then clutched at my hammering heart. "A very bad rage problem. The cure is probably yoga. Yoga seems to cure everything. Maybe I should head back and enroll in some yoga classes."

That was...effective. Not low profile, but effective.

This time the pride rang through his thoughts loud and clear. Also giddiness. The vampire part of him had loved the show of force and violence.

"I don't know if I'm happy that you can understand me again, or severely worried that my ethics committee is a creature distinctly known for a lack of ethics."

Both, I should think.

"Yes. Probably. Let's find that freaking river before we meet any more bullies. I don't want to know what I'm going to do next. It'll probably make me faint. Or worse, make me giddy like you."

Both, judging by the display a moment ago.

"Do me a favor. Stop thinking."

I didn't like his soft chuckle. He was getting way too much enjoyment out of my newfound talent for savagery.

The problem was, like them or not, I'd need a bigger dose of these new talents soon enough. The demons I'd just gone up against were probably level twos or threes, creatures that could readily be summoned to the Brink. Even the tough one earlier had only been a level four or so, even though he'd clearly had some special powers. These were the flunkies. The hacks. The ones who couldn't make it in the big leagues. Except for a couple of new magical traits I hadn't seen before, they were nothing.

Anxiety made my stomach churn.

If these were the lackeys, what would I find across the river?

CHAPTER 15

WE PASSED THE charred remains of the demon that had been in the wrong place at the wrong time. All it had probably wanted to do was trade a trinket or something, and instead it had witnessed a psycho thumping demons with their own extremities.

"You're just relaxing and taking it easy, huh?" I asked Darius quietly as we made our way. A pair of growls sounded somewhere to the left beyond the rock, followed by snarling and hollering. A fight had started. "Letting the girl take care of everything."

You are doing a wonderful job. I would hate to get in your way and prevent you from kicking heads.

"Super. I can see that you'll forever remind me of that. In my defense, it was a tense situation and I wasn't thinking. Or in control."

Yes. It pulled at my primal side in...pleasant ways. Almost as alluring as ripping off arms and chasing demons around with them...

"Oh good. I needed to know that, thanks," I grumbled. "And it was just the *one* arm."

I slowed when the path opened up in front of us. My heart, which had nearly returned to normal speed, started to thump faster again. We were coming on an intersection. I worried I'd see demons in it.

"The good news is…" I said as I stalked forward, my power throbbing. I felt the earlier demon chant vibrating through me. *Blood! Blood! Blood!* "At this rate, no one will try to present me to my dad. They'll ship me back to the surface as quickly as possible for fear I'll kill them all."

Or want to fight you in a show of bravado.

"Don't help, please." I gingerly touched the rock wall and felt a prick on my palm. Too sharp to flatten against—not that doing so would really help me.

Figuring I just had to go for it, I summoned all my power and stalked out into the space with a confident swagger. My sword pushed against my back, wanting to be taken out and swung around. The weight of my gun reminded me that demons could also be shot.

Stillness greeted me.

I let out a relieved breath and looked around.

Jagged rock walls on all sides, nearly uniform in height. We'd come from one prong of a fork in the road. I turned to look at the other prong, along which the scuffle from a moment ago must've taken place. No one walked out. Either they'd been going the opposite direction, or they were dead.

The pathway in front of us led away right. No hovels peeked over the walls, and no voices floated our direction.

Plunk.

I gritted my teeth. The leaking roof was starting to get on my freaking nerves.

Have you felt any of these demons? Darius thought-asked.

"What do you mean?" I started forward again, not wanting to curse my good luck.

The level-five demon in Seattle, and the one we called not long ago, seemed to feel your power. And you theirs, correct?

I thought back as we hurried along. "Their power made mine throb—either the fire or the ice, depending on their type of magic. But ever since we got down here, my power has become a beast all its own."

They should feel your magic.

"At first I thought they couldn't, but maybe they do. As you've seen—safely from the sidelines, I might add—I am constantly noticed. I should invite them to tea so I can ask if it's my power they are feeling or my mug they are seeing. Or both." I analyzed the rock walls, which were reducing again. There wasn't any apparent rhyme or reason for their fluctuating size. "Why did they put in walls, anyway? Why create corridors that essentially lead to the same places? It's not like these are streets with homes, and the occupants want privacy. They've made it so you *have* to stay on the path. You can't go over the walls unless you want to cut yourself up. It feels like we're rats in some science experiment in the Brink. I don't get the reason for it."

Being that the creatures in this section of the edges are extremely volatile, maybe privacy is exactly what they're after. The fewer demons each sees, the fewer problems there will be.

I frowned, because maybe, but there weren't exactly tons of nooks and crannies on the paths. Hiding wasn't really a legitimate option. Besides, the paths just dumped out into the open. Privacy en route to the meeting didn't mean much if you didn't also have it while conducting business.

The rocks around us fell away. Another step and the imagery around us changed dramatically, blanking out my thoughts. I turned around with wide eyes as Darius pressed up against me. Behind us, the corridors of rough rock walls had disappeared, replaced with a desolate landscape stretching as far as I could see. Gray stone had turned to hard mud or clay, run through with cracks.

I turned back around, gripping Darius's arm.

Directly in front of us, a single pier led into the smooth water of the river. It stretched out in front of us until it disappeared behind a thick layer of gray fog. No ripples or current disturbed the surface. Desolate beach ran along it, and just like behind us, there wasn't another person or creature as far as the eye could see.

"Only one dock," Darius said out loud, clearly wanting to interrupt the unnatural silence.

"Right in front of us." I patted my gun for comfort. "Was that the only path to get to the river, or would that pier have magically appeared in front of no matter where we'd entered?" I looked around again. "This smells like mind-fuckery to me."

I walked along the beach, watching the dock as though it would follow. It stayed right where I'd left it. So did the fog, not shifting and rolling like normal fog. The dried mud under my feet didn't feel as smooth as it looked, nor did it give way like that substance normally would have. In fact, the hardness felt like the stone we'd just left.

I stopped and looked up. The canopy of rock from the edges of the underworld had been replaced by limitless gray sky, the same color as the fog. Seeing it stretch forever, like the beach, like the new canvas of dried desert behind me, gave me vertigo.

Yanking my gaze away, I looked back toward Darius.

The bottom dropped out of my stomach.

He was gone. The spot he'd been standing in was empty.

I glanced to the side. The dock was lined up with me. It was no longer where I had been.

"Holy tater tits, Batman." I broke out in a cold sweat, fighting the urge to sprint back in his direction. If I did that, and he was just obscured by fog or an illusion, I'd miss him, and in this place, it was entirely possible I'd never find him again.

Plunk.

I froze. And looked up.

The gray sky was there, same as before, but that had been a drop of water. I was sure of it. Which meant the leaking rock ceiling was up there somewhere.

An illusion. That's all this was. Trickery of the eye. Magic intended to do what those walls had done: force us on a certain path.

Mental fuckery, like I'd thought before.

I closed my eyes, focusing on my connection with Darius. I could feel his beating heart, pounding rhythmically deep inside me. Strong and sure, it wasn't at an elevated speed, which meant he wasn't freaking out like I was.

Could *he* see *me*?

Instead of opening my eyes and looking around wildly, like I'd just done to no avail, I looked internally, feeling the natural homing device assured by the bond. It was a beacon that would allow me to find him anywhere. In any world. We would never be lost from each other.

I walked like a blind person, waving my arms in front of me to keep from bumping into anything. With my luck, a pole would randomly appear just so I'd knock my head against it. If there was YouTube in this place, the residents would go to town thumbs-upping that little nugget. It would be right up there with the whole head-kicking debacle.

A slight hum filled my body as I neared what should've been Darius's body. His heartbeat stayed strong and steady. Another few steps and a flare of delight fluttered my heart and flipped my stomach. Being that this was the first time I'd been away from him since the bonding, even just a little bit, I wondered if that would always happen when we reunited. It was nice.

I opened my eyes.

The pier was back in front of me. Darius was not.

"Darius?" I called.

I am here. You should be right beside me. I am reaching for you but not feeling you. I can hear you in my mind.

"Does your heart not react when you freak out? Because you should be freaking out—not that I'm judging." I was totally judging.

I saw you disappear. This place seems to be an illusion, tricking our minds. It also seems to have some metaphysical power. The change in our proximity has put us on a different plane. Or the same plane but in a different space. Perhaps it's meant to isolate people before they go over the river.

"You're talking nonsense. Okay, look, we need to get back in the same acid trip. Do you have any experience doing that?"

Drugs do not affect vampires in that way.

"Dang it. Don't do drugs, they said. They'll ruin you, they said. Well, now look." The dock lurked across from me, taunting me. Ready to move around like a ghost when I wasn't looking.

Rage sparked again, and this time I let it fill me. Fanned it higher. I didn't like being punked. If this place wanted to mess with me, I'd mess with it right back.

"Let me know if anything happens on your side." I set fire to crawl along the dock, feeling things out. Magic radiated from that direction, complex and comforting. It was equal parts fire and ice, blended in a breathtaking way. This magic couldn't be unraveled by a mere touch. In fact, it needed counter magic—I would have to work in opposition with its structure to tear it apart.

I spent a few more minutes studying what I was feeling, trying to make sense of it. Identify it. Then I pushed my magic out all around me, mixing the two sides as best as I could despite the fact that they wouldn't peacefully blend.

The world lit up around me. Fire and ice interlaced in the sparkling, complex fabric of this entire illusion.

"My father is an absolute master," I said softly. I knew this was above me, and it would take too long to even attempt to carefully unweave it. I'd have to do what I did best. Try to blast through it. Which was good, because my appreciation didn't stop the rage boiling within me. Something else, too. Confidence. The desire to command. To control everything around me, even though I clearly wasn't doing great with controlling myself.

I waved my hand through the air, operating on impulse. Letting my power lead me. If I was going to crack up, I might as well go big.

Swirls of ice flurries played within the magic, followed by sparks of fire. I threw an explosion into it, shaking the ground and punching a hole through the void of gray. The visual winked, and everything blinked black. When all the light was lost, a blue tint appeared, showing a lightning-quick glimpse of the world beneath the illusion. Stone beneath my feet, pockmarked and uneven like before. Pier after pier down the way, the edge of each two feet apart from its neighbor. Rolling, boiling wisps of fog contained within invisible walls, allowing me to see past it now. Rock walls hacked at so as not to reach out into the beach illusion area.

The river did have a current. A fast one.

The illusion blinked back in place and I felt blinded.

I curled my magic into the fabric of the illusion and short-circuited it. There it was again—raging river, the line of piers.

As I watched the water, a twisted body—*and is that a broom?*—floated along. Maybe someone hadn't possessed the right magic to cross the river and finish up their...sweeping?

I blinked and shook my head. I was probably seeing things.

One thing was for certain. This was all for show. A grand hoax to make it seem cooler, or scarier, than it actually was. To make people feel more alone than they really were.

My dad was a showboat.

He had me going, too. He'd gotten me good, the tricky devil.

Reagan?

Oh yeah.

I worked my magic without thinking. Without planning. I set my goal—bring Darius back into my acid trip—and let intuition guide me again. Fire slid over my body. Ice throbbed up from my middle. I forced them outward until they wove together in a halo around me. Then I shoved that halo in the direction Darius should've been, punching through the tapestry of the magical illusion in order to reach the reality beneath.

The world around me throbbed. Not just the illusion I'd been marooned in. All of it. The whole damn thing.

Blue flared on all sides, showing the magical blueprint of the spell, and then the whole thing peeled away. Demons stood on a large platform of stone, looking around in confusion. The piers showed up again, side by side, probably forty or fifty in all. Figures sat in the boats docked at the ends, rocking in the current. The fog wafted in front of them, a magically created fence mostly see-through at this point.

All the figures in the boats turned as one, and stared in my direction.

"Oh crap."

I reached out, grabbed Darius by the arm, and yanked him toward me. "Hang on to me while I try to put this back."

"Yes, hurry!" he said.

Now his heart was hammering.

CHAPTER 16

I HAD NO idea how to reconstruct what must've been my father's work, so I pulled all my magic back into myself—all except for the halo I'd formed around Darius and me. I chewed my lip as the world around us throbbed. Blue light flared, still showing people looking around in confusion, before the illusion finally rematerialized.

"I have no idea what any of that was, but I'm a rock star when I let my split personality take over." I wiped my forehead.

"You are a natural, Reagan, like a handful of mages in the world. What you aren't, however, is subtle. Or even remotely good at strategic thinking."

I started forward. "That sounded like a giant thank you for bringing you back to your lady love. Almost like groveling. Jesus, man. Get a grip. I don't need thanks. I'm happy just to be awesome."

I didn't have to look back at him to know he'd narrowed his eyes at me.

The dock felt like real wood—it had probably started that way, but magic had made it indestructible. I had the impulse to jump to the one I knew waited beside it, my eyes wide open, just to see what happened. But it wasn't worth the risk. I'd probably miss and get wedged between them in that dark, murky water. Given the creature I'd seen floating in it, and what might or might not have been a dirty broom, it had to be a hotbed of underworld bacteria.

Our feet thumped softly as we walked down the pier. I put my hand into it and felt prickles along my skin. "What do you feel?"

Darius did the same and flinched. He extended his hand again, slowly. It disappeared into the fog. "It is painful, but tolerable."

"Maybe this is the real gate to the underworld, only allowing those with demon blood to pass."

Wariness crossed his features. "We will now find out if Ja was right."

"Or if she was trying to kill you by sending you down here?" I grimaced. "That probably should've occurred to me. It would've been a good reason not to bond."

"Which is why I didn't mention it."

"Since you know everything, obviously."

"Yes."

He'd missed my sarcasm.

I stepped into the fog. Darius walked in after me.

Immediately, his eyes tightened and his jaw clenched, clearly in pain. He kept pace, the sound of our feet on the boards muted even more than before. Wisps of white slid across my skin, lightly stinging.

Plunk.

I balled my fists. "If those drips continue the whole time we're here, they will slowly drive me insane. I'm not kidding." I thought about what I'd just said. "More insane."

A few more steps and the fog cleared, revealing the boat at the end of the dock. From my previous efforts, I knew that it—and the other boats we couldn't see—floated in the center of the huge river. Its bow was pointed upstream. Within it, sitting placidly at the back and staring straight ahead, was a creature in a dark gray robe with a hood covering its head. I could just see its human(ish) face, now noticing the grayish skin and missing eyes.

I did say *ish.*

It could see, though. Either the hollow sockets were also an illusion, or it had sonar or something. The boatman had looked right at me.

My dad was definitely a showboat. A real flair for theater, he had.

"How are you doing?" I asked Darius.

Still standing, he thought.

Yikes. I wondered if it was as bad as Dizzy's spell

breaking his hands. I didn't want to ask for fear it was worse. I really did put the guy through hell. I'd have to get him a fruit basket or blood bag or something after this was all through. Maybe a back rub.

"How about now?" I asked, not advancing toward the boat just yet.

"I'm fine now. It feels the same here as in the edges. There is also still air. I wonder if that will change."

I did, too. Why else would I have inherited the ability to survive without breathing?

"That fog must be what keeps people out." Darius turned and studied the gray, stagnant mass. "It's strong magic, like the illusion anchored to this place, but it's still just magic. It can be worked around with enough power and skill."

"Like...by mages, you mean?"

"Yes. Lucifer is mighty, but he is not untouchable. Neither is the elf royalty. I've seen them undone by an incredible dual-mage team. Brothers. Absolute naturals. Who, consequently, were banned from the Realm after their trick. They changed the layout of the castle. I don't think anyone knew that could be done until that point. Natural mages such as those are extremely rare. Only a handful exist, that we know of, in the world. Form two naturals into a dual-mage team, and they could undo this fog, cracking this kingdom open like an egg."

"Wow. Don't dream *really* big, do you? Should I

mention the flaw in your plan?" I paused for a beat, and when he didn't answer, continued. "Mages can't get through the gate to the edges."

"Where there is a will, there is a way."

"Right. Well, good luck with the whole supernatural world domination thing. Think those dual mages will help out?" I stared at the creature in the boat. It hadn't turned our way, though our murmuring voices must've reached it. "Also, do you think that thing can hear us? If it has super hearing like a vampire, it might be able to make out what we were saying, and I doubt you want your plans foiled before you even begin."

"It has not so much as twitched in our direction. And no, at this distance, with the muted quality of this place, and with how low we are speaking, it shouldn't be able to hear us. Not that it will matter."

Confident much? I had a feeling the other side of the river would cut that right out.

"That mage pair no longer exists," Darius said, still not advancing. "One of them, the older of the brothers, died somewhere in Europe. He was on the council of the Mages' Guild, but it's rumored he didn't like the direction the guild was going. He tried to amass support to reject certain changes. Soon after, he went on a business trip with a few of his followers. He never came back."

"And his followers pled ignorance?"

"Only one follower lived. You can guess which position he now occupies."

"Yikes. I barely know those crooked bastards, and I hate them." I braced my hands on my hips, because I needed to make a move soon. I was stalling. I knew it, Darius must've known it, and the deaf-mute in the boat probably knew it. The faker.

"The younger brother, Emery, went off the grid after that. He went rogue. He pops up now and again, but when he disappears and doesn't want to be found, he can't be."

I thought back, because this sounded familiar. "Is he a handsome guy?" Darius's look darkened. I threw up my hands. "Not that I'm interested. I just remember Callie mentioning a powerful mage that was off-grid."

"Why did she mention it to you?" Jealousy tinged his words, and I couldn't help a laugh. Learning to feel again came with some unpleasant side effects, it would seem.

It occurred to me that the troubles in the magical world were much more strained than I'd originally thought. Each magical faction was at odds with another. I didn't like that Darius was making plans to get involved, even if I knew he'd attempt to be stealthy. There was no way I wanted anything to do with any of that. I needed to keep my head down and get out of here without getting discovered, now more than ever.

After that, I could work on talking Darius into a nice, quiet life without demons and intensely powerful mages. I didn't want to set off a magical war like a powder keg.

As always, that was easier said than done where it concerned me. I was a bad idea playing out at the best of times.

"So I could snap a picture if I ever saw him and pin it up on my wall. No biggie," I said. "Anyway, let's do this. We can't stand here all day."

Darius's stare held mine for a moment before he finally tore his gaze away and directed it at the boat. "At some point," he said, "one of these boats must be gone when someone arrives to use it."

I walked forward. "Yeah, I don't know how that works." I hadn't thought to look when I was messing with things. "We can ask Mr. Patient, there. Assuming he can hear at all."

I stopped beside the boat, which did not bob or move. A rope attached to the side of the boat had been looped around a metal tie down on the dock, though maybe that, too, was just for show.

"Hi," I said tentatively.

That was English, Darius thought.

I didn't know how to speak the demonic language on cue. Or even if there was more than one.

"Can I have a ride?" I stuck my thumb out like an

idiot before ripping it back down.

The creature in the boat continued to stare straight ahead.

I stepped into the boat. It rocked like I'd expect from a normal boat, and didn't at all expect from the magical boat. My weight tilted it, sending me sprawling. I banged my knee on a wooden seat and fell against the side, getting splashed for my efforts.

I wiped away the water—which felt normal, if dirty—and sat up quickly. "My bad. I wasn't expecting that."

The creature continued staring straight ahead, right past me.

Darius stepped in a moment later, annoyingly graceful even when the boat pitched. He smoothly sat down.

The creature came to life, if that was what you would call it. Its head turned slowly until its eyeholes pointed at me.

"Who are you?" the creature asked in a flat, sandpaper voice.

"I am the egg man," I said seriously.

Darius slightly shook his head. He probably also rolled his eyes.

"Egg man," the creature said. Its head slowly turned to Darius. The suit wasn't hiding him from the boat captain. "Who are you?"

Darius stared at him for a beat. "I am the walrus."

I couldn't help myself. I was a Beatles fan. "*Goo goo g'joob.*"

"Walrus," the creature said, ignoring my soft singing. It switched its sightless gaze to staring between us. "Where do you go?"

Before I could say "Across the river," Darius said, "East shores, regio Festum."

"I really need to look at that map," I said softly, then snapped my mouth shut, in case mentioning a map was as much of a tell as pointing a huge arrow at my head with *spy* written across it. It wasn't like this was a theme park and people went around handing out maps.

The creature reached out with a bony hand—and I mean *bony*, as in "not covered with skin"—and unstrung the rope. The boat calmly drifted away from the pier, but I felt a subtle rocking and bumping that didn't match the smooth expanse around us. But I'd seen what these waters really looked like; the magic was strong to keep us this level.

"Do you ever throw anyone overboard?" I asked the creature.

It didn't answer.

We drifted away from the dock quickly, reminding me of the fast-moving current I had seen. No other docks showed themselves.

"Because you lot don't seem impressed with

strangers," I continued, analyzing it. The eyeholes weren't gory. They reminded me of a doll's eye socket after the marble had fallen out. Creepy, sure, but not necessarily icky. "If someone died in that fog, you'd get up and toss them over, wouldn't you?"

It continued to stare.

The nose was tiny, a little button that wouldn't be much good for smelling. The lips, full but leathery, curved halfway across its face, the mouth too big. When it threw on a smile, if it ever did, the effect would no doubt be startling.

The dock fell out of sight and the fog evaporated into the air. Barren beaches seemed to stretch on forever on either side under the limitless gray sky. The boat hung in visibly motionless water, yet I continued to feel the minuscule bumping and rocking.

My body said, *You are floating.* My eyes said, *You are sitting still.* My social perception said, *Mr. Undertaker is making things awkward.*

A drop of liquid splatted against the creature's forehead. As though we had run into it. As though we were going at high speed.

It didn't react to the projectile water splat. Like it had never happened.

"I feel like I'm dreaming, but I know I'm awake, and it is really stressing me out." I leaned forward and stared at my feet. "Is this a long journey?"

Just like before, I received no answer.

Darius reached over and took my hand. Like a hound dog salivating over a bone in its master's hand, I watched his thumb trace across mine. Then slide back. Over. Back.

It wasn't the touch that was a comfort, so much as seeing his finger move while feeling the movement. That made sense.

I had to keep myself from looking around at everything that didn't make sense.

"The boatmen are insane." I jumped when a drop of water hit the back of my head. "They have to be. I'm well on my way, and I haven't been here long."

You will get used to this, mon ange. *Have patience. New vampires go through a similar mental culling.*

Mental culling?

I didn't ask for specifics. It wouldn't help. I needed to get out of this damn boat. It was bending my brain in terrible ways.

Time ticked by. Too slowly. I watched Darius's thumb and focused on the movement, until I noticed a change. It was subtle at first, a slight movement in my peripheral vision. Shortly thereafter, I noticed we were drifting closer to the opposite bank.

Hell, maybe the bank was drifting toward us. Anything was possible in this horror show.

I looked over my shoulder, relieved to see a pier like

the one we'd left. The boat stopped at the end, waiting patiently for Mr. Undertaker to come to life and refasten the rope.

The creature's head turned to me. "Safe travels, Egg Man." Then to Darius, "Safe travels, Walrus."

"*Goo goo g' joob*," I said miserably.

"No fog," Darius said as we walked along the pier. Was it me, or did I hear relief in his voice?

"I'm apparently pretty powerful, regardless of how well I know my magic, and still you felt a lot of pain going through. How could someone bonded to a lesser-powered demon make it?"

He shook his head and looked back the way we'd come. Mr. Undertaker was still there, staring straight ahead. Waiting. "I can't say. It might have something to do with age. I doubt Moss would've been able to cross, even with the bond, and if he had, he would've needed to recoup for much longer."

Ah. So while I'd been stalling with the chatting, he'd been shaking off the fog burn. Interesting.

"So, maybe Ja was just that much older." We neared the end of the pier. Oh, goody. Another never-ending beach.

"That's the thing. She wasn't much older than I am now when she went into the Dark Kingdom. She didn't seem overly concerned about the fog when we talked."

"On average, women do have a higher threshold of pain. Maybe you're just a wimp."

He frowned at me as we reached the end of the pier.

"Okay." I took a deep breath. There was no telling how long I'd have the opportunity. "Let's get through the illusion veil. Once we're inside, we'll hunker down and take a look at that map. I need a game plan. Then we'll run at Agnon and the sect that's got him, kill them all, and get the hell out of here. And so help me God, if the damn ceiling drips on me in there, I'm going to punch someone."

"With whose fist?" Darius's lips quirked into a lop-sided grin.

Another thing I would never live down.

I stepped off the pier and jolted as my foot sank into the ground.

Correction: I jolted as I stepped onto hard mud that shouldn't have had the give of wet straw.

My vision warred with my sensory perception as I forced myself forward. My boots shone at the tread, indicating wetness that went with the soggy feeling of sinking. By sight, we still traversed hard, dried mud.

A few moments later, we stepped through the invisible line. The barrenness of the beach disappeared, and a new scene took its place.

I stopped dead for a moment as my brain tried to adjust. And failed.

Darius didn't prod me forward, but grabbed me around the waist and hurried out of sight.

CHAPTER 17

AN ENORMOUS CIRCUS tent rose in front of us, blasting neon from every surface. We had a side view of a gigantic green Ferris wheel with a big grinning face on the spoke, rolling over and over. Flashing lights outlined a loop-de-loop roller coaster, which seemed to emanate screams. Fireworks exploded in the distance, pinks and purples and greens and blues.

The pathway leading up to all this strobed color in little squares, blinking quickly. Above it all, permeating everything, was the *bim-bom, bim-bom, bim-bom* of circus music.

"I don't like this," I said with a dry mouth.

We stopped behind a camping-sized yellow tent and crouched into freshly layered sawdust. Darius pulled off his backpack and unzipped it.

I crawled to the edge of our cover and peered around. An elephant with shaggy, clumped fur rolled by on four independent beach balls. Its tasseled hat didn't need a string to remain on its head. Beyond it, strutting around with a big stomach and a weird cackle, was a clown. *A clown.*

My eyes went wide and I yanked myself back. "Look, I can handle demons. Fire, brimstone, damned souls—all that I can handle. But clowns? I don't think I can handle clowns. Especially evil-looking clowns like that one."

Darius unrolled the parchment.

"I mean…" I palmed my forehead. "I expected a dark kingdom, not a circus on crack."

"You okay?" Darius asked.

I gave him an incredulous look and shoved my finger in the direction of *Cirque du LSD*. "Are you serious with that question?"

A smile graced his lips. He clearly didn't have a newly realized phobia of circuses like I did.

"From what I understand, on the outskirts and less-traveled parts of the Dark Kingdom, Lucifer allows the sects free rein. If the sect likes circuses, and they have the magical ability, power, and space to create one, they can. As you see. Also remember that the more powerful demons can change form."

I knew that, but an elephant with weird fur rolling around on beach balls?

I rubbed my eyes. I needed to stop fighting all this. One thing seemed certain: it wasn't going to get any better. If anything, it would get a whole lot worse. "Okay, fine. So what's next?"

Darius turned the parchment so I could see it. Clearly marked was the sect of the demon who'd made the map. That demon had also indicated a preferred point of entry, which was titled South Shore and had a note in Latin pertaining to paradise.

I gave Darius the side-eye. "We could have gone to paradise, and you chose the insane circus?"

He ignored me. "If we had landed there, the demon's sect would have been on the way to our destination." He traced a dotted line to a circle in the middle of the map.

"Our destination is very close to the castle, which I assume has my fa—Lucifer in it."

"We need to use a code name."

"Grand Poobah?"

He frowned at me. He was doing that a lot lately. If he wasn't careful, his face was going to get stuck and I'd have to dump him for losing his perfect looks.

I chuckled. He frowned harder...probably because he didn't hear the joke. "Sorry, I'm still adjusting to the mind-fuckery from the river, and now—" I hooked a thumb over my shoulder. The *bim-bom, bim-bom, bim-bom* combined with the swirling colors and crackling fireworks in dizzying ways.

"Actually, you look human, so calling him your father is probably better. Anyone overhearing will assume you are trying to track down an incubus or similar. That won't raise suspicion."

"Fine. Look, there are no real notes on here regarding which places are okay, and which we should avoid. So without a guide, we should take the shortest path. That'll get messed up somehow, because it always does, and then we'll improvise. But sitting here, planning for the unknown, is ridiculous."

"Do you have the map in your mind?"

I looked away and tried to recall it. The image came to the surface, crystal clear. I looked back to be sure, and smiled in elation. "I wonder if I'll remember people's names now, too." It was something I was notoriously bad at.

"One can only hope." He rolled up the parchment and stashed it in his backpack. "As you said, we will take the shortest path, yes?"

I suddenly realized what that would require. "We have to go through the insane circus."

"Yes. Try not to kill anything with your power. Do it with your sword, or not at all. Rumors of you will be circulating already. That'll bring challenges."

"Do you think the boat captain will talk?"

"And say what? The Egg Man wasn't seaworthy, but the Walrus seemed to do just fine?"

I narrowed my eyes at him. "It wasn't the sea that was the problem. Mostly. And I meant where he dropped us."

"He wouldn't talk to you, but...under threat, who is to say?" Darius slung the backpack over his shoulders and rose from his crouch. "Any demons following us are the least of our troubles. Ready?"

No, but I'd never be.

I rose, took out my sword, and followed him around the small tent, the cousin of the mammoth big top looming in the distance, moving away from the river and deeper into the circus. More tents, all bright colors, dotted the way. Sawdust littered the ground, some fresh but most older and squishy, like what I'd felt on the beach. Regardless, it was going to get in my socks, and that was the *worst*.

A tall woman strolled out in front of us with a hairy chest highlighting her large breasts, six fingers on one hand, and a mustache that curled at the edges. It looked like the demon had mixed a few of the "freaks" from the classic freak shows.

She glanced our way before throwing her arms wide and creating claws with her hands. "Hah!" she yelled.

I gripped my sword's hilt a little tighter, ready to jab her, but she swirled away, flaring her colorful skirt as she did so.

"I have never been so keyed up in my life." I let out a shaky breath. "This is really fucking with me, man."

"You will at least blend in."

"Please don't say I blend into this crowd. That is not

good news for my self-esteem."

We picked up the pace. A clown ran past, different than the one I'd seen before, wearing giant red shoes with claws sticking out the ends. Its face was mostly white, but some of the paint had rubbed off and black-spotted green skin shone through. Teeth that ended in points punctuated the clown's silent scream.

A roar shook the ground, beastly and deep. A giant lion, nearly as tall as I was, padded after the scary clown. It shook its mighty mane. The edges glowed with the colors flaring all around it.

Bim-bom, bim-bom, bim-bom.

I pulled Darius to the side, because we didn't need to tangle with something that had a scary clown running from it. As we moved, though, the lion's nose twitched. Its giant head swung our way.

"Run!" I yelled.

Another roar shook the ground.

I didn't wait for Darius to give his assent. I took off in the direction of the clown. If I got lucky, I could catch it and trip it. As long as Darius and I weren't the last in line, we were golden.

Another roar rattled my bones. Darius was beside me a moment later.

It's coming after us, he thought.

"No shit, Sherlock. What'd you think it was going to do, give us a cuddle?" I weaved in and out of the tents, hoping to lose it that way. In my peripheral vision, I saw things flying forward. A glance back and my blood ran cold.

The lion was bowling through the small tents, flinging them every which way with such force they fell to our sides. Papers and other debris, whatever was in those tents, flew around us. There was a solid *thunk* of an old-school typewriter as it sank into the ground five feet away.

"That doesn't even fit with the theme!" I hollered, angling right to get out of the tents.

I thought you usually ran at attacks.

"That is a freaking giant lion, man! I'm not trying to go head to head with a lion with nothing but a sword."

You are not being rational.

The lion roared as it burst out into the open strip leading to the huge circus tent. Demons of all shapes and sizes, most fitting with circus theme, including a little boy with a big lollipop and a forked tongue, scattered.

"All the other demons are taking off, and you think I'm irrational?" I picked up speed, but I heard it right behind us, shaking the ground with each step. It didn't look big and heavy enough to concuss the ground with footsteps, which meant there was an illusion afoot, and the real creature was probably gigantic. All the more reason to run.

Another roar and all the tents leading up to the circus arches tumbled through the air like paper in a tornado. The ice magic within me throbbed right before something swatted my backside. The lion shared a few of my magical tricks. Wonderful.

I went flying, just like those tents, ass over end.

"It's powerful," I said as I hit the ground and rolled. Darius tumbled beside me, for once not looking like a graceful elder vampire.

Let's go. Hurry! he thought frantically.

Like I needed to be told.

We jumped up as one and sprinted for the circus gates, the huge golden archway glittering manically with the reflection of lights.

Bim-bom, bim-bom, bim-bom.

The lion's roar drowned out the music as we raced through the arches. A collection of women dressed in red performance suits rolled by on a unicycle, one stacked on top of the other, fanning out to the sides. Honestly, it was pretty impressive.

"Eat them," I yelled over my shoulder at the lion, pointing at the stacked women. "They have a better presentation."

The lion got to the gates and pulled up short, letting out another hearty roar, this time sounding frustrated. We ducked behind a Chinese pagoda-looking thing, the big top at our backs, and glanced out.

The lion paced the gates, sniffing and staring. It wouldn't pass through them. The demons that had scattered before still hadn't come out of hiding.

"All the demons in there are afraid of that lion, and that lion is afraid of whatever is in here," I said softly. "Where have you brought us, Darius, and how the hell are we going to get through?"

CHAPTER 18

THE OBVIOUS ANSWER was not to go through the enormous circus tent, but to go around.

The sect seemed to have thought of that.

One side of the tent had pits dug a hundred feet out and going as far back as I could see. Some of those pits were obvious, but—as I quickly found out—some spots that looked like solid ground fell away to spikes of doom.

The other side of the big top ended in a steep cliff that dropped off into nothing. The gorge also spanned about a hundred feet. Someone must have dug it out, because there was no natural reason for there to be a huge drop-off between the two sides.

Clearly they wanted people to experience the circus, or die.

Back near the archway, the lion had wandered off. It had probably found someone new to chase.

"Why don't we head back to the boat? I bet one will be there," I said, squinting as a means to block out the music. It didn't work. Go figure.

Ja mentioned this area was considered the wilds, and it was the best place to get in unnoticed.

"Ja might also have been trying to kill you, remember? She downplayed the whole fog thing."

We will encounter one or two powerful demons in any of the entry points, and encounter more concentrated sects of power as we get deeper in. There is no easy way to accomplish our tasks, Reagan.

I knew he was right, which made me grumpier.

Fresh sawdust was sprinkled on the well-kept ground in a direct path to the entrance of the circus tent. A monkey wearing a tutu idled by with its hands raised, chirping. Another ten feet down the path, rope lined with colored plastic flags rose along either side of the path, wide at first, then narrowing.

Off to the side of the flap sat a ticket booth with a lone attendant, a bearded cheerleader standing a head taller than Darius.

"How many?" came the attendant's deep, scratchy voice.

One was on my tongue, but what if they saw through Darius's suit? They'd probably be more offended by an attempt to break the rules and sneak someone in than they would be by having a vampire in their midst.

On the other hand, admitting to two was pointing out that I had a friend. An invisible friend. Who was lurking around somewhere. Spying.

No one liked spying.

"How many?" the cheerleader asked again.

A presence behind us had me glancing back. I did a double take. Two torsos (and heads) connected at the chest and reduced down to one set of hips and legs.

"Uh huh, that's happening," I said, turning back. "Two."

Without asking for payment, the cheerleader slid two black tickets across the wooden booth. It looked beyond me to the conjoined twins.

"All righty, then." I edged away, trying to play it cool. I held both tickets and continued through the flap of the circus tent. Light spilled out from within, and that ever present *bim-bom, bim-bom, bim-bom* rose in volume. It was said that you could never get too much of a good thing, and clearly, this crowd loved that monotonous music.

Would anybody notice if I burned this whole she-bang to the ground?

Hesitantly, I continued on until I saw what was in there. Then started back-pedaling, bumping into Darius and making it no farther.

What is the matter? he thought.

Outside, I'd gotten used to the constant flashing of hysterical color. All of that cut away inside. The interior of the tent was decorated with lines of alternating black and white, spinning around the tent—small at the top, growing larger and larger until they splashed down at the bottom. Rows of bench seating, also alternating black and white, led down to the empty, round, black performance area on the bottom. Spotlights of brilliant, dizzying white flew around the enormous space.

"Seriously, would anyone notice if I burned all this to the ground? That is now an honest question."

Darius's hand on my back, pushing me forward, was not the answer I was looking for. *Let's walk around the top and get out any way we can.*

After a couple steps he bumped into me, as though pushed. I glanced back to see Two Heads looking around in confusion. Both sets of eyes came to land on me, and a flash of anger took over. "Hey!" it said.

"Sorry, buddy." I took a step back and gave an *olé* gesture, clearing the way for him. "After you, please. I insist."

"How many tickets did you get?" One set of eyes dipped down to my hand holding the tickets, and the other looked around. "I don't see no friend of yours."

"He's shy." I slipped the tickets into my pouch. "He'll be in soon."

"You know what they do to those who are greedy."

"Feed them to the lion?"

"Yes."

I nodded with a frown. "Not a lot of originality in

this place, huh?"

Both faces gave me a confused look that turned into hostility. "I will be watching you."

"And coming from you, that's saying something."

He moved down the aisle toward the performance area at the bottom. I thought he'd stop at the first few rows, clearly excited for the show. Instead, he continued on, crossing the circular area and disappearing through a flap in the back.

My stomach turned over. "Not good."

We had best go.

Yes, we had, because if we didn't, I had a feeling we'd be part of the coming act. I couldn't ride a unicycle, and I certainly couldn't do it carrying a bunch of scantily clad women. I'd be found out or ridiculed, and I wasn't interested in either.

We moved around the top, behind the last row of bench seats, making for an opening. Once there, I tried to pull at a flap, but wire held it fast.

Nothing my sword couldn't fix.

It was a testament to how dazed this place made me that I couldn't remember putting my sword away.

Hurry, Darius thought, and I felt a firm hand on my arm. *People are filing in now.*

His heart started to thump faster.

I pulled out my sword in a quick, practiced motion and slashed it at the wires. The sword cut through them as easily as it did Jell-O. I knew from experience.

I ripped the flap back as Darius thought, *Go!*

Before I could dash through the newly created opening, air condensed around me weakly and held me in place.

"Do I break out of this?" I asked Darius through the side of my mouth.

He didn't answer right away, and I knew it was because he was assessing the situation. Probably looking around to see who would notice, something I couldn't see from my stuck-in-the-air-and-facing-the-flap vantage point.

Do not break out. Let us go with the flow for now.

Easy for him to say—he was invisible.

"Grab the ticket from my pouch."

That will be noticed.

"So will the fact that I got two tickets for one me. That seemed to be a sticking point with my new friend."

The air revolved me until I was looking at a demonic face shrouded in blond hair. The only other oddity, as far as those things went, was that it had human male genitalia that ended halfway down its legs…in a hand.

"Normally I would say that you didn't try very hard, but you win the gross factor. That's really…something." I couldn't look away. Until the hand flexed into a fist. "Yikes. You give *cock punch* new meaning."

"You took a ticket. You must fight," the creature

said.

I expected shivers of fear. Instead, I felt shivers of excitement. *Am I smiling?*

Three Fists turned and made its way to the nearest aisle. The air, so weak that it almost couldn't hold me, dragged me behind it, scraping my boots against the ground.

"You will want to release me from this hold," I said in a rough voice while trying to keep control of my power. "It is making me angry."

It ignored me, thumping me down the stairs.

Close your eyes and focus on me, Reagan, Darius thought, following behind. *Focus on me. Don't let your power loose. Not now.*

I did as he said, sinking into the feel of his steady heartbeat. His comforting presence.

All the while, my rage thumped in time to *bim-bom, bim-bom, bim-bom.*

"We need to find a loving sect," I muttered. "Maybe a lustful one. Certainly a quiet one. The rage is getting out of control."

"That is why you are here, is it not? To let the rage out of control?" Three Fists hissed, and I got the feeling this was him excited. "Wrath. Violence. Blood."

"I just want to go on my way."

"You will, soon enough. Unless you can rise up and claim your worth."

I had no idea what that meant.

Three Fists used his air hold to move me across the performance area and through the flap. Darius followed. Several demons, including Two Heads, were crowded in a sort of holding area. The air hold released me and Three Fists pointed at a line forming to the side. "Wait in that line."

"Is someone going to give me instructions before I go out? I've never been here before."

"Wait in line. Go through. Kill the creature, or die trying."

"Simple enough." I shuffled to the back of the line, already a dozen people deep and continuing to grow. Darius shadowed me. "So all these people are waiting to fight some creature and hoping not to die?"

The creature in front of me, a plain-Jane demon compared with the rest of the lot, looked back. It must've thought I was talking to it, because it answered. "Are you fresh from the Brink?"

"Yes?"

It turned back around. "Did your maker send you here to prove yourself?"

"...Yes?"

It nodded. "It is trying to kill you. No one from the Brink stands a chance against one of its kind."

"Its kind being a demon, or being the creature we're about to fight?"

"Generally both. Humans are weak. Their pleasures might delight us for a moment, but mixing their blood with ours"—it spat, a glob of green—"is the worst offense. You are an abomination. Your human half will ensure you die a horrible death."

"You forgot to say *no offense* at the end of that. It's only polite, really." A roar drowned out the music for a moment, and even though it was probably a bad thing, I couldn't help but enjoy the reprieve. A crowd cheered. At least, I assumed that was what all the banging and thumping and scratchy or guttural yells meant. "And why are you here?"

"To prove to my sect that I am ready to rise in power."

"You think you can kill the creature, then?" Another roar drowned out the music. The crowd banged and jeered.

"No one kills the creature."

Three Fists came through the flap we were all waiting in front of and spoke to the first contestant. A ticket was handed over and Three Fists motioned the creature—who, like my half-blood-hating buddy, wasn't wearing circus paraphernalia—through.

"Right. Okay." I chewed my lip, thinking over the things I'd heard. "But you either kill the creature, or die trying, right? So that means you were also sent here to die. Hello, pot."

Another roar preceded a collective gasp, followed by wild banging and cheers. A moment later, Three Fists was back, looking for the next contestant.

That was fast.

Adrenaline coursed through me. I was about to go up against the creature that had made a lion quiver in fear.

"Did your creator tell you nothing?" The demon ahead of me glanced back while making a distinctly mocking sound. It made me want to punch it with Three Fists' third fist, if it could be arranged. "You must last for one cycle to claim victory."

"Ah." So Three Fists was a broad-strokes kind of guy. "How many people make it through?"

"A quarter or less of those who make the attempt. Have no fear. You will be added to the list of those who don't."

We stepped forward. "You like me, don't you? I can tell. No, no." I held up my hand as it glanced back. "Don't get freaked out. I have a sixth sense where it concerns demons. I can read you buggers from a mile away. You want to be my bestie."

It spat again.

The roaring creature moved through the contestants at an alarming pace. Only a few made us wait, causing the crowd to gasp and moan. Two Heads didn't make the cut. The cheering for those who lived was not nearly as loud as for those who probably died a gruesome death. It was clear what this crowd was into.

Finally, it was my new admirer's turn. It handed over its ticket, glanced back at me with a haughty sneer, and stepped through the flap.

The seats that I could see were filled with mostly circus folk, and some underdressed demons that clearly hadn't gotten the memo. I saw my new admirer walk out to the middle of the performance area and raise his hands before the flap drifted shut.

The roar (which I'd gotten used to) drowned out the music (which I would never get used to) for a moment, announcing the start of the fight. Time ticked away and a few gasps punctuated with roars echoed through the flap. The lackluster cheering announced a favorable ending for my bestie.

I had no doubt he'd hang around and watch me. He was a sweetie like that.

Three Fists pushed through the flap and faced me.

Reagan... Darius, who'd been waiting next to the flap, had gotten a look through it. The accelerated beating of his heart confirmed it wasn't good news.

"I sure wish I couldn't feel your heartbeat at times like this," I muttered as I handed over one of the tickets. I held my breath.

Three Fists narrowed its eyes.

"I'm ready," I said, zipping up my pouch.

Its eyes drifted down and stuck to my pouch. It held out its hand.

"Dang it." There hadn't been an opportunity for Darius to snag it. I dug out the other ticket. "Sorry," I said. "I thought my friend would be here. He's not, so I don't need that extra one."

Three Fists hesitated, staring at the tickets. Its eyes held suspicion when it glanced back up. "Who is this friend?"

"My friend. He's from the edges. You wouldn't know him. Helluva nice guy, if a bit of a flake."

Three Fists shook its head slowly. "You are being greedy, wanting double the time." A grin spread across its face. "We do not allow that. You should be tossed out in disgrace."

"Oh. Well, that's okay, then. Go ahead and toss me. I'll just head out the back, shall I?" I hooked a thumb behind me.

A pointy-toothed grin spread wider across its face. I wished I didn't notice all the flexing hands. "Humans have no honor. That is why you are here, yes? You hope to prove yourself?"

"...No?"

"I think it is." It snatched the last ticket. "Double the time. Granted."

No! Darius reached for the neck of his suit. He meant to take it off. *I will take my turn. It is enormous,*

Reagan. Obviously powerful. You cannot—

"Do not reveal yourself," I said through clenched teeth. "Don't you dare. I might joke that you are taking the cowardly way out—and if not, I meant to—but you are my ace in the hole. I might need a surprise counter-attack. Stick to the plan. If this creature nearly takes me down, help me then."

Reagan...

"Speaking your disgusting human tongue will not help you now," Three Fists said.

"I liked you a lot better when you were being help-ful." I unslung my backpack and put it down beside the flap. Hopefully speaking English, I said, "Grab this as soon as I go through the flap. Wait until the first roar to follow me in. This demon's able to carry things teleki-netically, so I doubt anyone will question the backpack flying. Just make sure to get it before someone else grabs it."

Reagan... He was pleading.

"Do you wish to remove that... What is it called?" Three Fists asked, pointing. "Fanny belt, yes?"

"Really? Even here?" I rolled my eyes. "It is a pouch, for fuck's sake."

"I was summoned for months at a time by a group of disgusting humans who wore them. I know the slang used by you vile humans."

"You're putting on blood sport, and you're calling

humans vile?" I rolled my shoulders and thought about opening my pouch. "Does magic work down here?"

"Of course. You are not the first offspring of a mage who summoned a demon for pleasure."

"Gross. You know, I didn't get this hostility earlier. This is a different side of you. Your grumpiness is showing. Are you tired?" I glanced in my pouch, making sure I remembered what all the various colors meant.

"Enough stalling. I will enjoy watching you die, greedy, disgusting human."

"You guys are really disgruntled about the whole double-time situation," I muttered.

Three Fists pushed through the flap and then held it open with its hand, watching to make sure I followed. I did so with a straight back and raised chin. Adrenaline pumped in time with my heart. Rage pumped in time with the music.

The crowd shifted in impatience. They banged on their seats or whatever they had at their disposal as I stepped onto the performance circle. A large demon decked out in a clown suit sat in a box I hadn't noticed off to my right. I felt a protective wall of air draping down in front of it.

Even from the distance, I felt the pulse of that demon's power. It was even stronger than Agnon, the lower level five from Seattle. It called to my ice magic, expanding it throughout my body. Unlike before, my fire magic rose as well, already more powerful than normal from being in the underworld.

I felt obscenely powerful. I felt *alive.*

I bowed, a grand gesture that felt right.

"A human," the clown said, leaning back. "Interesting. We haven't seen one of you since the Great Master enhanced the fog near the river. Your maker must've had substantial power. I can almost feel it. Who was it, tell me?"

That clenched it. Darius's suit did deaden the feel of my power. Maybe I'd remember to thank him if I ever got over this whole circus situation.

"I don't know," I said with a flourish, playing to the crowd. "He was a love 'em and leave 'em kind of guy."

"Hmm. Well. Please continue." He waved his gloved hand, and it was then I felt the presence behind me.

I turned and the first thing I thought was, *I'm going to blow my cover.*

CHAPTER 19

I T WASN'T A creature I could've expected. Not at all.

I had no idea how I'd missed it upon first entering the arena. My suspicion was that I had intentionally blocked it out.

Because it was a freaking dragon.

A *dragon!*

I wasn't sure if it was using that shape because it was massive and terrifying, or if it was actually the mythological creature. Being that unicorns were real, I had my suspicions.

Its scaly hide glittered and sparkled when it moved, like a writhing rainbow. With the lights shining down on it, throwing color around the room, I now understood the reason for the black-and-white decor. Heck, even for the color outside. This great beast was the attraction, and Clown Demon over there was hamming it up.

Great wings topped with hooked claws tucked against its sides. The large hind legs indicated its ability to launch into the sky, and the small front legs would probably soon be swinging at me, trying to rip me apart with the clawed ends. A great tail curved around it, the end spiked like a Brink dinosaur.

The thing took up a quarter of the performance area. All it had to do was stomp around and hope it squashed me.

Again. How in holy Hades had I not noticed it immediately?

"I bet my sword doesn't do a great job of piercing that hide," I muttered, reaching into my pack. "Well, then. Let's have some fun, shall we?"

The dragon roared its challenge. It spread out its mighty wings as best it could, given the space constraints, and bowed.

"Oh." Surprised, I bowed back. "That's nice."

It roared again and stomped toward me, fairly clumsy and odd. It wasn't a ground creature, I could tell. If it got into the sky, I bet all that awkwardness would melt away.

What was this majestic beast doing in this ramshackle circus?

"Blink once if you are being held prisoner," I said.

It rose onto its hind quarters and slashed at me with its front legs. Expecting that, I back-pedaled as fast as I could, putting away my sword. I was sure it had vulnerable spots, but I didn't want to dodge underfoot to find them unless there was no alternative.

Let's see if the Callie and Dizzy team can help me out, I thought.

I grabbed out the T-Rex spell casing, pinched, and threw it at the flap at the back of the performance area so it would distract the dragon that way and give me room to work. It flared pink light.

The dinosaur grew from the casing, three-quarters as big as the dragon and utterly lifelike. Its thick hide, a dark green, looked tough and kind of swampy. Its teeth gleamed as it opened its mouth to let out a mighty roar.

The dragon flinched, its focus abruptly shifting, now clearly unsure what the hell was going on. It regrouped quickly and spun, swinging its spiked tail.

I dove out of the way, barely missed, and spilled half of my spells. "Dang it!" I grabbed them in fistfuls and shoved them back in the pouch, pausing only to pinch a Weather Beater and throw it at the crowd.

Lightning rained from the ceiling, followed by churning tornadoes. Gasps and shrieks filled the air. A woman with a fistful of large hoops went flying through the air, the first to be caught by the spell. Her rings separated and arched through the air, a lovely blast of color.

I glanced up as the T-Rex lunged for the dragon. The dragon spun again and smacked the side of the T-Rex with its tail, making the dinosaur flicker. I heard a sound like a bug zapper. The dragon roared and backed up.

I threw another T-Rex out at the crowd, just to mess with everyone, and because they deserved it. Why not? If you didn't know the rules, you didn't know when you were breaking them.

A dog in a party hat flew past me. A zebra head attached to a demon's body flew by in the opposite direction. The dragon swiped again, undaunted by pain. The first T-Rex blinked out.

I heard yelling behind me but didn't pay any attention. The dragon was advancing.

An explosion rocked the other side of the tent, behind the dragon. Darius. Colorful fire flew into the air, then exploded again. I knew each explosion would spray little magical needles down on the crowd even as the lightning attacked them.

I zipped up my pouch, since Darius would cover for me, grabbed out my sword again, and rushed at the dragon. It lunged down at me, snapping its great, pointy teeth, and I slapped it in the face with my sword. The *clang* sounded like metal against metal.

I was right—even with my magic, my sword would not pierce that armor.

"This is a terrible thing to ask," I said in a collection of grunts as I ducked under its leg and rolled. "But do you critters shed and sell your scales? Because I would pay for that armor. I really would. Million-dollar idea.

Let's talk."

I hopped onto the knee of its back leg, surprised at how slowly it moved. When it shifted, bending back to snap at me, I sheathed my sword and jumped, grabbing the edge of its wing and pulling myself up. The wing flapped, as I'd figured it would, trying to shake me loose. I let go, the timing a little off, and splatted onto its back.

"Now what?" I asked it. It roared and beat its wings before pushing off with its legs.

"No, no, no! That was a rhetorical question. There isn't enough room for that!"

The sharp edges on the end of the wings fanned the crowd. Gashes opened up on arms, faces, and backs, whatever the wings could reach, before the dragon rose higher into the air.

"I should've thought that through." I grabbed wildly for something to hold on to, but my hands slid against smooth scales. Its neck was too thick for me to wrap my arms around. Its wings beat too frantically for me to grab.

I glanced over its shoulder, seeing Clown Demon looking up at me with a wide smile behind its ice magic shield. It was the only one still watching the show. The rest of the former observers were now running frantically, trying to escape the spells.

For now.

I winked at Clown Demon even as the dragon's muscles bunched under me. It was about to make a move, and I had a feeling that would lead to me being dumped off its back.

"Darius, if you don't want me to use my magic, you better get ready to catch me," I said, hoping that translated into his mind even though we were a good distance apart.

If I got past the dragon, I had a feeling Clown Demon would be up next, so I made fire spring up on the ground around its special box, out of sight of the demon and unnoticed by the pandemonium around it. I immediately felt the ice power creating the wall. Just like the work of all the other powerful demons I'd encountered so far, this concoction was complex, woven together meticulously. Deftly.

The dragon tilted, and I scrabbled for purchase. My fingers caught a lip between the head and neck, but I didn't have enough time to secure a hold. Instead, I slid off its back, across its wing, against its claw (which hurt something fierce), and off.

Weightless, I windmilled my arms. My fire magic kept working on the ice wall, counteracting Clown Demon's efforts. He was definitely powerful, but I was a good student. I sped up the effect as I winked an eye open and looked below me.

The ground rushed toward me.

I started an air buffer, quickly running out of time. Arms wrapped around me out of nowhere and scooped me out of the sky.

"Oh thank God, Darius," I said in a gush. "That would've been a rocky landing."

He threw a spell at Clown Demon as the last of the air wall disintegrated, and it hit the base of the box with a *thunk*. The demon's smile wilted and it leaned forward in its box. A vine instantly began to crawl up the box, sprouting fierce thorns.

"How have you done that?" Clown Demon bellowed. "Someone is carrying you! Yes, I can just see it." Clown Demon gestured. The small hairs stood up on my arms. It was about to hit us with some powerful magic.

"How long does it take that spell to work—" The vine shot up in front of Clown Demon, unfurling like a friend saying hello. The demon's brow furrowed as lovely red flowers bloomed in front of it. A moment later, they spat out something I couldn't make out.

The demon flinched and looked at its front, still clearly confused. It wiped its chest. Then swatted it.

Magical acid, I believe, Darius said. *It seems to work very well on demons. More so than I was expecting.*

"Did Penny do that?" I asked, mystified. That was a league above Callie and Dizzy.

"No."

He didn't elaborate as he ran. The *thwump* of drag-on wings beat the air overhead. It wasn't doing anything more than staying in place at the top of the arena, watching us.

"Think dragons can spit fire?" I asked as we ducked through the flap and into the area where the would-be combatants awaited their turn. All their faces were frozen in shock.

Ordinarily I would say yes, but then why is it here, in a sect that has Incendium magic?

I had no idea.

I vaguely know the direction we're going. I waited next to a circus member until the last possible second so I could get a read on its previous location. It is a hazy power, at least for me. That was why I wasn't waiting for you to fall.

"At least you got there before I went splat."

You wouldn't have splatted from that height. You would have bounced and severely broken something.

"Right…"

He turned a couple times as color slowly worked into the design of the enormous tent. I could tell when his knowledge ran out because he slowed.

"It's strange that we haven't seen anyone," I whis-pered as he paused at an intersection in the canvas halls. He was still carrying me, holding me tightly against his chest.

Do you think so? I am under the impression everyone turns up for the main show. And for the record, you made it through both of your time allotments and then some.

He chose the tunnel to the right and picked up speed again. As we moved through the back end of the tent, several living areas were sectioned off, probably for the higher-powered demons that didn't live in the smaller (now mostly ruined) tents at the front of the big top. A few turns later, which were totally random, regardless of what he said, we burst out through the back flap into blessed darkness.

If only that meant we were free.

CHAPTER 20

*A*RE YOU TIRED? *Do you need to rest?* Darius asked as we ran through the back lot of the circus.

Strange shacks and leaning buildings made of wood or stone suggested the kind of caravans that the circus staffers in the Brink might live and travel in. Few beings wandered around, but those that did were all costumed or disguised as circus animals of some sort.

I felt fatigue pulling at me, but knew I could continue on. I had a feeling that if I ignored the human side totally, I could keep going for much longer. Maybe never stop. Until I (possibly) dropped dead. It would be a one-time shock.

"I'm okay," I said. "You?"

"Surprisingly, yes." His deep timbre rumbled through his chest, and I was glad he was using his voice again. "I thought we'd have to figure out sleeping schedules, but at the moment I don't need it."

"I can run with you, you know. You don't have to carry me."

"I want to," he said simply. I suspected it was because he'd feared for me before the dragon fight.

Sounded fine to me, both because of the contact, which was comforting, and because I was lazy.

I thought over the things we'd seen and heard. One thing stuck out. "Clown Demon said he hasn't seen a human—which really means half human or less, obviously—since my dad enhanced the fog. Other demons seem to hate anything human, but aren't surprised to see us in their territory. Even beyond the edges. Don't you find that strange?"

He was quiet for a moment. The makeshift caravans fell away and the land turned wild, though not unpleasant. A strange sort of...grass, I would call it, formed a bumpy meadow. Twisted and gnarled trees rose to the sides and began to creep closer. It was like a pleasant hillside in a Jane Austen movie mixed with *The Nightmare Before Christmas*. Weird, but once you realized the gothic feel of it, kind of nice.

"That fog must've been put in long ago," Darius said, angling right as we raced through the trees. I knew he was altering course from the straight shot to our destination. And since my memory was freaking awesome now, I also knew he would skirt the edges of a place called Caritas. If my Latin, which was dicey, was correct, that meant affection, love, or passion. Maybe all of the above—Latin confused me. He was answering my wish for a momentary diversion from the violence.

"Demons are immortal unless killed, like vampires. Like gods. Some will have long memories and little concept of the passing of time. A human in their midst won't seem like many lifetimes ago to them. The term *enhanced*, however, suggests that the previous fog wasn't doing its job. Which would account for the difference between mine and Ja's experiences."

"Why's he trying to keep everyone out, do you think, including creatures he's fine with being on the edges?"

Darius shook his head slowly. "Ja spoke of the many delights in the Dark Kingdom. The beauties. Why go through the trouble of creating those and then hide them? Unless he's tightening the borders to keep the influx of other creatures from tarnishing his creations. The elves tried tightening the Realm's borders once. At least, that's what they called it. What they were really attempting was to wield an iron fist of control. With new species come new ideas, and that can create control issues for a leader. Make your people dependent on you, ensure they learn only the information you would have them know, and what a smooth ride you've created for yourself as a leader."

"Did they fail to realize that vampires won't let anyone have a smooth ride?"

"They learned that lesson the hard way, which was why their attempt failed. Miserably."

"I'll bet." I brushed my fingers against the base of his neck, thinking. "I think we are ignoring the dragon-sized elephant in the room."

"Was that creature real? Or a demon assuming the shape, like the lion at the front of the sect?"

"I don't know about the lion, but the dragon was a dragon. They might call it something different here, but it was a dragon. No demon could mimic those scales. My sword couldn't even scratch them. Do you think that fog is there to keep the dragons a secret, like the unicorns?"

"There has to be more to it than that. If it wasn't for the effect of unicorn blood, they wouldn't have to be guarded and kept secret."

"Not to mention the importance of the part they play in creating new vampires."

"That as well."

I watched the subtly changing landscape for a while, noticing the trees becoming denser and adorned with more foliage. "Whatever the reason for that fog, I doubt it's targeted at humans. That's not the thing that erodes at humans' mortality down here. The other heirs of Lucifer were able to get past it, but still ended up dying."

"I agree. Without that fog, humans might be able to get in for a time, but I doubt they would be able to stay for long. How long depends on their power level, I imagine, but only a certain type of half-breed human can survive down here. They must have a lineage of immortality on their human side. For you, it is the bloodline of the gods passed down through your mother's side."

"What about the other species with that bloodline? Like elementals? Why couldn't Lucifer breed an heir with them that would last down here?"

"Each species poses their own challenges for reproduction, but it seems, unlike strictly magical people, humans are able to handle almost anything."

"We can basically breed with anything magical?"

"A great deal of magical species, yes. As far as I have seen."

"Weird."

"Regardless, whatever Lucifer is hiding, I want to know what it is. Vlad is probably already trying to find out. Right now, I am leading the race. I want to cross the finish line first."

"Ah. So it all boils down to: you are competitive, and want to beat Vlad."

Darius was quiet for a moment as he ran through the trees, not once flinching despite a couple of last-minute saves from running headlong into various branches and a tree trunk. I, on the other hand, flinched a great deal. I wasn't used to running at those speeds without the adrenaline from battle pumping in my veins.

Finally he answered. "At the heart of it, yes. But I do wonder what is being kept from me. And how I can get in to discover it without being noticed."

"Your suit, obviously."

"I am wondering if the suit does less to hide me than you do. When the clown demon, as you called him, realized someone must be carrying you, he could see traces of me. Until that instance, no one even tried. The suit cannot fully contain what you are, so you're easily noticed. Before they can look around and notice me, you're ripping them apart in some way."

"You really need to stop with that. It was just a couple of occurrences, but I don't like to talk about..." I chewed my lip. "I hope the rage issue wears away when—if—I get out of here."

"You will get out of here. There is no doubt. The question is, will you make the situation worse rather than better?"

"Wow. Talk about a truth bomb."

"If you weren't with me, I wonder if people would notice me more easily. I'd be granted admission—it seems all one needs to do is get through the fog for that—but I wonder if I'd be met with hostility."

"And if you were?"

"Magic works down here, so most of the demons wouldn't pose a challenge. Some of the more powerful ones would. If they wanted me dead, especially if they were willing to work together to that end, I have no doubt they would make it happen. Which would greatly put you at risk."

"Why? I wouldn't be here with you."

"What would you do if a demon killed me?"

A stab of pain pierced my heart and spread fear, remorse, and then, as was usual down here, rage throughout my body.

"Yes, *mon ange*. You would blow apart the gates of hell and teach them what terror really looks like," he said softly, and gave me a squeeze. "Which would draw Lucifer to you. You would deliver yourself into his hands, since you are no match for him. Not yet."

"I'm learning, though. The magic. Their weaves are really complex, but with the memory upgrade, I am building on everything I'm learning. I feel like a bionic woman."

"Keep analyzing. Learn all you can."

The landscape changed. Gradually, the dark, muted colors of the forest morphed into tones of purple. The ground lost the grassy look and changed into soft tufts of something like lavender, all blooming. Puddles formed and merged as we traveled, eventually forming a small stream. Strings of leaves dripped down from the trees, some brushing the ground. Instead of green, like a weeping willow, they were all a vibrant shade of purple to complement the overall look.

"Wow," I said, amazed by the transformation. A haze formed over the ceiling, disguising the overhead rock like a sheer drape, but not covering it entirely. It felt like a decoration, not the bending and manipulation of reality itself, something that made me want to smile.

After another few minutes, glowing lights resembling stars popped into the haze above, glittering and beautiful. The stream enlarged slowly, now about two feet across. The tufts of flowers were crushed when stepped on, like I'd expect, but they sprang up again in Darius's wake. Beside the stream, the bank and rocks took on a grayish hue to counteract all the purple.

"Wow," I said again as Darius slowed. "This really is...beautiful. It's nice knowing that this side of my heritage isn't as...horrible as I'd feared."

Not all the trees wept, now. Some climbed high into the sky, the trunks and branches dark, offsetting the vivid purple leaves.

"Ja spoke of these places. They are for travelers to rest or idle." He stopped at the curve where the stream turned into a lagoon. Small rivulets and currents created movement in the water. "She spoke of them fondly."

He put me down and took my hand, entwining our fingers and taking it all in. It reminded me of when we were at the hotel in Seattle, sitting above the water and sharing a quiet moment.

Rustling caught my ears. I jerked my head to the

side and immediately went on high alert.

"Be still," Darius said softly. "These are peaceful zones. Fighting is prohibited. If a demon cannot calmly enjoy this place, it must move on."

"Remember that your information is super old."

"In a closed-off kingdom such as this, change is very slow."

Someone emerged from within the branches of one of the willow-type trees. I say someone, because the being was in human form. A man, in his mid-forties, with toned muscle and long, shaggy hair. He didn't wear clothes, nor did he have hair elsewhere on his body. His arms were a little too long, legs a little too short, and chest a little too broad. To a demon, I was sure those details were minute and unnoticeable. But to a human, it was jarring enough to make the onlooker stop for a moment to try and figure out what was wrong with the picture.

"Why would it choose a human form in the underworld?" I asked softly.

The being moved to the right, making its way around the lagoon.

I don't know. Darius had seamlessly switched to thought-talk. *Did you feel any power coming from it?*

I shook my head slowly. "But it's probably too far away."

I wonder if it's reminiscing about a joy ride it took to

the surface. It would have to be a powerful demon to create a form on the surface, as you know. That or... Darius's hesitation was long enough to jar my curiosity. I glanced at him. Tightness had formed around his eyes as he looked down at me. *Ja told me a rumor about these places. Often they are formed after Lucifer returns from a trip to the surface. Sometimes after he goes to the Realm, and sometimes after a journey to the Brink.*

I pulled him to the nearest willow-type tree so I could look inside. "That doesn't seem like a very exciting rumor." Certainly not enough for the tight eyes.

He personally creates these places, and it's said they are fashioned after someone who made an impression on him on one of those visits. Possibly that demon was soaking in the feeling of that person—and he created a form to go with it.

"Was Lucifer into both men and women?"

Made an impression *doesn't have to mean love affair,* he thought. *But as to your question, I do not know.*

It took me a moment to realize what he was really trying to say.

My heart stopped for a moment and an intense longing came over me. "Do you think he made one for my mother? They weren't together long, especially to an immortal, but do you think my mother is represented here?"

CHAPTER 21

I *DON'T KNOW*, mon coeur, Darius thought. He was calling me his heart. That was sweet. *His meeting your mother would be fairly recent to an immortal.*

I nodded, because even if Lucifer had created one, I wouldn't be able to see it. The whole thing was nothing but a rumor, so the only way I'd know for sure would be to ask my dad. And clearly that couldn't happen.

Shall we rest for a moment? Darius looked around the willow tree.

Layers of green-gray moss cushioned the dark brown, almost black trunk. Purple leaves fell like a layered waterfall from the branches, creating a lovely sensation of privacy.

But we couldn't stop to rest just because something was pretty. Just because I hoped one of these tributes had been made for my mom. But for a moment, I leaned against Darius and took it all in, letting the beauty infuse me and unwind some of the aggression that had suffused me. Dissipate some of the rage.

Muscles I didn't know had been tight slowly relaxed. Tension I hadn't felt in my shoulders loosened. Darius's hand let go of mine and came around my body, pulling me close. My feelings for him flowered, filling me with soft warmth. A smile drifted up my face and I put my arms around his middle, soaking in the feeling of contentment.

"Your rage speaks directly to my predatory instinct," Darius murmured. "As a vampire, it makes me feel alive. Makes me feel powerful. I have found an ally in you. Someone to run into battle with." He turned me toward him and angled my face up to his. He pulled off his mask and brushed his lips across mine. "But I love this feeling just as much. It speaks to my primal instinct to protect. It makes me feel human. Complete. Through you, I can access both lives I have lived—this one you see before you, and the one I once believed had died in the change. I love you, Reagan, now and forever."

I fell into his toe-curling kiss as passion flooded my body. I reached up to grab his suit and rip it off, but pulled back at the last moment. Instead, I shoved his chest and made him stagger backward.

"Sorry," I said, out of breath. I braced my hands on my knees and squeezed my thighs together, trying to relieve some of the new tension in my womanly bits. "I had a strong need to go for a ride, but I don't want to unravel the magic in your suit. Or, you know, leave ourselves open for attack while thinking about...other things."

His fangs elongated, and I knew he was barely in control. He nodded slowly, his body taut, fighting the urge to rush me and finish what we'd started.

"Okay." I threw him a thumbs-up, trying to ignore the hot coiling of my body. I turned to leave. "Let's keep moving."

I pushed the cascade of leaves to the side as a shape registered in my peripheral vision. Gliding through the air, silent and deadly, a sparkle of color twinkled against the purple backdrop before it disappeared from sight. A quick glimpse was enough to ramp up my heart rate.

I jerked back and my body keyed up, the serenity I'd felt in this place quickly replaced by battle-ready rage. "Did you see that?" I asked.

What? He moved up beside me and leaned forward, not disturbing the leaves. Which meant he couldn't see much.

I crouched, and he followed me to where the leaves thinned. The slice of sky that hung above us was purple and empty. "I can't be sure what it was. A large shape above us. Flying. I thought I saw color."

"The dragon?"

I clenched my teeth in frustration. "I really want to say yes, but I didn't properly see it. It could be anything."

His brow furrowed, like it did whenever he was

working out a complex problem. I couldn't hear anything, though. No thoughts were registering in my mind.

"Don't fail me now, magic," I said as sweat wet my brow. We'd be dead in the water if I'd somehow lost access to my powers.

What is the matter? he thought-asked me.

"Wait. I heard that. Why can't I hear your thinking? Is it my magic, or—"

I have worked out a way to keep some thoughts private, he interrupted, and that came through just fine. *Surprise.* He resumed his thinking pose, basically ignoring my presence.

"Great, fine. But let's talk this out. What are your thoughts, Mr. Strategist? Because if you've got nothing, we need to approach this my way. That includes busting out of here and killing things in a no-killing zone. Wait." I held up my hand. "What if it is the dragon? Can it come at me in here, or is it bound by the same rules?"

That was one of my many thoughts. I was wondering whether, if it is a dragon, it's the one we escaped from earlier. Are there many of them in the underworld? If so, do they normally stick together, or are they solitary? Do they band with demon sects willingly, or are they trapped? If it's the latter, can we offer it a way out somehow? What about other potential flying things?

Back to the dragon from the circus, since that is the likeliest scenario, I am calculating the amount of ground it must've covered so far, what that means for its speed, not to mention the quickness with which it was able to organize and head out. Taking those numbers, I can—

"Okay. Good call. You need more time to think. I'll sneak around and try to see it again to cut down on some of those questions." Before he could stop me, I ran through to the other side of the tree. No wonder the guy wasn't worried about mind-fuckery. He lived in a constant state of it inside his own head.

Taking care to go slow, I pushed the layer of leaves to one side and looked out, immediately seeing a demon sitting at the base of a different sort of tree, staring up and to the right. It leaned forward a little, to track whatever it was, and I quickly hopped out and followed its gaze. Empty sky.

When I looked back, the demon was surveying me.

I pointed at the sky, not sure if no violence also meant no talking. In this kingdom, it probably did. I took a chance, anyway. "Did you see that thing?"

It pointed at my legs. "Where'd you get human clothes?"

Not important, demon!

I walked beside the cascading leaves, my eyes on the sky, letting silence drift between us. I was hoping its thoughts would give it away. Nothing was coming, though. "Was it a dragon?" I asked.

"Those pants. Those are human pants. Where'd you get them?"

Apparently this thing didn't realize I was human, which was good news. It also didn't seem to care about the flying object, which did not help my information-collecting efforts.

I chanced a step out into the open, ready to dodge back in.

"I trade you for them," it persisted. "I tell what fly by."

What did it think I was, born yesterday?

Two more steps into the open area between the trees and the visible sky was still clear. Although the slice of sky I could see was small. I would need to get away from the trees to see into the distance.

Or just get the information out of my new pants-loving friend.

I turned to the demon. "These pants are worth more than your paltry information." I hadn't meant to sound so rough. "What else?"

"How about that pouch around your waist?" the demon said, standing. "I trade you."

"*Thank* you for calling it a pouch. That's great. But not on your—" I paused, remembering the old pouch I'd stashed in my backpack. The one that had seen me through some tough battles.

It would get a chance to help me out again. What a champ.

"Wait." I scampered over to my backpack and pulled the pouch out from the bottom of my bag. Lumpy and stained, it was not a prize like the pants, or even the new pouch, but beauty was on the inside, and I'd rip out that demon's heart if it didn't see that.

Whoa, girl, I thought, heading back. *Don't kill the thing that has information for you.*

The demon's eyes widened and it rubbed its hands together in excitement as I held out the old pouch. It was clearly not a poker player. It was also clearly keeping its thoughts to itself.

"What do you give me for it?" I asked, shooting glances at the sky.

"I tell you what I saw." He pointed upward.

I felt Darius's presence behind me, watching. It was time to go.

"Fi—" I cut off as stars blinked out in my peripheral vision. A shape interrupted the empty purple.

I quickly walked backward toward Darius's location in the willow tree.

The demon glanced up, and its eyes stuck to the shape overhead. Frustration and disappointment crossed its expression as it shifted its gaze back to me.

Trying to show that I was taking the unintended hint, I edged forward until I could get a peek without being easily seen from above. My blood ran cold.

A rainbow shimmered against the background, beautiful to behold. Great wings beat at the sky twice before the creature resumed its silent glide through the air. Straps crossed its chest, and I could barely make out something on its back leaning over its shoulder, looking down.

A clown in a harness on a dragon.

"This place is one giant acid trip," I murmured.

Clown Demon wanted vengeance. Or answers. Or all my shit. Any of those options spelled disaster for me.

"No dice," I said, turning.

"Wait! I give this." The demon grabbed the tail end of a snake that had worked out of its scabby skin on its side. It held it up.

"Good God, no." I grimaced at it. "Why would I want your pet snake?"

Its brow puckered. "Healer. Fair trade."

Take the snake, Darius thought. *We must go.*

I didn't want to touch the snake, so how was I supposed to take it?

The demon misread my hesitation.

"What else you need?" it asked in urgency, shaking the snake at me. Its eyes shifted to the pouch and it licked its black lips with a green tongue. "What else? Trade!"

Directions, Darius thought. *Hurry. We don't have*

much time before it doubles back.

After a hasty deal featuring a snake, exchanged information, and the realization we'd been speaking English all along—more evidence that I couldn't tell the difference between the two when I was hearing and saying words—we ran through the willow tree to the other side and looked up. All clear.

As fast as we can. Stay to the trees.

I ran beside him, doing as he said, but I couldn't stop myself from looking back. In the sky, floating along in the other direction, was the majestic body of our violent foe. Its wings pumped before it continued to glide, moving like a great bird of prey.

"If it turns around, we're screwed," I said, putting on a burst of speed.

It doesn't know we are here, and it doesn't know how fast we can run. We have time before they zigzag back in our direction.

We couldn't be sure they were zigzagging at all, since this place wasn't logical, but I let it go.

A demon sat forward as we passed, confusion written across its face. Two others popped out of a willow tree, interrupted from some intimate activities, by the look of it.

I had a brief curiosity about their reproductive abilities, but let it go. If there was ever *not* a time to talk about demon sex, this was surely it.

The purple tones around us darkened and turned muddy brown before sliding into black. Stars still speckled the sky, but that was the only light. Velvety moss turned into wild grasses that scraped my legs. I knew without testing it that it would rip up human skin.

"Are we sure we can trust that demon?" I asked as we veered left. My foot splashed into water. My other foot did the same, the land turning marshy. Not deep water, however, which was good, if annoying.

Considering how star-struck it was with your pouch, I would be inclined to say yes.

I sure hoped this wasn't the one time he was wrong.

SOME INDETERMINATE AMOUNT of time later, which felt like hours but was probably less than one, we slowed as we came upon our first sect on the new route. Shades of molten blue interrupted the black of the sky. A full moon shone through the clouds, shedding light on hard-packed dirt in strange patches, like it was shining through tree branches high above, although no trees surrounded us. Ahead, a huge church or gothic mansion—maybe a combination of both—rose into hazy bluish fog. The ground dropped away on either side into jagged cliffs.

A stream of thoughts invaded my mind: Darius working things out. Calculations, distances, a catalog of the architecture before us, the time it would take to go around it all, the probability the dragon would head this way, the likelihood of an attack by the sentinels posted at the entrance with rigid frames and weapons—on and on, round and round. Finally, it ground to a halt and he said, "Let's continue on as planned."

"All that just to keep moving as we were?" I angled right, like the demon had said. "And what did the architecture have to do with anything?"

"I like to notice the fine details in case they might be relevant in the future."

We snuck around a tree and paused, looking at the sentinels. Neither of them were looking our way, and we were too far away to see their eyes. Figuring they hadn't noticed us, or didn't care about us since we weren't approaching them anymore, we continued down the ravine, which, my pouch-wearing demon friend had promised, would lead to a secret path along the cliff face. It was a way to get around without having to go through, and the fastest way by far to get to the heart of the Dark Kingdom.

"Well, here's hoping it wasn't a whack job." I clutched the rocky side and started down the steep, narrow incline.

"It wanted a fanny pack. How sane do you imagine it is?"

"Not cool, Darius. My poor pouch sacrificed itself so we can get to our destination, and you're making fun." I shook my head and noticed a cut in the side of the rockface. This path had purposefully been created with sneaking in mind. My kind of people.

My foot hit a rock and kicked it over the ledge. I paused, listening. After an incredible amount of time, it *bonked* off a hard surface far below.

I flattened against the rockface for a second, looking down at my heavy boots. Only one and a half could fit on the path side by side. Rocks jutted out along the "path," and I'd have to contort my body to get around them. A couple hundred feet away, another rockface looked at us, wondering what the hell we were doing, no doubt. Below, the fake moonlight glittered on a sea of metal points, ready to stick anything foolish enough to take a tiny path along a cliff face and slip off.

"If I fall, I'm using my power," I mumbled, moving along.

"If I fall, I also hope you'll use your power. This is…treacherous."

A spot of black interrupted the moonlight.

I froze and grabbed at the wall. My foot slipped and my weight shifted, tilting me toward the ledge. Darius grabbed me and pulled me back, but his heel slid out from under him. I grabbed his arm and heaved with all my might, stopping his downward progress. He scrabbled up beside me again, and we stood with our backs to the rock, breathing heavily.

A large body glided above us, its wings spread and feet tucked under its body. The dragon's scales caught and refracted the moonlight in a beautiful kaleidoscope of color. On its back, looking over its shoulder, was that persistent clown.

"I hated clowns before, but now..." Rage pounded inside of me. I could tear that thing out of the sky. Pull it down and send it careening to the spikes below.

Easy, love, Darius thought, probably feeling me tense. *Any large use of power might alert the sect above us. They are not so far away, and they have sentinels.*

I knew that, I did. But my split personality didn't care.

The dragon pumped its wings, pushing a little higher into the faux-sky. The clown jerked its head left and stared at something. The dragon pumped its wings twice more, putting on a burst of speed.

A roar shook the rockface, and not from Rainbow Dragon.

"Another one?" I whispered, trying not to shake. That deep-throated dragon roar—I was pretty sure it was another dragon, anyway—rooted fear deep inside me, like that (now headless) demon I'd encountered in the edges. "They must not be super rare."

Darius didn't say anything, just breathed slowly in and out. His heart was beating erratically again.

I couldn't hold back the grin that spread across my

face. "That scares you, does it?"

Rainbow Dragon curved away from the sect, disappearing over the other cliff.

"That magic is powerful." I saw Darius gulp as he said it, and my smile spread. "I wonder if a mage can recreate it."

"You nearly peed yourself. Admit it, you are scared of something."

"I am scared of a great many things, and most of them concern your safety."

My smile slipped. "Foul play, getting gushy when I'm making fun of you. That's below the belt."

We looked up, but the overhang of the cliff prevented us from seeing anything. Rainbow Dragon hadn't circled back.

"Do you think it saw us?" I asked.

Darius shook his head, not yet moving along. "They would have to know to look for this path, which seems unlikely. They'd probably assume it was a cliff face."

"Let's hope so."

"Yes. Hurry, we don't want to be stuck here in case the other creature decides to inspect."

CHAPTER 22

TWO OTHER SECTS, a few lovely oases, and another indeterminate amount of time later, which was probably a half a day instead of the months it seemed to be, Darius and I came to a weary stop. We had just cleared the last tree in a sort of evergreen forest, and an endless desert stretched before us, flat and empty except for a couple dead trees that dotted the hard, cracked ground.

I braced my hands on my hips and looked back the way we'd come, desperate to lie down and take a nap. But here we stood, on the edge of the worst place to dodge a dragon attack.

"That demon didn't seem too smart, and so far it's been right, but it's starting to look like it had an elaborate plan to strand us in the middle of nowhere while that dragon flies overhead." I pictured the map in my head. "We are close, too."

Darius stared out ahead of us, and I knew he was going through our options. Thankfully, he'd stopped including me in his chaotic thought-fests. There was clearly a reason for his placement in the vampire hierarchy, and it wasn't just his age.

"We haven't seen the dragon in a while," Darius said.

"True." I rubbed the ground with my toe. The top flaked off, dry and brittle. "But if the clown thinks we're going to the castle, it might pass over this area. This is one of only a few entrance points on this side of the underworld. We've taken a lot of time getting around those other sects. And that's not even taking into account that there's clearly no cover *by design.*"

Silence fell again, and I waited for Darius to put those new tidbits into his think tank.

He shook his head. "It is impossible to tell how long it will take to cross."

"This has to be an illusion." I looked up at the gray-blue sky showering down yellowed light. Puffy white clouds hung above us, getting lower and smaller on the horizon, emphasizing the impression the desert went on forever. "Unless you were wrong about the underworld, and it has pockets of infinity like you say the Realm does."

Darius continued to stare out at the desert, not answering. He'd probably already thought about that. Then replayed his conversation with Ja, including all the little nuances most people wouldn't notice.

It was exhausting me, and I wasn't actually doing

anything.

"I can try to tear this down, like I did on the bank of the River." I pulled my lip through my teeth. "The trick is to imagine what I want to do and then let my dark passenger, A-K-A my power and the reason I'll end up in the looney bin, do its thing."

"Why would he put an illusion here?" Darius asked softly, squinting now. His wheels had to really be turning. "Is he trying to turn people away, or does he simply wish to watch who approaches his castle?" He rubbed his chin, something I'd never seen him do.

"Perplexed, huh?" I nodded and started forward. "Let's just handle this my way."

"That is exactly how you will end up revealing yourself." His roving eyes caught up to me.

"This is going to show my extreme ignorance on most things *magical worlds,* but…cameras don't work outside the Brink, right?"

"No, not that I have seen. Something happens to them when they go through the gates, even those powered with batteries. Light in the Realm is created magically. I assume the same is true of the light here, such as it is." He looked up at the glow above us that never wavered or changed wattage.

"I'd love to know how," I said, gesturing toward the fake sun. Despite the danger, I half wanted to see if I could use my magic and try and get the blueprints.

"As would I. In the Realm, it is usually a flame or an orb created with magic. Elf magic, pixie magic—there are a few creatures that can achieve the effect naturally. But the magic has to be stored in an appropriate container—it's tied to a specific source. I don't see that here."

"My dad has tricks."

"It would seem so. Ones he is not sharing with the elves."

"So if he doesn't have cameras, someone has to physically watch for travelers. I doubt there is scaffolding above us, so that someone would have to fly or sit on the ground. Sitting on the ground doesn't make sense, because they don't have phones here. The watcher would have to race us to announce our presence. I'd kill it before it put on the jets. So we're really only worried about flying things."

"Yes," Darius said simply. He'd thought of all that.

I continued talking through my thought anyway while I walked, I'd already decided; Darius kept pace with me. "We've only seen one flying thing. The dragon. Which…could be a problem. I didn't try any real magic on it, but it's a dragon. It might be impervious to my magic, or too far away for me to do anything.

"If it is our dragon friend and his clown sidekick, they won't try to tattle on us. They'll try to kill us and take our stuff. Which isn't ideal, I grant you, but I am confident I can think of something to keep from dying."

"And if it is another dragon? Is that why you were rubbing your chin?"

"No."

Oh good. There was a more perplexing situation at hand than a rogue dragon.

"I'm sure I could figure it out. Violently." I looked up at the sky. "Like I said, I can always try to crack this bitch open and see the guts. Just give me the word."

"Since when do you ask for permission?"

"You think ahead, right? Isn't that your claim to fame? So I'm letting you do your thing. Don't get lazy on me now."

Darius looked behind. We'd already put substantial distance between us and the lush green trees, but the horizon looked unchanged, the way ahead never ending. "The risk is not yet worth the reward. You showing that level of power so close to the castle…" He shook his head and glanced upward. "Not yet. How are you doing on energy?"

"I'm feeling the drain of all this traveling. I could use sleep, finally. You?"

"The same. I am amazed we were able to last so long without it. Longer even than in the Realm." He tsk'ed. "I should've asked earlier." After a pause, he said, "I almost wonder if we should go back to the cover of the trees and take care of that before we get too far out."

"This can't go on forever. It can't. It's more eye trickery. Impressive, though. If I wasn't stuck in it, I'd give the old man a nod of approval."

Darius's honeyed gaze came to rest on me for a moment, assessing.

"What?" I asked.

"Were you like your mom?"

"Somewhat. Why? Are you wondering how like my father I am?"

"Yes. It is a pity things are the way they are."

"Tell me about it. That is, if he's a cool guy. Or maybe he's mostly an asshole with a few good qualities. In which case, I'm good with the way things are. Except for the hiding thing."

He smiled at me and looked forward again. "Touché."

We fell into silence as the faux-sun blazed down on us. Our feet crackled on the brittle ground. I thought back to the map. To what I had thought was a relatively small section of nothingness between sects. I'd seen a few at this point, and many of them had turned out to be an oasis of some sort, or just a common travel way. Demons in those areas tended to mind their own business, and if they looked me askance, they went back to minding their own business as soon as I met their gaze.

I thought back to those demons, and how quickly

they'd looked away. "You don't think word of me has spread already, do you?"

Darius glanced over at me before going back to his scanning. "Why do you ask?"

"Did you notice any demons wary of making eye contact with other demons in the oases?

His gaze stopped moving, now pointed upward. "I did notice demons seeming wary of each other. Shifty-eyed, as you would say. You clearly looked out of place to them, but you didn't seem to raise any more concern than the others."

Small graces. "Demons didn't seem wary of each other in the edges."

"No." Darius slowed and put a hand on my arm. "I've noticed it more the farther we've traveled into the Dark Kingdom. I can't tell if that is normal, or if we are walking into something unusual." He raised a hand and pointed. "Do you see that?"

I squinted into the sky, not seeing anything but a few puffy clouds heading toward the distant horizon, which did not curve like anyone born in the Brink would expect. It tripped me out.

"My vision improved with the bond, but it's still not to your level. What is it?"

"A flying object of some kind."

I was so tired, I could only think of one possible response to that: *one-eyed, one-horned, flying purple people eater...*

He did another scan of the sky before going back to that one spot. "Yes. It is something flying. Either it is small and near, or large and far away."

I nodded, because yes, that was how perspective worked.

Darius pulled the flap away from his satchel and looked around. His gaze stopped on a dead, leafless, twisted sort of tree standing fifty feet away, leaning so hard I wondered how it hadn't already fallen.

"Are you going to try and work a privacy spell?" I asked, trailing after him.

"Yes. I want to see what's coming before it sees us."

Doing things his way really had its advantages.

We stopped by the tree. Spells worked best when they were rooted to something, and natural things worked best. But out here, since there was a distinct lack of *somethings,* I agreed that the tree would have to do.

We put one on each side and one above, though the one overhead balanced unsteadily as it tried to cling to the paltry branches. Usually for short term only, the spells would (hopefully) make the eye slip right by us, rendering us mostly invisible until the brain of the being observing us figured out something was tricking it and wised up.

I stared out through the purple film. Our side of the spell was colored, but the other side would appear clear.

It didn't take long for me to see what Darius was talking about.

"A vulture," I whispered.

"Three times as big as a Brink vulture, but yes, that's what it looks like."

And like a Brink vulture, it drifted lazily past us without flapping its wings. Unlike a Brink vulture, it was not riding a breeze.

"We're headed back into mind-fuckery territory," I said, tapping my gun and thinking about taking out my sword. "Do you see any more?"

"No. Not just yet." Darius whipped around and squinted. His hand fell on my shoulder.

I followed suit, and there it was, a giant bird soaring through the sky, looking at the ground with beady eyes (we were too far to see the eyes, but I'd back my imagination on this one).

"We were looking at a distorted reflection, used to trick travelers as to the whereabouts and proximity of the coming entity." A small smile graced his lips. "Genius."

I didn't have time to ask him how he'd figured that out. The bird was nearing us now. It did one pump of its great wings, pushing itself through the air. I bit my lip as it flew overhead, inky black wings fluttering. My magic swelled, urging me to shoot a jet of fire at it.

I dug my nails into my palms, desperately trying to

hold back with everything I had. Because who knew if there were more beasts coming right up behind this one? If there were, the others would see the whole thing and they wouldn't have to travel far to tattle.

The vulture traveled beyond us for another hundred feet or so before tilting, turning like it was approaching a dead end. It headed back toward the trees at an angle.

"Maybe it's leaving," I whispered.

Once it reached the tree line, it curved again, doubling back. It was scouting the area, looking for enemies. There could be no other explanation.

Feeling like the hunted, my power pulsed. Rage welled up. Then, strangely enough, love surged inside me, too, and the emotions swirled around each other. My magic mimicked it, more blended now than it had ever been. More balanced.

That did not mean I was in control of it. Not by a long shot.

"It has to go away," I whispered, half begging. "It has to go away, or I will kill it."

Easy, mon coeur. *Patience. It did not see us. The spells are working. It will move on. Even with bad vision, it only needs a couple sweeps to see all. We simply must wait.*

Sweat beaded on my brow. I chewed on my lip.

The vulture passed to our left, looking down on the great expanse of empty space. It circled a tree that was a bit larger than the others, as though trying to see every nook and cranny before moving on. Trying to find stowaways.

It acted like it was the most deadly thing in this part of the kingdom.

It wasn't. I wanted to prove it.

I squeezed my eyes shut as my power pumped higher. Round and round it rotated, begging me to do something. To assert my will. Prove my dominance.

My skin felt too tight. My blood throbbed in my veins.

At the same time, the rush of rage, paired with the deep ache of love, felt so *good*. So raw. I felt Darius deep down. Felt my sword pushing against my back. The weight of my gun. I cherished the memories of my mother. My gratitude and loyalty to Callie and Dizzy. Fire. Ice.

The purple film in front of us melted away, disintegrating before my eyes. My power pushed out around us, tearing down the other spells. Burning through our cover.

The vulture, passing to our right toward the distant trees, issued a loud screech. It pumped its wings, gaining speed. For one brief moment I thought it would head away. Thought it hadn't noticed. But instead, it folded up its wings and dove straight for us with an avian-type battle cry.

This bird wasn't here to seek and report. It was here to attack.

CHAPTER 23

*F*IGHT.

That one thought from Darius was enough to break my dam of control.

I stepped away from the tree like a commander joining the field of battle. I thrust a hand into the air. Air encircled the bird, the distance not a problem. Power roared through me, so sweet it cut. So pure it lifted me up.

Literally.

I rose into the sky and clenched my fist. The vulture screamed, stopping mid-air.

Another flew out over the trees, pumping its wings frantically, spreading its clawed feet to strike. Its speed was amazing.

I ripped the first bird out of the sky and catapulted it down for Darius to deal with. The moment I released it, it turned for me, not able to see Darius. It hopped forward, ready to beat its wings and elevate enough to use its mighty claws.

Without delay, Darius was on it, attacking it from

behind with his own claws out.

When I spun around to face its friend, the giant bird was twenty feet away and closing fast.

"Hells bells, they *do* move fast." I ripped up my hands. The bird lifted its feet to score me. I batted it away with air before enclosing it in a firestorm. My energy, low to begin with, felt the drain.

We must go. Now! Darius grabbed my arm and pulled, dragging me back to the ground.

"Why are they attacking us?" I said, spinning and running behind him. "Do you think word has spread about me?"

It was diving before it could be sure of who you were. No, it wasn't you specifically. I can only guess that we are on the doorstep of another sect, and they do not want visitors.

When I saw my new pouch-wearing demon friend, we'd have words.

We didn't get any closer to the horizon, but suddenly the light clicked off and our surroundings changed drastically.

Darius skidded to a stop so quickly I hit his back. My eyes went wide, my stomach flip-flopped, and my lungs burned, suddenly dry of air.

We stood on a bluff overlooking the middle of the Dark Kingdom. I'd expected a few things, but nothing like this.

Nothing like this.

A castle *a la Beauty and the Beast* rose up in the distance, large and majestic with pointy spires and various towers. Green swathed its base, dotted with color from what I could only assume were roses or other flowers. The air around it twinkled with fairy lights and the sky was dark and filled with a milky way of stars.

"Gorgeous," I said in a strangely raspy voice. It must've been the lack of air. "It has to be another illusion, though, right? Because it's hazy and seems much too close."

The bluff on which we stood seemed to be offering the wayward traveler, or someone returning from a long journey, all the wonder and majesty that was my father's home.

I blinked away the image, not allowing myself to be seduced by the loveliness. This wasn't why I was here, and like so many other things in this place, it was an illusion.

Ready? Darius thought, looking at me.

"Yeah." The wide path in front of us led down the hill and disappeared around a bend. A hedge rose up, and razor-sharp spikes gleamed within it. "That doesn't look friendly."

No. Let's try not to be noticed.

Easy for him to say. He was still virtually invisible.

We took off and drifted to the opposite side of the

spike-infested hedge, moving toward another bend up ahead. The castle's image dissipated. I was happy for it. I needed to keep my wits.

Darius crouched at the intersection up ahead, looking in both directions. I joined him, staying low and as small as possible. The path had formed a T, and I knew we had to go left for our destination.

He tensed to rise and I grabbed his shoulder to keep him put, hearing shuffling from the very direction we needed to go. He'd already hesitated, though, hearing it as well.

It didn't take long to see what was making the sound. A group of four demons crept along, huge creatures with thick, corded muscles. Insects traveled their bodies, disappearing into cracks and coming out elsewhere, like they were eating through rotting flesh. Two held large spears, and the others sported claws.

I felt their power pulsing, strong and cold, aching through my body in the most delicious of ways. These demons were packing some serious power. *Serious* power. And I was dragging like a college kid at the end of a week-long bender.

My hand was still on Darius's shoulder, and now I squeezed, worried. If I felt their power so clearly, would they be able to feel mine? It was only somewhat masked by my suit. If they looked our way, my only hope was that Darius's suit would mostly block me from view.

Otherwise, it was on like Donkey Kong, and they'd have a helluva lot more control with their magic than I did with mine.

The beings paused on the path, rigid.

I braced, ready to grab my sword, when a new feeling washed over me. Spicy sweet, prickling my skin and eliciting a moan of delight. Fire magic. Raw and pure; just as powerful as the demons we could see, but much more familiar. I couldn't see them, but I could feel them, another group of extremely powerful demons in the vicinity.

Darius wouldn't know a second set of demons were afoot. I thought as hard as I could. *We're about to witness a battle. We need to get to cover.*

At least I did.

He didn't move or indicate he'd "heard" me.

A group of three demons surged out from the path on the right. As they ran, spears burst from the hedge, preceding them in an advance attack. The spears didn't land.

Invisible hands swatted them away, icy power filling the air and bolstering my own magic. I could almost see the complex weave the demons used curling through the air.

A demon from the right shot a ball of fire at the original crew. It rolled and boiled along the path. The ice demons couldn't defuse it in time, and it sliced through one of them, chopping through a limb and singeing the side of its body.

A snake slithered from around the wounded demon's side before biting near the wound. The wound began to stitch together. Another slithered out of its leg, heading up to the shoulder. I watched in awe for a moment as the dang thing worked on growing the arm back! Holy crap. That snake wasn't such a bad find after all.

Ice magic rose up as solidified air, but the fire cut it down quickly. These demons were clearly on the same power level but with opposing magic, and they knew exactly how to use it on each other.

I watched in fascination, my need to hide utterly forgotten.

The two groups crashed into each other. A demon jabbed a spear forward with blinding speed. Its target angled just enough to miss it. The first retaliated with an attack of slashing claws. The would-be victim dodged. The aggressor created a sort of knife with ice. Fire burrowed through, breaking it apart.

Darius's hands were on me, shoving me away.

I couldn't tear my eyes away from the battle as another demon got its spear in its opponent and ripped it from side to side, not giving the snakes and also insects enough time to stitch it back together. Fire blistered the skin of yet another demon. Growls and grunts punctuated each new wound.

More fire-powered demons ran from the right, lending backup.

Go! Go! Go! Darius bodily lifted me and ran, pushing through the non-spiked hedge on our left and cutting through green grass stippled with wild daisies. It was a stark contrast to the vicious fight on the path.

"What are we walking into?" I asked, seeing magic rise up over the hedge as the demons continued to rip each other apart. "Is this one of the violent sects?"

I was led to believe the inner kingdom was one of outward peace and political maneuvering. If they need to fight each other, they take it to one of the sects on the outskirts, like the circus sect.

"Clearly things have changed since Ja was running around this place."

Clearly. Though I can't imagine Lucifer would allow his inner kingdom to crumble from this type of fighting. They are practically on his doorstep. He has to notice.

"Maybe he is refusing to pick sides and letting them sort it out?"

Possibly. I couldn't say. Regardless, we will use the distraction.

"We also have someone to blame the deaths on."

Exactly. We must get into the sect, find the leaders, and destroy them. From them, we can determine how many know your secret. As I've said, if this species is like most others, the leaders will not have trusted just anyone with the information. Foot soldiers will only get directions, not the reasons behind those directions. You will simply be a half human to most of them, not Lucifer's child.

Good, because these sects were huge, and there was no way Darius and I could take out an entire one on our own. I didn't even know if we could take out the leaders.

Darius pushed me, silently urging me to get running. We cut across the meadow, knowing from the map that the leftward path would wind away. Soon we were out in the open, the daisies and wild flowers not doing much to hide us. In the distance, stone buildings rose up over a metal fence with pointed tops and something resembling barbed wire twisting through the spikes. Everything was spikes here. They loved spearing people, clearly.

On the other side of the fence was a hedge of bushes with long briars ready to prick anyone who made it over. As if in an attempt to soften the buildings and perimeter, ivy sporadically crawled up the stone, dotted with bright pink flowers.

A roar sounded above us. I flinched and looked up.

Huge wings beat at the sky, attached to a dragon with shimmering, multicolored blue scales. It wasn't Clown Demon, but it didn't matter. It took a dive for us anyway.

"Darius, put distance between us!"

He didn't argue. He broke left, putting on the jets.

Thanks to the bond, I was faster than I'd ever been.

Unfortunately, I wasn't as fast as a dragon.

CHAPTER 24

I T OPENED ITS. mouth and issued a stream of blister-
ing fire, scorching the ground in a strip before
rolling over me. I cocooned my body in ice magic,
keeping the fire from burning away anything not fire
proof.

I reached the fence and stared at all the deterrents
that kept us from going over. I healed quickly, sure, but
if I vaulted over the fence at this harried pace, I'd get
torn up enough to make myself vulnerable for a while. I
couldn't afford that.

The dragon turned with incredible speed, agile
when in the air. It made another pass, raking me with
fire and setting the briars ablaze.

I glanced at Darius, not sure what to do. Which way
to go.

Before I could yell the question, another dragon
shape drifted over the stone buildings in front of me.
Red but with a pink shimmer, another great beast
moved through the air. These creatures clearly did not
need light to set off the glimmer in their disco-ball

bodies.

Its roar was deafening, deep chested and a little raspy. It pumped its wings as the dragon that had been plaguing me with burst after burst of ineffective fire rose into the sky.

Darius was next to me a moment later, putting a small vial to my lips. *This will help with your energy. We must hurry.*

The unicorn blood slipped past my lips and exploded in my taste buds. Joy and adrenaline pumped through my middle and blossomed, filling up my life force and heightening my senses. Power pulsed within me, giving me the same *skin-too-tight* feeling I'd had earlier, but this time it was even more acute. There was a pounding sensation—as if all that magic was ready to erupt. I felt powerful. Indestructible.

With tingling limbs, I turned to Darius. "What about you?"

He pulled me closer and bit into my neck. I moaned and dropped my head back. His serum mixed with the unicorn blood, creating an indescribable feeling of euphoria.

The dragons above crashed into each other, gouging with their feet and biting. They tumbled through the air and toward the ground before they broke apart, beating at the sky with their wings and roaring at each other.

Darius pulled away from my neck. A droplet of

blood dribbled down his chin, and he wiped it away with the back of his hand.

The pink dragon blasted us with an unexpected stream of fire, mid-battle with the other dragon but retaining the presence of mind to notice us at what were probably the gates of its sect. The blue dragon used the distraction to its benefit and flew forward with claws out.

I covered us with a hasty shield of ice magic. My magic coated Darius's suit and immediately unraveled the spells. I'd exposed him.

"I'm sorry, I just reacted," I said, pushing him along the fence. "But that fire would've scorched you. It was a hundred times hotter than the one at the gates.

"I understand, thank you. Come on, if we can get out of view, we can get over."

We ran around the corner of the fence and staggered to a stop. Up the way, a horde of twenty or so demons climbed or carefully worked their way over the defenses, dropping down into the briars and wading their way out. They were sneaking in the back of their enemy's stronghold while their cohorts created a diversion at the front.

A horrible screech announced the end of the dragon battle. I looked back in time to see the blue dragon do the flying equivalent of limping away. The pink dragon watched it for a moment, not following. A moment later, it swung our way, looking along the fence.

The land was wild, but the brush and trees had been cleared for a good hundred feet leading up to the gate. We'd never make it.

Darius pushed us away from the enemy demons and back around the corner. *It's coming. Cover us with your magic.*

I did as he said, seeing the pink, shimmering beast soar through the sky. The fire came as expected, washing over us but not doing any damage. The dragon saw the enemy a moment later and sounded a trumpet-like call, beating its wings for speed and taking off after the demons that were already across the fence.

"There'll be a battle here in no time. Let's get moving," I said. We chose a spot and started to climb. Metal ripped at my suit and tore my skin.

While they do have defenses, these sects don't have the added security like the others at the outer reaches of the kingdom. No gorges or traps with spikes. They have merely a fence and some cleared land.

The trumpet call boomed above us.

"And a dragon. Don't forget about the dragon."

Yes, but... Darius flinched as a metal burr from the barbed wire nicked his leg. Blood welled up. *One dragon can't replace some of the things we've seen.* He threw his leg over the spikes at the top of the fence and slipped. A point cut into the inside of his leg. He grunted and scrambled to get a better hold.

"You okay?" I asked as fire rained down. The dragon wasn't getting the hint that fire didn't hurt us. I wondered about the fire demons. Were they basically fire proof, too? Because if so, what was the point of using a dragon against them?

These defenses speak of a violent species in a not as violent area.

"What's your point?" I grimaced as the spike at the top of the fence scraped my leg. Searing pain vibrated through me.

Two things. One, if they don't usually fight, what is causing this? And two, when will Lucifer put a stop to it?

The dragon passed by again, dropping quickly from the sky. Its feet reached for me, intent on grabbing me and forcing me off the fence.

I punched it with air, knocking it off its flight path. It screeched and rose again, hovering over me for a moment before sounding the trumpet.

"It probably has no idea what I am." I threw my other leg over the top of the fence. "This is going to hurt." I dropped down into the middle of the bushes. Briars dug into me, scratching and tearing. Darius joined me a moment later, grunting as he made his way out.

We have to get cover.

"Whatever gave you that idea?" We limped to the

nearest stone building, moving as fast as we could. Rounding the corner, we ran smack into two demons, clearly summoned by the dragon's calls.

One of them hesitated a brief moment, its eyes going wide in its malformed head. Darius took advantage, his fingers turning into claws as he swiped. The other demon launched forward with an air knife. I dodged the thrust and kicked it in the stomach while ripping out my sword. The air knife came at me again as the other demon lost its head to Darius's efforts. I slashed down, cleaving the demon where its neck and shoulders met.

A surge of air pushed toward me from the side. I turned, bringing up my sword, but my power got there first. Roaring out of me, the fire broke through the ice magic and kept going, rolling through the air and piercing into the demon like a knife.

The demon screamed and jolted, succumbing.

Darius grabbed me by the arm and pulled me, running over the demons we'd just killed.

"My power is acting on its own volition," I said, my lungs burning. They weren't used to exertion without air.

For now, use whatever is at your disposal. We'll figure it out when we aren't running for our lives.

Fair enough.

We ran between the buildings. The view was such that we could see the courtyard at the end of the corridor. Demons warred, using power, weapons, or their own claws. Yelling and grunting competed with clangs of metal.

Darius pulled me to a wooden door on the other side of the corridor. The lock clicked and he pushed the door open, rushing in with me following behind. His claws extended as he set upon the startled demon inside. Two blinks and the demon was slumped on the ground.

"We need to heal and come up with a plan," Darius said, shrugging out of his clothes.

I shut the door and did the same before looking over my wounds. As I'd expected, my skin was ripped and torn from the run in with the fence and the briars. Nothing too bad, but a few places hurt like the bejeebus.

"Here." Darius passed over another vial of blood.

I took it greedily before he transformed to his monster form. Another explosion of energy and power vibrated through me. I dug in my pack for my leathers. Something slid past my hand.

I flinched back before I remembered what it was. Then hesitated.

"Oh ew." I reached in again and extracted the snake, grimacing as it wriggled.

Something solid hit the outside wall. The clatter of metal announced someone had lost their weapon. The battle was in full force.

I put the snake onto my leg, wondering if it would work on human skin. Without warning, it bit me, its fangs digging into my flesh.

"Ow!" I started to yank it off, but the pain had already numbed. The gash next to the bite started to close up right before my eyes. "Oh wow. This works."

I let the snake roam my body. It bit me near the deep cuts and just slithered over the smaller gashes. The healing ability was insane. When it was done I offered it to Darius.

He shook his head and pointed at the worst of the problems, already nearly closed up. His monster form wasn't as good as the snake, but it was close.

"Now what?" I asked, returning the snake to my backpack. I finished putting on my leathers and strapped on my weapons again.

He hovered near the door. *We skirt the battle, try not to reveal your magic any more than we have to, and find the leaders of this sect.*

"A human running around this battle is going to draw notice."

Hopefully not with all the fighting. They'll be focused on survival. They won't have time to notice you. He loosened the straps of the backpack, something that didn't look easy with his claws, before putting his satchel and clothes in it. He would be using his monster form. This fight was about to get uglier.

I ran out ahead of Darius, sword in hand. At the end of the corridor, I threw a spell that created a riot of noise and light right in the middle of all the fighting. It exploded, throwing a demon up and over the crowd. The light flashed like a strobe, and some demons flinched away or jerked up their hands to cover their faces. Others stabbed those that gave in to fright.

We ran along the wall on the outskirts of the battle. A demon stepped into my way, and I thrust forward and stabbed it in the chest. Darius launched at another, hitting the demon's upper body with his clawed feet and knocking it over. Then he raked his claws across the demon's face and stabbed its throat before jumping on to the next one.

I slashed another demon in the back as I got moving again, making it arch and reach for the wound. One of its enemy demons descended, taking the opportunity for an easy kill. I left them to it.

We ran down a side corridor and turned left. Darius kept looking up, directing us toward the building looming over the rest. A creature with three legs ran our way. Darius got to it first, ripping and tearing at it like a wild thing. He hardly slowed, continuing on at a fast pace.

More fighting and clangs came from the right. Darius ignored it, continuing straight. We ran down another corridor, the design like an above-ground ant colony made of stone. I got the feeling it was supposed to make a stranger lose their way. Darius never faltered in his directional choices.

Five demons stood in the courtyard at the base of the tallest building, large things without weapons. Which meant they didn't think they needed them. Their eyes came to rest on us, and their power instantly welled up, thick and heavy. I felt it pushing and pulling at me, giving mine the boost to which I'd grown accustomed.

"They are powerful," I said to Darius right before the air condensed around us.

Kill them. He raked his claws through the air, shooting sparks as he cut through the ice power.

I blasted two demons that were standing close to each other with hellfire, cutting down the air around me as I did so. They squealed as the fire ate away at their bodies. Darius ran at the others, spearing one with his claws as a wall of air swung toward him.

I finished the two I'd blasted. I wasn't taking any chances.

An air impact shoved Darius across the ground and toward a stone wall.

I broke up the power and struck the demons back with an air and fire one-two punch that I pulled out of my ass. The effect was like hitting them with a giant paddle embedded with spikes. I felt them try to dismantle it, but they couldn't counter both types of power, so their efforts were ineffective.

That seems like the Great Master's power, I heard from one of their thoughts.

I hacked at its neck with my sword and Darius full on ripped the other's head off. No wonder he liked when I let my rage show.

The door they'd been guarding burst open. The wood slapped off the stone wall. Power the likes of which I'd never experienced wrapped around me and lifted me into the air. I couldn't move. Couldn't understand the weave. Didn't know how to break into it even with my mixed power.

A huge demon with wings folded close to its red body stepped through the door. A tail with a triangle at the end flicked out from behind it. Its eyes glowed white from within a bony head. All it needed was a trident and it could be a cheesy Halloween costume.

"So it is true," it said in a rough voice as it sauntered out of the door. "An heir does exist. And she has delivered herself to me. How convenient. It saves me so much tedious effort."

Its gaze swung to Darius, who was suspended ten feet away.

"And she has somehow brought her vampire lap dog into the Dark Kingdom." It *tsked.* "I detest your kind. We do not need any more of your half breeds. Killing you will give me no end of pleasure."

If Darius was as confused as I was by the half-breed comment, he didn't show it. The demon lifted its hand, and air turned into a stake directly in front of Darius's heart.

CHAPTER 25

"**N**o!" I SHOUTED. "If you want my cooperation, you'll leave him be."

The demon studied me for a moment as two other demons ran into the courtyard. They slowed in jerky movements when they saw the dead littering the ground.

"What of Tensess?" the red demon asked the others, not looking away from me.

"It killed our ambassador," one of the demons answered. "It wants your head."

"Does it, now? That isn't very friendly." The red demon paused for a moment, considering. "Send someone to attend to the Great Master. Take him gifts. Try to keep him put, and unaware of our activities until we have Tensess's head. Release our full arsenal. Tensess has no idea what it has unleashed."

"Yes, conspector." They turned and ran.

"I have been at odds with our neighboring sect for centuries. They are always under my skin." The demon turned and walked through the door. We followed it through the air as helplessly as kites on a string.

Can you get us out of this? Darius thought.

I closed my eyes and felt the magic around me. Solely ice magic but so expertly woven, and backed by so much power, it almost seemed like an inanimate object. Even hacking at it with fire wouldn't disturb it. This demon was out of my league.

Miserably, I shook my head. We were in a fix here, and I wasn't sure how to get us out of it.

Two floors up, the red demon opened a wooden door and poked its head in. "Call the Five. I have important business to discuss. It cannot wait. And have them bring in that sniveling Agnon. We need all enlightened parties in one place."

That would have been good news if I'd had a hope in Hades of breaking out of this hold.

An affirmation had the red demon pulling back and shutting the door.

"What's with the getup?" I asked.

The red demon entered something like an elevator shaft that had no elevator. We drifted in beside it like balloons.

"This, you mean?" It ran its hand in front of its chest. Its tail flicked.

"Yeah. It's a little cartoony for the leader of a sect this close to Lucifer."

Its smile pulled at its cheeks, showing a mouthful of

rotten, brown, pointed teeth. At least, they looked rotten. The demon was probably hamming it up for my benefit. What a sweetie.

"You call him by his real name," it said. "Amazing. Either you have no fear, and are therefore stupid, or you are playing games. I wonder which it is."

"I can't really get a reading on you. Was that rhetorical?"

We rose through the air, up through the spacious shaft. This thing was its own elevator. I hated how cool that was.

"And you speak our language. More amazing still. That will make things so much easier. Tell me, who taught it to you?"

"Oh no." I shook my head. "This isn't some one-sided Q&A. If you want answers, you have to give them. I'm still waiting for your reasons for looking so ridiculous."

"Stupid, then. I see." We reached the very top floor. I looked down and my stomach threatened to revolt. There was a void of empty space below us. A lot of it. And we were totally under this demon's control—we would go splat if it wanted us to.

Darius had been right, though. The most powerful thing in the sect (hopefully) made its...office? Hall?...on the highest floor.

I mentally checked in with the vampire, and was

absolutely astounded to realize his heart was beating regularly, strong and slow. Either he was going dormant until he had an opening to revolt, or he thought I would come up with a way to save the day.

I hoped it was the former. No ideas were coming to me as of yet—all I could think to do was study that magic and hope something came to me.

We drifted after the demon into a large rectangular room with huge rugs covering the stone floor. In the first half of the room couches and chairs were clustered together for easy conversation. The second half seemed like a king's chamber, with a large wooden chair at the front and smaller chairs lining the walls leading up to it.

The red demon took the chair at the front while Darius and I were forced to split up, each controlled by a different surge of air. I was brought to a stop front and center, facing the demon, while Darius was put off to the side.

"So." The demon crossed an ankle over a knee and leaned back, reminding me of a human. I wondered how much time it had spent in the Brink. "You have come to me."

"Surprise!" I said.

"You realize your worth, I take it."

"To you? Yes. To my father?" I hesitated.

"Maybe you are not so stupid after all. There is some debate that he won't be as thrilled to discover he has an heir as we had previously thought. He has been let down in the past. But so far, you are holding up just fine. Look at you. Not even the hint of the death rattle humans always seem to develop in this airless part of our world. That bodes well. Then there is your mother."

I couldn't help the shock of longing that came over me, something that aways seemed to happen when she was mentioned out of the blue.

"Yes. We know who your mother is. Why do you think we had to grow those accursed flowers along our walls?" The demon snorted. "She loved natural beauty, so I hear. The Great Master has decided we should incorporate more of that within the kingdom. *All* of us should, not just the insufferable love seekers and sex worshipers. What are we, elves?"

Warmth welled up inside of me. My father didn't just remember my mother, he had incorporated one of her loves into his home—and not just in some glen for weary travelers, in the whole kingdom. That was sweet, even if it was probably a short-term situation. Darius was right; for an immortal, the twenty five years he'd been away from her was a blink of an eye. At least his affection for her had been genuine. That was nice to hear.

Shuffling sounded behind me. I craned my head, but I couldn't get a good look at the moving shapes I saw out of the corner of my eye. That was, until they filed in and took seats.

Six of them in all, and five the expected knobby, bony, or otherwise gross form of a demon. The last was a tall, skinny thing that reminded me of an elf. It skulked in behind the others, bent and broken.

My old friend Agnon. It needed more time to heal, because it looked pretty miserable. Or maybe that was as good as it was going to get.

"What is this?" one of the demons asked.

"We are needed elsewhere. We do not have time for captives, however strange," another said.

"For those of you who doubted, it seems Agnon was telling us the truth all along. This is the heir." The red demon gestured toward me grandly.

"*This* is the heir?" one of the demons asked, rising. It stalked up to give me the ole once over. "It is but a human."

"It is *part* human, as Agnon has said." The red demon uncrossed his leg. "Agnon was also correct about her magic. She has both types. I saw her use them together, but it seems she hasn't yet fused them. She is in her infancy."

"Clearly." Another stood and walked around me. "What is she, a hundred human years? She knows nothing."

"A hundred? Really?" I glowered at the demon that had said that.

"So it is the heir. So what?" said one of the demons that hadn't bothered to get up. "If we present her to the Great Master now, we might risk his displeasure. We are not sure he still values an heir. Not after the son died."

"And if he does?" the red demon asked. "Then we are holding an invaluable prize."

"We can always test the waters before presenting her," said the one standing in front of me. "If he seems favorable to the possibility, we go ahead as planned. If not, we kill her and be done with it."

"In the meantime, we can train her," another said. "Use her."

"Because I'm going to be on board with being used." I shook my head. "You guys need to take a lesson from the vampires on how to properly manipulate someone." Hisses filled the room. "Not a fan of vampires then?"

"We are in agreement," the red demon said, ignoring the vampire comment. And Darius. "We must take her elsewhere to train her. We cannot have her so close to the castle, nor can we risk knowledge of her getting out until we are sure she is ready. And wanted."

"We no longer need Agnon. Its purpose has been served," the demon in front of me said, turning toward the red demon.

"I agree. Guarding it has become tedious." The demon flicked his fingers.

"Wait! I know her. I have seen her in action. I can help you train her. She trusts me," Agnon wailed, dropping to the floor with a bowed back. "Please."

A spike of air drove through its back before expanding, breaking its body apart. I crinkled my nose. Sure, I'd come here to kill Agnon, but that was kind of messed up. And here it had thought it was a valued member of the sect. Probably.

"We have a battle to attend, but before we go, I want proof the heir has the power you claim." The demon in front of me turned back, now with an air of expectancy.

My body lowered until my feet hit the floor. The air around me released, leaving me standing on my own. Not like that would help. I knew the demon would just grab me up again if I tried anything beyond the dolphin show they were asking for.

"Show them," the red demon commanded.

I crossed my arms. It was a little *sullen teenager* for my tastes, but under the circumstances, I didn't have any better options.

"That's right." The red demon leaned forward, its eyes gleaming. "The vampire is needed to assure your cooperation."

Darius grunted as a slice of air pierced the center of his chest, just missing his heart.

"No!" I yelled.

Do not let their treatment of me influence you, he

thought.

"Okay. Okay!" I begged. "I'll show you. Leave him be."

"You see? We do not need to manipulate you. We simply need to know your weakness." The red demon smiled, and this time its teeth were white and dripping with crimson blood.

"We're not going to get along, you and I," I said, calling up a ball of fire on one side, and lifting a chair with air on the other. My power crouched inside of me, controlled. *Of all the times for it to wait for me to initiate rather than just exploding out and taking care of the problem...*

"Weak," one of the sitting demons said.

"She can do much more." Air struck Darius again, in multiple places, ripping pieces out of his flesh. A spike hovered against his chest in line with his heart, poking his skin. As I watched, it started to turn slowly, burrowing its way in.

Adrenaline dumped into me as I felt his pain. As his heart started to hammer.

I love you, he thought. *You have been the highlight of my long life.* The softness of his farewell, the reverence, tore at me in a way I could barely comprehend. I could feel his resignation. His certainty that he would die. If not right now, eventually. They would torture him to get what they wanted out of me, and when he was no longer needed, they would kill him like they had Agnon.

He was happy I would live. I could feel it. His only regret was that he would have to say goodbye so soon.

Agony soaked down into the very fiber of my being because he was right. Everyone in that room knew it.

Unless I could do something.

No more hiding. No more fear of what my power would turn me into.

It was time to own what my father had given me in all its splendid glory.

I laughed, a purely demonic sound that I must've picked up somewhere along this journey. Power ripped and tore at me, pounding. Rising. I opened up to it, toppling my reservations and letting it consume me.

The rage was first, sending my fire into a frenzy. It traveled beneath my skin and licked at the air. Violence and anger boiled inside me, dragging me under. My vision pounded red. My fingers itched to kill.

Not yet, my power whispered at me, like a passenger sitting on my shoulder and murmuring into my ear. *You aren't complete yet.*

I ground my teeth and held on, remaining open. Inviting all the soul-eating power into my body, and allowing it to fill me however it would. When I felt my humanity slipping away, I didn't flinch back. I didn't slow it down. I kept going, realizing now all the subtle defenses I'd developed over the years to keep myself safe from this humanity-eroding power. Not anymore. I had to trust in my mom's heritage. I had to trust that my father's power wouldn't destroy me.

"Do my bidding," the red demon commanded. "Show me your true power!"

Its command drilled into me, but I felt no urge to comply—no, my power coiled, ready to prove my dominance. They thought my father was scary, did they? At least he was sane.

Not yet, my power whispered again, holding back.

The dagger of air twisted into Darius's skin, leaking blood down his front. He stood still, not thrashing or showing signs of panic, but the tightness in his eyes and his clenched jaw showed just how much pain he was in.

Not yet...

I squeezed my eyes shut and held on.

"What are you waiting for?" the red demon yelled.

"I have no idea." Stuffed full of violence and the need for retribution, still I listened to that inner call—I let myself remain open for more magic to pour in. That was when I felt it. A rush of love so deep and great that I fluttered my eyes open and looked at Darius.

He was staring at me, in pain, resolute. Waiting for the end and feasting his eyes on my face. The feeling hadn't come from him.

"Almost," I said softly, letting my eyes close again. I was almost there. I could feel it.

Another rush pumped into me. Sex. Lust. The need to bang everyone in the room. Which was gross. I would ignore my split personality if it said to do that...

"Do you feel that?" one of the demons asked, its voice grating on my ears.

The emotions and feelings twirled as still more magic filled me, pumping in from somewhere unseen. If I'd had the presence of mind to gasp, I would've, because suddenly I could feel where everyone had just been. Whether loitering in the window to watch Darius and I do battle with the five demons we'd fought outside; or in a building across the sect, organizing the fighting effort; or at the dragon paddock, checking in on the momma and its baby.

"They have a baby dragon," I said without meaning to.

Thoughts flitted around me, not taking shape. Except for Darius's. I read his loud and clear.

Goodbye, my love.

"Nope." I shook my head and opened my eyes.

Now, my power whispered.

CHAPTER 26

I ROSE MY hands into the air, feeling my power swell in a sweet, savory, though horribly violent way. Shivers covered my body. Excruciating pain brought me to my knees, surging and boiling my insides and scraping across my skin. All the elements of the underworld—violence, rage, sex, and even love—crashed against one other. Raked across my bones.

I hung my head as the red demon yelled at me. I didn't catch its words, but it seriously was starting to get on my nerves. Could it not see I was going through something here?

I clenched my teeth and hung on, refusing to stop what was happening.

Heat infused my blood. Then cold. One after the other, flash boiling, then freezing. The two halves of my power coiled around each other, twisting and tightening. The pain from the onslaught of extreme temperatures intensified.

Then, with a final blast of agony, my power fused together.

I grunted and collapsed to the ground, my strength momentarily fleeing. Relief and joy blossomed within me—for the first time ever, I felt balanced. I had always been so afraid of the anger and desire for destruction tied to my powers, I hadn't recognized or allowed in the good elements. Like any world, there was good and bad here—they were two sides of the same coin—and my powers embodied all aspects of the underworld.

I could marvel later. There was work to be done.

Summoning my strength, I climbed to my feet. Fire exploded out from me, washing over Darius and ripping away the air digging into his body. I thrashed through the magic holding him, hacking it apart. I threw the backpack at him and yelled "healing snake" before batting away a burst of air from the red demon. I could feel the weave of the spell. Understand the intention. It was meant to subdue me.

"Now. Where were we?" I picked up a chair with my power and ripped it across the room. One of the demons threw up a defense. I tore it down before smashing the chair into it. I tried to blast another with hellfire, but a strange weave of the fused magic came out instead. It cut through the sucker like a knife through water, way better than hellfire and impervious to the demon's attempts to block it.

"Uh oh, the human learned a new trick!" I laughed manically as they started to run. Crazy always freaked people out. Not even demons were immune to that basic life rule.

I bent my newly fused magic into a prison and trapped the red demon inside, even as I chased after the others. "Where ya going?"

I dragged a stream of power across one of the demon's bodies. The demon fell in two halves on the ground. I grabbed another with a burst of air as it was jumping into the do-it-yourself elevator. I pulled it back as a blur of movement interrupted the pandemonium.

Snake roaming around his monster-form body, Darius joined the fray, moving like a man with a purpose. Or, more accurately, a predator with a vendetta. He had to still be in pain, but he was clearly ignoring it.

He slashed the demon I'd kept from escaping, leaving ragged tracks down its body. When the demon hit him with a solid wall of air, Darius raked his claws through it, sending up sparks, refusing to be pushed back.

Yes, a predator with a vendetta. He was pissed.

I threw up a wall of fire and ice to keep everyone in the room—and anyone else out—and left Darius to it. He needed to take out some frustration, and those demons weren't nearly as powerful as the red one. An elder was a good match for them.

After turning slowly, I stalked back to the red demon, feeling his attempts to pick through my magic. He was making excellent progress.

"So. Here we are." I stopped just outside of the cage and spent a moment fortifying the weave. It would be a constant back-and-forth battle, because the demon began picking it apart again almost immediately.

"I am impressed," it said, its voice grating. "I did not think you had access to this level of power yet. You hid it well."

"Nah. You were right. But there is no better way to bring out the best in a woman than threatening someone she loves. That was your bad."

"I am not the most powerful demon in this kingdom, you should know. Many of them have abilities that exceed my own. Should your father not protect you, you will be at odds with those that wish to use you."

"Which is a great reason to get the hell out of here, am I right?"

Reagan, we need to end this and leave.

I glanced behind me at the torn demon bodies littering the ground. The snake still traveled Darius's body, randomly biting before moving on.

"Right. Okay." As I turned back, the cartoon red of the demon dissolved into a leathery brown that matched my pants. Its wings grew, pulled even more tightly into its body so they didn't touch the magical bars, and its tail shrunk away. "I think I preferred the red."

"We can come to an understanding," it said. "You have cleared away my advisors. You've made room for a new leadership. We can forge it together!"

I collapsed the bars one at a time, hitting its body. It fought me, thrashing against the magic and pushing it away. The bars that struck it didn't slice through it as easily as the woven magic had destroyed the other demons.

I hit it with another blast of fused hellfire as the bars finished beating it. Still, it struggled to get up. The thing was a tank.

Darius rushed forward with claws and fangs bared. I beat him there with my sword, something I *wasn't* a novice with. The sword drew fused magic into the blade and I slashed down. It sliced through half the demon's neck before it stopped, needing another draw from my power. I gave it more, now feeling the drain of energy. Darius raked his claws down the demon's chest, making it thrash. I cut again with my blade, *finally* getting it through.

The room fell into silence.

"Dang it, that thing was hard to kill." I wiped the sweat off my forehead and sagged. I was thoroughly drained and utterly exhausted. "It could've been lying, but it said it wasn't the most powerful demon in the kingdom. Besides my father, obviously."

I would believe it. The most powerful would be granted the choicest spots within the kingdom, and that would be nearer Lucifer.

"Well, this one was almost too much, and that is with me totally letting go. If he'd had better advisors, I would've been screwed."

There are not an unlimited amount of top level fives. Those with the most power seek it for themselves and collect weaker people under them. You see it in every world, with every species.

"That's good, I guess. Regardless, we need to get out of here. We've gotten what we came for."

Yes.

He didn't change back into his human form, and the snake kept working. Darius needed to keep healing. The poor guy had really gotten the short end of the stick in this whole affair. I said as much.

I will get to spend more time alive with you. I would endure much more for that privilege.

I sure hoped not. I wasn't worth it. A sentiment I didn't voice, both because I'd seem like an ass, and because he'd just argue with me.

At the do-it-yourself elevator, I paused. "Unicorn blood. I'm not holding up very well, and you're probably heavy. I'll end up dropping us to the bottom."

You'd do better to take us out of a window.

Yes, I would. That was true.

This guy had all the good ideas.

Darius turned so I could get at his backpack. With his claws, he wouldn't be able to pick out one of the small vials.

You cannot take unlimited quantities of that, he thought as I took off the cap. *Too much, and it will confuse the mind instead of clearing it.*

I paused. "I'm not at that point yet, am I?"

No. Or I would've stopped you.

Right. Duh.

I downed the blood and felt the zing of energy. Underneath that, though, I still felt the pull at my limbs. I didn't have much left in my tank.

"We can do it." I shot him a thumbs up to project confidence I didn't feel and ran around looking out windows. From this height, I couldn't see the ground directly below. "Eenie, meenie..."

After breaking the largest one, I stuck my head out and looked down. A roof stretched out below us. All the better. At least it wasn't a straight fall.

"That'll do, pig. Let's go." I stepped up onto the window sill and looked back at him. "This is no big deal. I've levitated a dozen times in my life. This is just another day."

I clenched my teeth and stepped out, falling five feet—and losing my stomach—before I caught myself with magic. I rose back up, supremely focused and not even daring to look at Darius. With his monster form and the snake situation, I was afraid the gross of it all might throw me off my game.

"Okay. I'm coming back over." I hovered toward him with my eyes on my feet, focusing on my power and *not* focusing how high I was off the ground.

Ah crap, I am really *high!*

"I sure wish I could take deep breaths," I said in a level voice, turning so my back was to him. "Okay. Climb on."

Climb on? Would you not rather hold me with air?

"No, because I might accidentally crush you, or lose my grip on you. I have more power now, but I'm still not an expert at using it. If you're hanging on to me, my survival instinct will take control."

A human arm came around my shoulder. *Thank God, he changed form.*

The snake slithered across my stomach.

I really could've done without that.

I continued to focus as his other arm came around me. His legs wrapped around me next and his weight pulled me down. I lost the feel of hovering and we free fell like a sack of potatoes.

"It is okay." Darius spoke in my ear softly. "Do not panic."

The timbre of his voice, and the assurance, calmed me.

But cracking an eye open to see how much time I had to fix this situation scared the bejeebus out of me again.

"I got it. I got it." We turned ass over end. "I don't got it!"

"Relax," he said. "Have faith."

My power whispered to me. Urging me to do something.

"I liked it better when you did it for me," I yelled.

"What's that?" Darius asked.

"I'm not talking to you." I clenched my fists and focused on hovering. On slowing our descent and then stopping us in midair.

I peeled my eyes open. The roof looked back at me from twenty feet away. It didn't get any closer.

"Nothing to it," Darius said softly.

I shook my head as I slowly lowered us. The guy had no idea what a loose cannon I was. Sure, the power was technically fused, and that did give me more control, but that didn't mean I could leap from tall buildings in a single bound yet. I would fall out of a few and almost land on my face before I got the hang of it.

I'd just proved that.

Our feet hit the roof and we paused for a moment. Below us, demons ran every which way, some being chased, and some heading out in more organized groups. In the distance the pink dragon rose into the sky, a stream of fire scouring the ground under it.

"Let's try to blend into the chaos and run out of here," I said.

"Hide your power."

Now that the suit had been neutralized, I wasn't so sure I could. Which I didn't mention. We'd succeeded in our mission, albeit messily. Getting noticed now would ruin everything.

I ran to the edge of the roof. His monster form met me there. One story. Darius swung off of the ledge and landed gracefully, like a cat. I tried the same thing, slipped, and fell in a lump. I caught myself with air before impact, then ripped the air away and landed on my butt. I glanced around quickly to make sure no one had seen me.

Now I would stop using my power.

We ran into a crowd heading toward the path leading out the front. A demon glanced our way and did a double take on me. Then flinched away when it saw Darius. It started to slow.

Darius jabbed its side with his claws and ripped forward. It staggered.

"We're under attack from this side," I yelled over the dying demon's shout. Staggering to the ground beside it, I stabbed it with a spear of power, hardly noticeable. Hopefully, they'd buy it, caught up in the fever-pitch of battle, and they wouldn't think too hard about how he'd come by his wounds.

When the other demons flocked our way, looking for the threat, I lurched up and into another crowd, running parallel. Darius joined me immediately. Another twenty feet and we cleared the corner of one of the large stone buildings. The roar of battle assaulted us from the side, smacking into our forces. Fire rose up around us, the power a blip compared to the demon in that high tower.

Without thinking, I tried to counter with ice, like the power of the defending demons whose ranks we'd joined. Instead, the fused power lashed out like a whip. It tore a strip off the demon's face.

Oops. Yet another example of how terrible I was at keeping a low profile. Would I never learn?

Darius shoved me back toward the path, where the battle raged on. I couldn't tell the demons apart. Which of the leathery, scabby, knobby demons were our pretend allies?

Did it really matter?

I pulled out my sword as we ran out of the sect grounds and onto the main path, following another cluster of demons. Chaos ran rampant. A screaming demon shoved a spear at me, but I blocked the blow and countered with my sword. Darius ripped into another. We tore through a one-on-one demon battle, and put on a burst of speed.

A roar shook the ground. I looked up, knowing I'd see a dragon, and trying to judge how best to dodge or duck to ensure it grabbed someone else if that was its design.

Upon seeing the magnificent beast soaring above us, I staggered into Darius. Huge—double the size of the others—it shimmered black with hints of blue and an occasional flare of red. As beautiful and graceful as I had come to expect, it beat its wings before swooping down low, cutting through the fighting. It didn't shoot fire, or try and score anyone with its claws. Instead, it knocked people around, breaking up the clusters of battle.

A smaller roar announced the arrival of the pink dragon. It soared above the melee, but as soon as it got a look at the black dragon, it frantically lifted itself up and away.

The black dragon hovered for a moment, the flap of its wings audible, drowning out the shouts, yells, and clangs of battle. The fighting slowed. Crowds started to disperse.

Dread pierced me. Only the dragon of one person could stop this kind of carnage.

Lucifer.

CHAPTER 27

C LEARLY THE DEMONS from the sect we'd just vacated hadn't done a great job of holding Lucifer off.

"Run like hell," I said to Darius, now shoving through the outer edge of the gawking crowd.

Something else flew above the crowds, not as big as a dragon, but a great bird of sorts. As it glided by, a shock wave of fear pulsed through me, stilling my heart and making me stop with my mouth hanging open. When the winged thing stopped above the largest cluster of—now frozen—fighters, I finally got a good look at it.

The flying demon had arms and legs like a man, with three toes that almost looked webbed. Like everything else in this place, its fingers ended in claws. The great wings, black against the sky, beat steadily, keeping it hovering in the air. Its hooked ears reminded me of horns, but if they were, I couldn't see them from the distance. A tail whipped out behind it.

The crowd pushed away, giving the demon plenty of

room to land. This was one dangerous mother trucker.

"Go, go, go," I said, all action again, pushing at Darius.

We kept our heads down and weaved in and out of people, hiding at the back of the crowd against the hedge. At the bend in the path we'd abandoned before, I heard, "What has caused this? Where are your conspectors?"

I slowed without meaning to, hearing the enchantment in that voice. Not able to help myself, I looked back...

I expected to see a wall of demons.

Instead, as though I'd made it happen, a tunnel had opened up through the shifting sea of underworld creatures. A ways away, within a circle of empty space, stood a man clothed in form-fitting jeans and a white shirt. They were clothes Darius might've worn, and obviously created with magic because I doubted there was an abundance of human clothes in this place. He had slicked-back black hair and a lean but muscular body.

"Get your conspectors. Bring them to me," the man called in a voice that carried. I heard it as though he was standing right next to me. Felt the magic powering it. Saw the weave that expertly blended the two halves of magic until they were one.

It could only be one person.

Darius pulled my arm as the man turned, showing me some of his face. Even from this distance I could tell he was handsome, with poise and a confident bearing. He stood among the demons as if he owned them, fully in charge. At ease, though he'd just interrupted a grizzly battle.

Come, Darius said, pulling me along.

I had the fleeting impression that the man was turning toward me, but I stepped behind the wall of demons once again, out of sight.

"That was my dad," I whispered as I ran on wooden legs. "I felt it."

Almost certainly. We must go.

I shook my head against the longing to meet him, more powerful than I would have expected but probably typical of adult children in similar situations. Okay, only similar in the never-met-your-father way. I picked up speed, staying tight to the hedge. When I looked back, I saw a few demons glancing our way, more running toward the neighboring sect—probably to get their master. The pink dragon was flapping in the air at the edges of the battle, its head pointed right at us.

"I hope that black dragon doesn't let the pink one go flapping around." I pushed in tighter to the hedge. I certainly didn't want the black dragon to see us go.

We ran out the way we'd come, up the hill and toward the beginning of the illusion. Except when we got there, we didn't find a desert. Or a lovely green field dotted with wildflowers. We found a wide pathway that led to two arched doorways. Fire raged within the frame of the one on the right, and on the left, fluffy white clouds drifted across a bright blue sky.

"I feel like I have just sat down to a poison duel with a Sicilian," I mumbled.

What? Darius frowned at me.

I shook my head. He needed to watch more movies. "Basically, the fire door looks terrible. You'd assume whoever set this shebang up is trying to steer you to the blue door—and you do not want to do what they want you to do. So then you take the fire door. *But,* what if they realized that you'd think it was a trap, and they knew you'd take the fire door, so in the end, it's the blue door that is safe?"

His frown became more pronounced.

"If you'd gotten the *Princess Bride* reference, you wouldn't be confused right now." I glanced back the way we'd come. The sect had disappeared, replaced by a vision of a path crowned with glistening arches of ice that abruptly ended in an inferno. Flames curled up from a huge pit, reaching into the black sky above. "Nice."

It is impossible to say which path goes where. He looked back and forth between them, and back the way we'd come. *But we do need to choose. They will have discovered the dead conspector by now, and when the other sect swears they didn't kill them, someone will mention the human and vampire escaping. They'll come looking for us.*

"I'd go fire." I pointed, as if he didn't know which I meant.

I can withstand larger quantities of heat now that we're bonded, but I'm not sure I can withstand that degree of fire.

"Given that the dragon kept trying to fry people, I don't think just anyone can withstand fire. This is probably just for show."

Darius started forward, hard-faced. Without hesitation, and not much of a heart uptick, he walked straight into the sheet of flame and disappeared.

"We probably should've done that together," I muttered as I hurried after him. For all I knew, we'd be sectioned off into two different places.

No heat surrounded my body. The flame didn't lick my skin.

"My father the magic man." The illusion cleared and I bumped into the back of Darius's nude human form, standing on a wooden pathway that cut through clear blue water to a large, multi-roomed hut on stilts. There was no other path but toward it. Light pink and purple clouds hung low over the setting faux-sun in the light blue sky. Absolutely gorgeous clear water stretched forward into infinity.

"Keep your eyes up," Darius said as he started forward.

"I wonder if the vultures in the desert belonged to one of the sects in that battle." The waters moved like a calm ocean, with ripples and small waves.

"Up, I said."

I yanked my gaze up from the water and glanced at the sky. Nothing awaited us. The hut loomed closer.

"It is likely," Darius answered. "Though which one, I couldn't say. I would've expected those birds to be in the battle."

"With the dragons? They wouldn't have lasted two minutes."

Darius didn't answer.

"I wonder if Vlad knows about the dragons," Darius muttered. "Those creatures would dominate a land battle in the Realm."

"My father would dominate a land battle in the Realm."

"You only say that because you haven't seen what some of the elves are capable of. Or a host of fae."

And I didn't want to. I wanted to go home, have a glass of wine, sleep for a decade, and go back to my old life hunting marks that had very little power or sense. This was too much work, and a war in the Realm sounded even worse.

Something was hunched beside the front door of the hut, just out of the glaring light spilling out onto the porch. I slowed with Darius, who clearly saw the same thing, twenty feet from the door, head moving as if scanning for a surprise attack.

"Should I just kill it?" I asked, looking over my shoulder. The bigger problem would be something coming behind us.

"Let's approach."

"I'm your Huckleberry." I frowned. Because he wouldn't get that reference, either. Ridiculous. How was I supposed to relate to the man when he didn't speak in movie quotes?

The demon hunched a little more as we neared, holding its hands in front of its scabby chest like an old woman worried about a burglar.

That is the demon Callie and Desmond called, Darius thought.

I squinted into the shadow beside the door, my eyes playing tricks because of the light streaming out of the building. A gray knobby thing stared back, not stepping forward.

"Honestly, I saw that demon before my memory got an upgrade. It doesn't look much different from all the others we've seen."

Darius glanced behind. *We don't have time to dwell. Find out what it wants, beware of a surprise attack, and kill it if you can.*

"Aye, aye, sir."

When we reached the front of the hut, Darius continued forward, scouting the building. I stopped beside the demon, my power at the ready.

"Heir," the demon said softly, not inching toward me.

"Everyone else who knew that information is now dead."

"I'm bound to you. I can tell no one of what I know, and I cannot rest until you are safely out of these lands. Please, let me guide you. Only then can I be released."

"We're clear." Darius's voice echoed through the hut.

"What do you mean, released?" I asked, edging in through the door.

"Mistress Banks impressed upon me to guide you. This trinket led me to you." It turned over a clawed hand to reveal a round imprint on its palm. "But the magic near the castle changes. I am not of the type able to go through to the other side of the inner gates."

"How'd you know I would come out here?" I asked, edging a little farther into the hut.

"This is the entrance closest to the sect to which you were heading."

It occurred to me that both doors from the ones we'd had to choose from would've led to the same place.

A crackle drew my gaze toward the area from which we'd come. Subtle blue lights, a shade darker than the water, flashed.

"Does that mean someone is coming through?" I asked as I jog-stepped deeper into the hollow hut.

"Yes. Do they follow you?"

"Of course they follow me! What do you think I am, subtle?" I wrapped the demon in air and tugged it behind me as I ran, my footsteps echoing. Darius waited on the other side with his satchel strung across his bare chest, looking up.

"We gotta go." I ran past him with the demon bouncing along behind me. If I'd focused more, I probably could've kept it suspended a little better, but I was tired. It was lucky I hadn't killed it.

"I still see no vultures." Darius dug into his satchel, and I hoped he was looking for a miracle. A moment later he caught up. A quick glance behind us revealed he'd thrown up a privacy spell. Why he hadn't gone for a more violent solution, I didn't know, but there wasn't time to amend the situation.

"Where to, guide?" I yelled at the demon.

"At the frung pond, we will go right." Its directions were interrupted with a couple grunts when it bounced.

"What's a frung—" The illusion of the pretty bay washed away to reveal a grassy area surrounding a small pound. A frog jumped from a lily pad upon our sudden entrance, disappearing into splash-less water. The water didn't even ripple. "Frog pond, did you mean?"

"Frung. That creature that just jumped." The demon pointed a gnarled hand right. "That way."

Darius worked at his satchel, his eyes darting behind us.

"I'll kill you if you are trying to trap us," I told the demon, unsure. Since we'd come out in a different place than we'd gone in, and everything was disguised by layers of camouflage, I had no idea where we were.

A fact presented itself in my Memory 2.0.

"Wait." I held up my hand, thinking. "You said there is only one entrance near the sect I was originally headed to."

"Yes. And you came through it. I hoped you would."

"But we went in through a desert illusion."

"The landscapes change, though the locations of the sects, oases, and throughways remain the same. Had you come to me, I would've—"

"Let's go." Darius had coated one spell on top of another and lobbed them behind us. I felt the vibration from the distance, though I couldn't see any shimmer. A nasty, invisible spell that would blast anyone attempting to follow us.

"We came from that way when we entered the desert area." I pointed, still discombobulated.

"That is usually the faster path if you need to go around sects, and often safer, but there is unrest," the demon said. "Fighting has not yet broken out, but my sect is expecting it to happen at any time. We are not involved, but even still, we are protecting our borders."

"What is stirring up all this trouble?" I asked as Darius nodded and headed right. "And why do you speak English when no one else seems to?"

Something we can discuss later, Darius thought as we ran.

"Just because a demon doesn't speak English, or French, or elvish," the demon said in a collection of grunts as it bounced along, "doesn't mean it can't. It just means it will not lower itself to do so."

"Is that like the fact that I *could* keep you from hitting the ground, but that answer makes me not want to?"

The demon didn't respond.

The terrain changed into a bumpy sort of path lined with smoothed rocks, the sides ever closer together, and a ceiling that jutted down in areas, making me feel like it was about to squish me. A blast sounded behind us, rattling my teeth. I glanced back, but a rock blocked my view.

"Faster, Darius," I said, pushing for more speed.

I will need blood soon.

I nodded, though he couldn't see me, and tore

around a corner after him. It took me a second to realize there was another way we could've gone.

"Is this right?" I asked the demon, slowing.

Darius half staggered and reached over to brace his hand on the rocks. He did need blood.

"This way leads to a lustful sect." I could hear the sneer in its voice. "The other to a sect that usually identifies more with a human's version of love. Either way is safe enough. This one is faster."

Darius jogged back the way we'd come, reaching into his satchel. Instead of putting a spell on the entrance to the path we were on, however, he put it on the other.

"Clever. Though they might realize you are fooling them." I narrowed my eyes as I considered the many-layered possibilities.

Darius set the spell before stopping in the entrance of our path and setting another.

I smiled and nodded at him. "Right. Better idea. You're so smart."

"You are becoming giddy," Darius said as he laid the spell. Something else nasty.

"Yes, I am, sir. I am half delirious. But that just makes me more dangerous, I am sure of it."

"More oblivious, at any rate." He closed the flap on his satchel and started to run.

I tore off after him, noticing his lack of grace, which surely meant he and I were in the same boat. There was no telling how many days we'd been up for, but the real problem was the amount of energy we'd been expending nonstop.

The rock corridor opened onto the peak of a cliff, surrounded by a collection of other cliffs. Red stars twinkled above, below, and across the way, not relegated to the faux-sky. The cliff kitty-corner to ours rose higher than the others. Water surged over the top and enjoyed a free fall before cascading down the cliff face. A demon made its way along a path cut into that cliff face, similar to the one we'd used on our way in. It disappeared behind the rushing water and spray.

"The entrance is behind that waterfall?" I asked, motioning for Darius to grab the waistline of my pants so I could scoot toward the edge and look over. I didn't want to fall over the side.

The water disappeared into a pool of blackness my night vision couldn't penetrate.

"Yes. The fastest way is to go through, however unpleasant. We will then be one neutral sect from the river."

This seemed faster than the way we'd come, though that might be because we'd told my pouch-wearing friend that we didn't want to go through any more sects.

I motioned for Darius to pull me back. "Do they just let anyone go through?"

"No," the demon said. "We must request admittance."

I ran my hand across my face, uncertainty pulling at me. "How long would it take to go around?"

"We would then need to pass through four sects—"

"No." I slashed the air with my hand. "Going through is not an option for us. Can we get around?"

Still hunched on the ground, it rubbed at the mark on its palm. Its excitement about serving the Great Master's heir seemed to have faded, but when the dual-mage team set out to bully someone, they really got the job done. It was their attention to detail that had me listening to the demon at all. They would've made sure to bind it to my good health and well-being, ensuring it did right by me and didn't try to set me up.

The problem was, what it thought would help me might actually imprison me or get me killed.

"We could get around, but it would take much longer. We'd be open to the sky for most of that journey."

"Dragons," Darius said softly.

"The number of dragons they will use depends on how much you are wanted," the demon said, looking back the way we'd come. "Maybe none. Maybe the fleet. It depends on if they suspect you or not."

"We are a human and vampire wielding magic in a time of high strife. They'll want us." I hung my head. "Okay. Let's head over to the demon sex club and hope they admit us."

CHAPTER 28

THE SPRAY OF the waterfall didn't splash my face, but the rumble nearly deafened me as we passed under the surging waters. A glistening gate that wasn't actually wet pushed into the smooth rock of the cliff face. The metal door stood open, and as we neared, the water rushing overhead fell silent. A strange hush fell over the hollow.

A tall being emerged from the doorway with pointed features and snow-white hair cropped short. Green wool draped from a skinny frame and brushed its blunt toes, eight in all.

"Trick or treat," I said.

"What are you?" it asked in a silky voice I did not expect from a demon.

"Oh, a little of this and a little of that. How about you?"

"We seek passage through your territory," the demon shackled to me said in a flat tone. I had no doubt it was trying to hide its disdain for the lust demons.

"And why should we grant it to you?" the gatekeeper asked.

"Look at this guy." I indicated Darius. "How many guys have you seen that are as hot as this guy? You've got lust brewing in there, right? Well, here you go. He can rev up a monk. You're welcome."

The creature took a moment to assess Darius before its eyes flicked over his shoulder. They narrowed. The creature stepped to the side to look beyond us.

I followed its gaze and felt my stomach seize. Through the small gap that looked out into the space between the cliffs, I could see something glimmering fly into the space between all the cliffs.

Oh yeah, they'd send dragons. Already had, by the looks of it.

Adrenaline pumped through me as I turned back to the gatekeeper. "Let us in. You won't get another chance to do so."

My shackled demon scurried behind me.

The gatekeeper's eyes flicked to the cowering demon, then back to me. A glimmer sparked in its eyes and a strange sound rumbled deep in its throat, almost like a cat's purr. "You have great passion."

"That's not where I was going with that threat…"

The demon's gaze moved beyond us again and a stray thought—*Who do they seek?*—drifted from its mind. When its eyes came back to me, I could easily guess the next thought. *This creature?*

"We are celebrating the change in the stars and do not usually let outsiders through. But you captivate me." Its gaze roamed over Darius. "Your essence intrigues me." Back to me. "I feel the pulse in you. The aching desire. It excites me."

"Ew."

"You may come." With that, it turned and walked farther into the sect.

"The change in the stars?" I asked Darius quietly as I followed.

"They have a ceremony every time they change the color and placement of the twinkling lights," the demon said, not lowering its voice. "They have so little importance that they create celebrations over made-up situations."

"Our time is not spent fighting and spying on our neighbors," the gatekeeper said dismissively as it led us through a tunnel. The sides branched out into little catacombs where figures were either lounging or engaging in lewd acts. Regardless of how icky my logical mind found the situation, a tawdry feeling filled the air more the farther in we got.

I wiped my forehead, trying to dislodge the memories of bonding with Darius. Of his slick body pressed firmly against mine. The feel of him inside me. Again and again. The grind of our movements.

"How much longer?" I asked weakly.

The gatekeeper turned with a sly grin, now walking backward in front of me. "You feel it, do you not?"

Sounds filled the air as the fervor rose. We turned a corner into a plush, spacious setting where mostly human forms writhed. Coupled or in an orgy, sticking with one or moving around—it didn't seem to matter. The area was alive with activity.

"Good grief." I had no choice but to slow, moving in step with the gatekeeper.

It ran its hand through the air, indicating the goings-on. "Care to participate? You can stay in your current form to do so. As you see."

I felt Darius's hand low on my hip. A backward glance revealed he was also feeling the effect, and if he scooted up, the effect would poke me in the back.

"We're good. Let's move on." I meant to slap off Darius's hand, but the weight of it felt good. Tingles spread across my skin and my lady bits tightened up, craving him.

Not the time, mon ange, Darius thought, the words dripping with sensuality. *Let us get out of the Dark Kingdom and I will devote as much time to you as you'd like.*

I grimaced and, with effort, removed my hands from his sensitive areas, not sure when I'd turned and plastered myself to him.

The gatekeeper wore a huge smile. "It feels good to

give in. Almost as good as it does to fight the urge. Stay a while. You will find what you seek."

"A wild ride, you mean?" I gestured at it to keep moving. "I live in New Orleans. There's a wild ride around every corner if you just open your eyes."

Speaking of eyes, they followed us, many painted with lust and desire. The gazes that surveyed my body felt like a physical touch. Darius's hand remained firmly on my hip, low and heavy. If I turned just a little, it would...

Almost there, love. A little longer.

I stopped stroking and uncurled my fingers from around his manhood. Like last time, I didn't remember relenting to desire. "My bad."

"It is easy to get caught up—"

"I got it," I said to the gatekeeper. "You don't have to keep pointing out the obvious."

A drumbeat sounded somewhere above us, and when I looked up, I saw faces peering down from the ledges—some laughing, some desirous. Many of the demons had taken the shapes of magical species that couldn't get into the underworld at all, let alone this far in. Most of the shapes were wrong in some way, like a wolf head on a lion's body, or a human head and limbs with an ape's body—actually, come to think of it, maybe that last guy was making fun of humans...

I shook my head and clasped my hands in front of

me so I didn't inadvertently grab Darius again. "How is it you are keeping the hand on my hip from wandering?" I asked him.

I deal in passion as a trade. I inspire lust as a normal course of my existence. These demons are similar to vampires in that way. The feel in this sect is welcoming.

Welcoming. That was one word for it.

I re-clasped my hands. They'd tried to go wandering again. At least they were only headed for Darius. That was a plus.

The catacombs twisted and turned, a new offshoot around every corner. Demons wandered or idled, always interested in the newcomers unless already entertained. My demon guide didn't seem to notice the palpable feeling of sex in the air, and Darius didn't bend, even a little. It was just me, constantly having my hands removed from Darius's person—without realizing how they'd gotten there in the first place—until I was walking with both wrists clasped in one of his large hands.

The gatekeeper thought that was hilarious.

"It is a pity you couldn't stay." The gatekeeper stopped at a gated archway leading out into the darkness speckled with twinkling red lights. No waterfall tumbled over this gateway. "But it seems you must run."

"Yes. Thank you for letting us through. And don't worry"—I hooked a thumb over my shoulder at Darius—"I'll jump him at the first available opportunity."

The gatekeeper's smile spread. "You belong here. You should return. I think it will do you good."

"I belong everywhere, and nowhere." I hadn't planned to say that, but it seemed to fit. To stop any other random things from popping out of my mouth, I gave a salute and started forward. "Thanks again."

"Beware the dragons. They are tenacious." The gatekeeper laughed and drifted back into the sect.

"A bit strange, that one," I muttered. "And not at all curious. That's a plus."

"Only a fool would want to get involved with someone being chased by a dragon," my grumpy guide said.

"And guess who gave me a map to the underworld?" I turned back and pointed a finger. "You wanted me to meet you here, so that makes you a…"

It glowered at me.

Darius put a hand on my shoulder and stopped me beside the exit. Like the entryway, the ledge looked out over a pit surrounded by cliffs. An overhang protected us from the sky, but that wouldn't last long.

Without warning, he moved in, holding my head in his strong grip and bending to my neck. I barely kept from flinging him out over the drop in surprise. A moment later, I couldn't help a low moan. Already feverish with longing from the trip through the lustful sect, I sank into the feeling of him. Grabbed various parts of him. Tried to get him into my body with an abandon that would horribly embarrass me later.

The demon is right beside us.

And that was why.

I whimpered as his serum spread bliss through me, pulling him closer, as close as I could. His hardness rubbed in all the right place. But he wouldn't let me go whole hog. I'd thank him later, I was sure, but was cursing him at the moment.

He finished and pulled back, and for the first time I felt pleasure burning through him. Not only that, but the deep ache of love that mirrored my own.

"We are wasting time," the demon guide growled.

Body burning and warmth running through me from all that was Darius, I didn't want to hurry anymore. I didn't want to run. I wanted to go back into the lust sect and take some me time. Well, us time, really. I was tired of all this drama.

Almost there, mon chere, Darius thought, probably feeling my listlessness through the bond. He rubbed a thumb softly against my cheek. *We are almost out of this. Just a little longer.*

Now that we had air again, I sighed. It really buoyed my mood.

I nodded and pushed forward. "Let's go fast."

The demon led the way as we ran along the ledge and down the slope. Darius and I had a map in our head, sure, but it didn't have the fine details that the demon guide seemed to know. For example, at the bottom of a steep set of stone steps, a nearly hidden tunnel offered us some respite from the skies. We sprinted through it, as fast as the demon could go (which wasn't as fast as us). At the other side, the demon stopped abruptly and looked up.

"We are too late," it said.

CHAPTER 29

I PUSHED IT to the side and took its place, looking into the dark sky. A multicolored dragon drifted by with a demon on its back.

A demon dressed like a clown.

"Holy blue balls, why hasn't it given up already?"

"That dragon belongs to a vicious sect that offers others the chance to fight the beast to prove their skill," the demon guide said.

"I know. I bested it, and that clown has been trying to find us ever since. We'd thought we'd given it the slip, but clearly not." I chewed my lip and gazed across the wide open space at the next sect, which seemed open and not as laden with defenses as many of the others.

"A few best it, and they go on their way, so I've heard." The demon rubbed at the mark on its palm.

"I hate doing things the normal way." I hunted for any other signs of an aerial presence and didn't see any. Not yet. The dragons from the other side of the lustful sect could have no idea we'd gone through it, not if the sect usually turned people away during the change in the stars. Eventually, though, they'd expand their search, and if we hung out here waiting for the determined clown to get lost, we'd give them time to catch up.

"Okay, how's this for a plan?" I ran out into the open, dragging the guide demon with me. Darius caught up a moment later, and while he didn't say it, I was pretty sure he was thinking, *Are you crazy?*

The stony ground turned quickly to lush, unevenly trimmed grass, spongy to run on. It stretched all around us with a few tufts and a couple lone flowers dotting the flatness.

"We can go around this sect easily," the demon shouted behind us. It had to be thankful for the change in terrain.

"Should we angle left or right?" I asked as a shout issued above us.

Clown Demon leaned over the shoulder of the dragon and pointed down at us.

Darius threw something into the air. A huge starburst of light blasted through the darkness, making me look away with blinking eyes.

"A little warning next time?" I asked as I tried to see through the spots in my vision.

Harried flapping drowned out the shouting from above. I chanced a look up in time to see the dragon swooping low, or maybe falling.

"Reagan, take care of this," Darius shouted.

I ran my hand in an arch and swatted the dragon with air, smacking it off-kilter. It tilted wildly, throwing its rider, who somersaulted twice before landing in the grass.

Darius was off, speeding toward it with claws (and probably fangs) elongating. He was on the clown in no time, ripping and tearing. But it was a powerful demon.

Darius went sailing, hitting the ground with a hard thump. Clown Demon was up, running at the vampire with magic unfurling around it. A weave of air surrounded the vampire as he catapulted to his feet. He raked at the magic with claws, tearing a hole in the weave and unraveling it before running forward to meet Clown Demon.

I sent a blast of my blended magic and swatted Clown Demon, making it roll across the ground. Darius probably could've handled it, but we needed to hurry.

Darius launched onto Clown Demon as it came to a stop, his claws digging into the other. An object went flying.

A snake.

That was why Darius's first strikes didn't end the fight before it had begun.

The vampire straightened, the fight finally at a close.

"I did not know vampires were so powerful," my

guide demon said, now being bodily dragged through the grass. I'd somewhat forgotten about it while dealing with the dragon.

"You haven't had many dealings with elders, I take it," I said, hitting the dragon with another burst to keep it from diving at Darius.

Darius was already on the move, running toward us with claws (and fangs) still out. The dragon shrieked when it realized what had happened.

It blew a sort of trumpet, long and loud, vibrating through my bones. When the noise died, it pumped its wings and rose straight up into the sky. Ready to dive bomb.

I readied myself for another slap of air. It kept rising, not looking down at us, until it reached a dizzying height—

Then it tilted its wings and sped away.

"What's happening?" I asked, my power ready for action. Darius put a hand on my back to keep me moving. "Does it realize it's no match for us, or is this dragon trickery of some kind?"

"You have freed it," the demon said, lying on the ground. It apparently didn't even want to bother standing up. "Death cuts the tie of loyalty."

"Are they violent pets, or..." I started running with Darius, once again pulling the demon behind.

"Disgraceful to call them pets. They pledge their

loyalty to one they deem worthy. They are allies. But their loyalty is to one being, not the sect. Where the being goes, the dragon goes. Often a demon that can secure a dragon has its pick of sects to join. Many become leaders eventually, accruing followers based on the status of having a dragon, even if the leader's power isn't sensational. As you saw."

"Where do they live when they aren't shackled by loyalty to a psycho clown and his mind-bending circus?"

"The Great Master sees to the solitary dragons, or those in their mating cycles."

My father, the dragon keeper. That would be a cool thing to have on a business card. Although Reagan "unicorn blood drinker" Somerset didn't sound half bad, either.

We ran alongside a paltry fence that could easily be torn away or jumped over. No spikes or barbed wire deterred those who were up to no good.

A moment later, I saw why.

"Is that a goat?" I asked in disbelief, staggering with surprise and fatigue.

"It is similar to a Brink goat only in appearance." The demon sounded disgusted again. My ignorance was really standing in the way of its whole hero-worship thing.

A little bigger, maybe, and with more fur, but otherwise the creature standing in the pen munching on grass looked like a goat. Same weird eyes, same curved horns, and same presence that made you pat your pockets to make sure you didn't have something in there it might want to eat.

"Is it an animal, though, or a demon doing a great job looking like a goat? Oh my God, is that a *llama*?"

"These aren't animals that exist in the Brink," the demon spat. "But yes, they are animals."

"Dude, you need to get out more. That's a llama. Snobby bastards."

Darius glanced over with a grin. "What do you have against llamas?"

Demons tended the animals and the grass behind nothing more substantial than the wired enclosure. They glanced up as we passed, but didn't show any other interest. Beyond them loomed a large structure almost like a barn, in good shape. Animals bayed in the distance.

"I had a llama growing up. It wouldn't give me the time of day, even though I was the one who always fed it. Ungrateful..." I leapt over a roll of hay. "Do the animals eat?"

"Of course the animals eat." The demon was growing tired of my questions, I could tell.

I let it go. It wasn't that important in the grand scheme of things. Nor was it important to dissect why these animals looked so similar to those in the Brink. Or why they had them in the first place when demons didn't eat or drink milk.

I probably had more questions about the animals than about anything else I'd seen thus far. Just when I thought I was getting a handle on the place, something else weird cropped up.

A knot of worry eased when we crested a berm and the landscape changed. A boat waited at the lone dock stretching into the still river. I turned back to the demon, and saw nothing behind us.

"Darius." I grabbed his arm, and we walked back out of the illusion together. From the corner of my eye, I caught the demon trying to scamper away. "Wait a minute there, hoppity." I wrapped it in air and, ignoring its screeches, dragged it back. "Where are you going?"

It looked at the mark on its hand, which had been fading but now glowed back to life. It hunched. "Magic in progress is severed when you enter the river. My task is completed."

"But you can't tell anyone about me, right? Be honest, because I will know if you're lying." I wouldn't know any such thing, but there was a good chance it would believe me. I was the heir, after all.

"The confidentiality bond as it pertains to the summoning is still in effect," it grumbled. "I will be punished for leaving without approval and having no reason for doing so."

"Yet you wanted to guide me initially. Guide me in secret, I might add. That doesn't add up." I narrowed my eyes at it. "You lying little devil."

It crouched to the ground and worried at its mark, looking up at me. It didn't say anything, but then, it didn't have to.

"Kill it," Darius said without inflection.

I should have. It had tried to set me up in the beginning, just like we'd thought. If we'd taken the path it had laid out for us, it would have brought me to its leader in the hopes of gaining a boon. What a sniveling little…

On the flip side, Callie and Dizzy could mark it to help me. My goal was never to come back to the underworld, but it never hurt to have insurance.

"Go," I said, dissolving the air. "Remember my…" I tilted my head. What was the word I was looking for. "Leniency?"

"Mercy," Darius murmured.

I snapped. "Mercy, yes. Remember my mercy. Now get gone."

It took off like a shot, clearly wanting to quickly put as much distance as possible between itself and me.

Without delay, I turned around and did the same thing, hurrying into the illusion of the river while holding Darius's hand so we didn't get separated. We ran down to the dock and climbed into the boat.

This creature had the same vaguely human look and grayish skin as the one that had given us a ride initially.

"Hello, Egg Man," it said.

"Are you the same guy we had before?" I asked it, because how else would it remember my supposed name?

Its face turned to Darius. "Hello, Walrus."

Darius nodded in greeting.

"Where do you go?" the creature asked.

I looked at Darius for an answer. Strategy was his department.

"The way we came in," he said.

Without hesitation, the creature untied the rope and the boat calmly drifted away from the side.

I blinked at Darius, wanting to ask a few questions. Like, why did he seem so confident it would know? And did it, in fact, know? And was this the same one as before?

Plunk.

I flinched and ducked away before groaning. "Not the drops again."

Silence filled the empty expanse as we made our way across the river. Darius, still nude and seemingly not disturbed that his bare butt was resting on an often used and probably rarely cleaned seat, stared off to the side patiently. The creature stared between us, also patiently.

I fidgeted and tried to keep from jumping over-board. I really hated this ride.

"Question." I pointed at the creature. It didn't look at me. "Are you a tattletale?"

Silence.

"Do you keep a captain's log of passengers?" I tried again.

Silence.

"If I throw you into the water, and no one is there to hear it, will the splash actually make a sound?" No one answered, so I had plenty of opportunity to think about what I'd just said. "Actually, will you even make a splash?"

I was tempted to see, just for kicks, but there were no oars. If this thing went over, we'd probably be stuck on this accursed river forever.

Another couple drops from the ceiling later, we drifted toward a dock. The creature tied up the boat. No fog greeted us from this side.

Huh.

The creature's head turned to me. "Safe travels, Egg man." Then to Darius, "Safe travels, Walrus."

I hopped off the boat, shaking my head. I couldn't even summon the enthusiasm to sing the last lines of the song. Despite Darius's assertions, I had *not* gotten used to the crazy that was the river. It just wasn't right.

Without balking, we walked up the beach and through the illusion we'd seen before. This one didn't change the second time around like that other one had.

"I wonder if you could've walked on that water," I said randomly, thinking of the illusion of the hut on the ocean.

Something large drifted above us. The roar shook my bones, bubbling up fear from inside me.

A black dragon.

The black dragon.

CHAPTER 30

"**W**HAT IN THE hell is it doing *here*?" I screeched, starting to run.

Darius grabbed my arm, probably worried he'd lose me in the layered illusion. *Do not use your power. We have to blend in.*

No kidding, but could I stop myself from protecting us the only way I knew how when it was a matter of survival? I wasn't sure.

"Should I go naked like you? I can burn off my hair. That might make me look as odd as the rest of them…"

"No. Keep moving." We stayed near the edge of the passageway, scraping our backs on the jutting, sharp rocks. The tail of the dragon disappeared overhead.

Demons hurried toward us or moved with us, glancing up in panic. One crashed into Darius and careened to the other side of the corridor, scraping against the rock.

Its eyes hit mine as it pushed away. A rare helpful demon, it said, "Go back the way you came! They only bring in dragons to burn the place out!"

He scurried toward the river.

We ran forward into a cluster of demons, all equally panicked. Another roar made everyone flinch. Someone grabbed at Darius's satchel, a thief taking advantage of the distraction.

Thieves should know better than to get grabby with a vampire.

Darius snatched the demon and swung it around, bashing it against the rock. Then he flung it to the ground and kept going as though nothing had happened.

A hollow of creatures opened up around us, giving us more room. That probably wasn't good.

The black dragon drifted overhead, and I looked up through my eyelashes, trying to see if anything or, rather, *anyone* rested on its back. Empty. Thank holy buckets of goo.

"Maybe dragons can't sense power," I murmured as we hunched and crowded in with the demons in front of us. They tried to get away, but we persisted, running behind them, basically herding them the direction we were going.

Don't chance it, Darius thought.

Everyone slowed into a cluster as we all reached the big open area where I'd slayed the huge demon. Only a few brave souls walked through it, hurrying from one side to the other.

"What does the dragon want?" I asked a strange creature beside me. It didn't look much like a demon, but I had no idea what it might be. Gargoyle?

"I don't know. I didn't even know dragons existed!"

"It's looking for someone," a demon in front of us rasped.

"Will they find someone else by accident?" I asked.

"Yeah. This is the start of the raid. Anything that can't go back across the river will be killed. Usually they don't bother with this area, but when they do, they clear it out. Won't want anyone on the outside hearing about dragons. The news can't get out with everyone dead." The demon looked up, its fear plain.

"Then why don't you head toward the river? Why doesn't everyone?"

The demon glanced back over my shoulder. "Too late now. I gotta stay alive long enough to sneak back over."

I followed its gaze but only saw a mass of cowering creatures, hunched together, as though trapped and waiting for a golden opportunity to escape.

I didn't know why it might be too late, but it didn't matter. I wasn't going toward the river, anyway. And I certainly wasn't the kind of girl to wait for the enemy to come to me.

"Darius, let's light this place up with magic and make a run for it."

"Wait. You got magic?" The demon in front turned around, giving me its full attention. It pointed.

I punched it in the face.

"Don't draw attention to me and I won't kill you," I seethed.

It ripped its finger down. "You're that human that beat two turns with the dragon," the demon whispered. "You got magic. That sect has been looking for you."

"They found me. The clown is dead. Take a hint."

The demon shifted. It looked around and then back to me, not moving away. It took hints like it minded its own business—not well.

"Where'd you get all that magic? You got any for sale?" the demon asked.

Two other demons hovering near us glanced over. Darius leveled an assessing stare at the demon willing to buy. I had no doubt a side business featuring large payments to the dual mages and demons acting like mules into the underworld could come out of it, but we didn't have time to hang around.

"We gotta—" I cut off as yelling and shouts rose over the murmurs. Everyone looked back, me included.

"Told ya," said the demon with a future as a magical mule.

The crowd around us shifted, their movements harried and jerky. Through opening gaps I saw demons running toward us from the corridor, fear smeared across their faces.

"Raid!" someone shouted.

The dragon roared somewhere to my right. A stream of fire raked through the trader space in front of us, blasting us with heat. Two demons flailed in the fire, scorched in the spray.

Screams of agony and the clank of metal filled the air, and the chaos was, sadly, headed our way. Large demons with weapons surged forward, pausing now and again to deliver a killing strike. An insect-looking creature climbed up the wall, whining and flinching as the protrusions pierced it. It didn't get far before one of the armed demons ripped it down. Suddenly the corridors surrounded by jagged rock walls made sense. They made it easy to corral, then take down, prey.

"We gotta go," I said, urgency speeding up my heart. I unzipped my pouch and dug out a handful of spells. I handed them over to our potential new business associate. "Pinch," I yelled, taking one out and pinching it. "And throw quickly."

I lobbed it behind us. An explosion sent a leg flying.

"Do it quickly. They won't all work without words. Ignore those that don't and move on. Stay alive, and the vampire will get in touch with you." I had no idea how, but that wasn't my problem. I hooked a thumb Darius's way before shoving the demon away from me. "Go! Save yourself. Kill people. Do whatever you do."

The dragon rose to the left, pumping its great wings. It turned toward the river and spewed a stream of fire. I grabbed a still, strategizing Darius and yanked him forward, pushing my way toward the edges of the crowd and waiting next to the main drag.

A few demons ran through the space, making a break for it. More joined until the place was filled with panicked creatures. I pushed Darius to the side near the wall as the dragon turned. The throb of power filled the area.

The gush of fire blistered the air as it raked down the main drag. Without overthinking it, I covered Darius and I in a protective bubble, ignoring the press of the crowd. The dragon turned, blasting those who'd made it across the clearing.

What better time to follow them?

"Let's go." I ran across the blackened stone of the trading area, putting distance between us and the task force. On the other side, I ran until the walls were higher and we couldn't see the trading area, before stopping and digging into my pouch. The beat of wings, much too close, announced the dragon was doing a flyby.

Darius dragged me to the ground and moved closer to the wall with me. A demon sprinted our way, looking up as it did so. A moment later, it jerked its arms over its head and ducked. A blast of fire consumed it, the flame spreading out along the corridor and washing toward us.

I threw another protective bubble over us, realizing that my ability to do so had to be something else imparted by my father. *Thanks, old man.*

Something screamed up ahead as the fire burned everything in its path. My breath caught as a glimmering black body and one wing appeared above the wall just down the way, the dragon checking out its handiwork. I clutched Darius, shrinking as best I could, watching the body. Seeing a front foot, then the back. Waiting for the head to appear next.

The rush of fire sounded, but not in our corridor. The dragon was cleaning out the one next to us.

"Go, go, go!" Staying low, ignoring the scrape of the wall against my arm, I ran, stepping on or jumping over scorched remains. We turned a corner and straightened, the dragon out of sight. For now.

"Spells," Darius said in a tight voice. He was feeling the pressure.

I grabbed a volatile spell, squeezed it, and lobbed it as hard as I could toward the dragon.

Darius threw his over the walls.

A blast of light exploded. The dragon trumpeted. Wings flapping drowned out a yell.

A pink haze ballooned up from Darius's spell. It solidified and then burst, spraying spikes.

We took off running, staying near the wall, constantly looking up to make sure the dragon wasn't coming our way.

Another spell went off, flashing red across the dark ceiling. Then blue. Our potential business associate was trying out his new arsenal.

That was good for us.

A demon stood in our way, cowering and blocking a small offshoot path. It was in the direction we needed to go.

"Move!" I shouted.

It stared at me, mute. Not complying.

I raked my special hellfire across its middle and kicked my way through, with Darius right behind. There was no room for cowards in this band of thieves and cutthroats. Not if we wanted to live.

That path dumped us out on another that led to the magical stairs. We were almost there.

I tried to look back for some sign of the dragon, but the walls were too high. We had to go up, though, and get out. If we stayed here, they would find us. Going back was not an option.

But if we went up, the dragon was sure to see us.

Darius ripped me around to face him. His bruising kiss fluttered my eyelashes. He stared down into my eyes and looked all the way down to my very soul. "I love you more than sunlight, Reagan Somerset, and I *will* see you out of this world and safely home, where I intend to kiss you every night for the rest of all eternity. Do you understand me?"

"Yes," I said fervently, clutching his wide shoulders.

His brow scrunched in determination and he nodded before stepping away. He dug into his satchel, to the bottom, and butterflies filled my stomach at the thought of the dangerous spells he stored way down where it was hard to grab.

Another roar shook my bones. People screamed. The crackling of fire sounded to the left. Shouts and yells, closer now. We were running out of time.

Darius placed three casings into his open palm before closing his satchel and digging into his backpack. He pulled out a vial of blood.

"If your mind goes hazy with this, just try to operate on your survival instincts. Don't think, just do. You need the boost, or we'll never make it." He handed it over.

I upended it into my mouth as Darius stepped away, murmuring something I couldn't hear. He crushed the casings in his palm, paused for a beat, and then threw them with all his might.

"Let's go!" he shouted, and reached for me.

I let him hold my hand until I could yank the zip on my pouch closed. I shook out of his grasp. "Only silly girls in action movies hold hands when they are running for their lives!"

I took off toward the stairs as the ground started to shake. Something hit off my head, and for once, it wasn't a drop of water. It was a rock.

More came down, the ceiling shedding, and a crack ran through the stone underfoot. The rock walls to our sides made a weird sort of grinding noise.

The shaking keyed up a notch, and I staggered to the side, losing my balance. Darius lurched the other way, reaching for me.

I batted his hand away as I righted. He was more graceful than me and clearly not used to falling. I, on the other hand, was an old pro. It didn't bother me one bit.

"Let's go, let's go!" he yelled over the groaning.

Rocks rained down freely now, bouncing off my head and striking my shoulders and arms and feet. The crack in the ground enlarged as another started up.

An explosion knocked me to my knees, jolting the ground under me. Another pushed me forward onto my hands.

Darius pulled me up by my arm and shoved me in front of him, staggering like a drunk.

"What the hell was that spell?" I hollered as we neared two waist-high beams that denoted the base of the stairs. I grabbed Darius with air and let fire burn around my feet. Yes, I'd agreed not to use my power, but I wasn't about to let us die. Besides, with all the chaos, who would notice? "Not even Penny has that kind of power."

"When the natural mage surfaces, it's usually to make money. I am unusually generous with him. It keeps him coming back." He looked behind us. "Go fast!"

I lifted us with air and basically flew up the steps, moving my feet like I was running, hoping no one would be the wiser.

"Hurry!" Darius shouted, his hand hitting off the air as he tried to clutch my arm.

I hazarded a glance back, because even though I was reasonably intelligent, I rarely proved it. The dragon pumped its wings, rising into the sky, not flinching as the rocks rained down. Looking straight at us.

"Oh sh—" I put everything into it, hightailing it up the stairs and hauling Darius with me.

I quickly learned that, when fear and panic were raging through me, I couldn't levitate as quickly as I could run. At least not yet. I set us down, lined the stairs with fire so we could see, and we took two stairs at a time. The flap of wings blotted out the pounding of my feet. My muscles screamed from exertion. Darius's heart hammered.

"Where the fuck is the fucking door, Batman?" I yelled, grinding my teeth.

The dragon's roar assaulted my senses and shook my body. I glanced back and saw its huge talons reaching for me.

We need a miracle... Darius's thought looped around my mind.

The claw touched my side, and the foot closed, nearly surrounding me. It wanted to capture, not kill me.

My father's dragon was about to capture me. Did he know?

My toe hit a step and I tumbled forward. Darius grabbed my arm and yanked. The world tilted. Sucked at me.

My face hit the hard ground. Darius landed on top of me before quickly rolling off. I jerked around, staring wide-eyed at the horizontal line in the sky. The gate.

We'd made it.

"Holy—" I sucked in a breath, relief flooding through me. "Crap."

His hand moved over mine. "Yes. We made it."

We took a moment to just breathe, but all too soon, reality returned. We had gotten through, but that didn't mean they wouldn't come after us. Did it? "Should we run? Will they come through?"

"I don't know, but let's err on the side of caution. Unless it is day in the Brink. I've lost all sense of time."

I was up and running before he was. We didn't worry about passing any wide-eyed creatures, and we didn't. Soon enough, the black of the sky leading to the gate melted into the burnt orange of night. It would be night in the Brink. Thank all that was holy.

A while later, we stood at the gate. Adrenaline surged through me. My heart raced. Laughter bubbled up.

I stepped through first, waited for Darius, and then threw my arms around him. My laugher grew louder as Darius turned to me. He stroked my face. A small smile curved his full lips and his honeyed eyes sparkled. "We made it."

A tear squeezed out. I took his hand. Yes, we had. Miracle of miracles, we had accomplished the impossible, and made it back in one piece.

CHAPTER 31

T HE NEXT DAY, I rubbed at my sandy eyes and wiggled a little closer to Darius. We'd headed straight to his house in the French Quarter, and I'd barely found the energy to climb up the stairs. We had gone straight to bed. No food, no canoodling, just sleep.

I glanced over at the clock and did the thinking equivalent of scratching my head. Could that be right?

It had been nearly twenty-four hours since we'd hit the bed. Holy crap.

I ran a hand across Darius's defined chest, relishing in his heat, in the steady beating of his heart, which I felt in his chest and through the bond. I had made it out because of him. Hell, I'd made it *in* because of him. He'd been right: I had needed him. Without question. He had just the right amount of knowledge, ability to strategize, intelligence, and daring to shine down there.

I was really lucky.

And really horny. The jaunt through the lust sect hadn't completely left my system. A lot of the underworld hadn't completely left my system. There were parts I actually missed. That I'd like to visit again. I hadn't expected that. I hadn't expected the peaceful feeling in some areas, and the adrenaline rush in others. I hadn't expected to belong so well.

It was not meant to be. My home was here. In safety. With Darius.

I let my hand trail over his six-pack and under the covers, then slid my palm against his velvety skin. He breathed out and turned his head to me. I claimed his lips while stroking. He reached for me, pulling me tightly against him.

I threw a leg over his hips and straddled him.

"I enjoy waking up to you," he said, pushing his hips upward. I moaned into his kiss, rubbing against him until he was ready, then pausing so we could properly line up.

"Me too," I said.

I fell into his kiss. The feel of him.

Sitting down was bliss, flipping my stomach and eliciting a long moan. I moved against him. A fervor came over me, and I needed him in a way I couldn't put into words.

His hands drifted up my chest and cupped my breasts, teasing my nipples as I swirled my hips. A moment later, he lowered a hand to below my stomach, working me to a fever pitch with his tricky fingers.

I let my head fall back with a loud moan. This felt

ten times better since the bonding. Magnified from our normal lovemaking.

On the edge, my body gloriously tight, I squeezed my eyes shut. An explosion of sensation rocked me, making me cry out. He shuddered a moment later, crushing me to his chest.

After taking a moment to come down, I asked, "Do you need to feed?"

"Yes. After you eat?"

"Sounds great. How long do I have you for?"

"Eternity."

"No, I mean, until you have to work. I assume you missed a lot of…whatever it is you do."

He slid his hands down my back and to my butt. He lifted me away and then immediately pulled me back, ready for more. "I have no idea, since I don't know how long we were down there, but I will make time for you, Reagan. I will always make time for you."

I didn't mention that he was a vampire, and really had nothing but time. It was a nice sentiment. I didn't want to ruin the moment for once.

He thrust into me, lighting up my senses. Then again, so deep and right. Faster and faster he moved, pulling me down as he pushed up. My body wound up, gloriously tight. Wetter than normal.

I frowned at that stray thought, but it wouldn't shake loose. Half of me soaked in the delicious feel of him. Of the emotion attached to this action. Of our love. But the other half of my brain realized something wasn't the same. It reminded me of sex with a human…somehow.

An orgasm hit me, making me clench my teeth. More hot wetness invaded my thoughts.

Something was definitely different.

"We need to eat," I said, moving off him as I tried to identify what was weird.

"What is the mat—" He cut off, staring down at himself.

I followed his gaze before checking my lady bits with my fingertips. "Is that what I think it is?"

He went unnaturally still.

I touched the gooey stuff. Stuff that vampires shouldn't be able to produce. "I am *really* glad I haven't stopped the birth control, or I would be freaking out right now. But is that for real? Did you ejaculate?"

He sat up slowly. "How is this possible?"

Something the red demon had said smacked into me. I repeated it with perfect recall, since my memory was freaking awesome now. "We do not need any more of your half-breeds." I shook my head. "Does that mean what I think it means? Is Lucifer closing the gates to keep species like you from breeding naturally within the magic down there?"

Darius's face came around, his eyes shining. "I'm

not sure. Hindering the reproduction of magical species would certainly weaken their power. If we hadn't discovered the unicorns, vampires would be slowly dying out. That would please the elves. I'm not sure how it would affect Lucifer. But Ja didn't mention it. This could be another effect of the bond. And while it seems I can ejaculate, that doesn't mean I can produce offspring. I must do more research. Track down and talk to older vampires."

"Yes. Track down people and ask questions, because we are not doing research using reproductive Russian roulette, I'll tell you that much. I can barely keep myself safe. No way am I bringing kids into the mix."

Darius stared at me for a long moment, the emotion overflowing in his eyes. I threw up a hand and hopped off the bed. "Don't tell me what you've always wanted and didn't think you could have. I don't want to know. What I *do* want is food. Lots and lots of food."

I was back to ruining the moment.

Darius let the matter drop, thankfully. Because while it was a very big deal to him, it was a return to normality for me. I'd dated a few humans, after all. I knew how the birds and the bees worked. I just didn't need them working on me, now or probably ever. Not with the life I lived. The possibility that he could reproduce, as strange as it was, didn't change anything. Except cleanup.

The next few days we didn't do much but eat, sleep, make love, and avoid calling the dual mages, because I was a huge coward. Callie was going to *kill* me. I did send them a note saying I was okay and I'd meet them soon for an in-person apology and thank-you, which I hoped to walk away from alive.

I shivered. No, I was not looking forward to that meetup.

It turned out we had been in the underworld for four days. Always moving, often fighting, and no sleep for four days. No wonder I was done in.

Finally, after five days of recuperation in Darius's residence, where I was waited on hand and foot by a very surly Moss, I was ready to head home. I wanted to resume the life I'd risked my freedom for. I wanted my own space.

The town car stopped in front of my house and Moss's eyes flashed into the rearview mirror. He didn't move to get out.

"No, no. I got it. Don't go to any trouble." I pushed the door open. "I'm a lady of the modern era, after all. I can open doors myself."

I shut the door behind me and watched the black town car pull away before turning toward my house. No Good Mikey was sitting on someone else's porch step down the street from our places. No one ever complained when Mikey sat on their porch. They knew better.

"Hey," I said, sauntering over and leaning against the banister. Paint flaked off and drifted to the ground.

"Hey," he said, looking me over. "You're clean. That's new."

I glanced down at my new hand-stitched leather pants and designer black tank top. Darius was predictable and ridiculous. "I took a shower."

"I see. Still no eyebrows."

"We can't have everything."

"And a larger, more noticeable fanny pack."

"Are you into fashion all of a sudden? Since when do you notice what people are wearing?"

"Since you've been gone. All I've seen are normal people wearing normal clothes. The difference is staggering."

I squeezed my lips together, half frowned, and did heavy eyes—all that to say I wasn't impressed. He grunted and stood. Clearly he spoke Face.

"What'd I miss?" I asked, falling in step with him and heading toward our houses.

"Several break-ins, all to your house."

"Well, at least you start with that. I usually get that news as an aside from Mince."

"Do you want to hear this or not?"

"Sorry." I made a show of zipping my lips.

He huffed. "First came the usual: those people

bringing groceries or whatever they do. Next came that old couple you always have hanging around. I didn't know it was them, though. I heard the news from Shotgun Joe."

"Who?"

"The neighbor in back of you."

I hadn't known his name. I kind of wanted to go back to that time, since something told me he hadn't earned it by doing crafts.

"I kicked my way in there to see what the hell was going on," he said. "Startled the old man. *Didn't* startle the old woman. She hit me with something fierce before I could even get my gun up. Didn't see it coming. Like a chokehold or some shit. I woke up at the bottom of the porch to Smokey arguing with them, telling them I was your neighbor." He rolled his shoulders. "At least I didn't piss myself. Chokeholds can do that."

"Wow." I didn't mention that chokeholds also required touching. Physical choking, if you will. I was pretty sure he didn't want to admit he'd been hit with magic. I was good with that.

"They were legit, so I tried to let them be, but the old woman forced me inside and practically poured whiskey down my throat."

"She's a bully at the best of times. She does it to everyone, don't worry." I felt a familiar pang of guilt. I needed to meet up with them. I couldn't stall anymore.

That would only make them madder.

"I'm not the type of guy who gets bullied. I *do* the bullying," Mikey said.

"Well, it seems you've met your match."

He huffed out a laugh but didn't comment. I was pretty sure he now had a soft spot for Callie.

"Right, fine." I stopped in front of my porch, newly swept and with the chairs placed *just so*. Darius's people left no chair untampered with. "After that?"

"A suave-looking mamajama. Real sleek and easy-like." He slid his hand through the air, like he was passing a bill over a saloon countertop.

"What are these words and weird body movements you're using?"

"He came with another dude. Short and shifty-eyed. That second guy didn't seem like nothin' except for the high-dollar suit, but he had a messenger bag draped over his chest. That seemed out of place. High-dollar bag, but still, I've seen witches sneak into the cemetery with that kinda thing."

Magical drifted out of his thoughts, and I gritted my teeth. I'd been practicing shutting out people's thoughts, because while demons—and Darius—had figured out a way to keep their thoughts to themselves, non-demons didn't know there was a need. I didn't want to hear what people keep private. Too much baggage.

"So Mr. Suave and his well-dressed sidekick busted into my house?" I asked.

"No. Walked in. It was locked. Those other dudes always lock it. I've checked. But this guy just sauntered through."

The small hairs rose on my arms. Clearly it was a vampire and a well-paid, and therefore high-powered, mage.

"Suave, you said? Debonair?" I already knew who it was, but needed to be sure before I thought about *why* he had come.

"Yeah." He slid that imaginary dollar across the dusty bar again. "Real easy-like."

I rolled my eyes. "What did they do?"

Mikey sat down on the second step and looked through the opening of the cemetery across the street. "I didn't want to go in after them. After what happened with your older friend, I figured I should call someone."

"I hope you didn't call Smokey…"

"No. I called that old broad. She had given me her card." He rubbed a spot on his cheek that I was sure had a scar at one point. "I figured she'd know what to do. I thought she'd come barreling down the street with her husband in tow talking placidly about killing things. That guy is nuts. Anyway, they rolled up real slow, stopping down the street where I usually hang out. She had me give her more information: appearance, dress, walk. Even after that, she didn't burst in with guns blazing. She almost seemed timid."

Crap. It was definitely Vlad. No one went in blazing where he was concerned. Not even me.

"Did you go in with her?"

"Are you kidding? She said not to in a very *calm* voice. I know that voice. That's the voice of a woman about to cut a bitch. I'm not trying to mess with that, her shit"—he meant magic—"and that rich dude and *his* shit? Girl, you gotta screw loose."

I held up a hand. "I'm not blaming you. So what happened?"

"Nothing I would have expected, as I said. She went in, no bangs or explosions happened, and then the suave dude came out." Mikey scratched at his neck and shifted uncomfortably. "Here's the thing. I was at the side of my porch in the shadows, staying real still and quiet. Nobody else noticed me. But this guy...he walked out like he did"—there was that hand gesture again— "and stopped. His shifty-eyed friend kept walking, but he stopped. Slowly, real fucking slowly, okay? He moved just his head until he was looking right at me. Right fucking at me." Mikey half jumped and half shifted, then shivered and rolled his neck. I'd never seen him move so much.

Definitely Vlad.

"He stared at me for a moment, right at me, and

gave me a little smile. Reagan, it was the worst fucking smile I have ever seen, and I've seen some shitty fucking smiles. Serial killers don't smile like that."

Vlad was the ultimate serial killer, so yes they did, but I didn't want to tell Mikey that. He probably already had nightmares.

"And then he just kept on going. Walked down the stairs as if nothing had happened." Heavy silence hung down on us for a moment. "He knew it was me who ratted him out."

I nodded slowly. It made sense. The question was, would anything come of it? I'd have to ask Darius. Vlad picked and chose what he cared about. I had no idea how that selection process went. I also had no idea why he was wandering around my house with a mage. Trying to find out more about my secrets, no doubt.

"They got in their Honda and drove away. A second later, I was forced into your house by the old pair for more whiskey."

I held up a hand. "Wait. A *Honda*?"

"Yeah. He wasn't driving the kind of ride your guy likes. Gray Honda. Accord, I think."

"And he was dressed nicely, with another nicely dressed guy with him?"

"Yeah. He *stood out,* know what I'm sayin'? But the Honda was plain."

"Huh." I thought on that for a minute before shrugging it off. Another question for Darius. "Anything else?"

"Isn't that enough?"

"If you only knew, Mikey. If you only knew." I trudged back to my house and up the steps, my good mood from the last five days draining away.

Once inside, I poured myself a glass of wine and sighed, taking a moment to enjoy the comfortable feeling of my own house and all my stuff.

I sat down on the couch and sipped my wine, thinking about turning on the TV.

A knock jerked me awake.

I blinked and looked around wildly. *Where am I?*

Another knock.

My living room came into focus. My TV, the screen black. The wine spilled down my new shirt, across my new hand-stitched leather pants, and into the cracks of my really expensive couch.

Awesome. I'd fallen asleep.

A strange sensation had me tilting my head as the lock turned over.

I couldn't place the emotion, but I did place the intruder, who had just stopped in front of a hovering ball of my hellfire, guaranteed to split a sucker in half with minimal effort.

Whoop-whoop.

"Reagan," Moss said, his voice frayed at the edges.

I sat forward, struggling to process what was going on. How could I still be tired after all the sleeping I'd done? And why had I let Moss so totally into my little world of magic?

Another issue for Darius. Poor guy. I was racking up quite a tab on his behalf. Although, let's be honest, he was now above Vlad on the knowledge scale, so I'd call that even.

"Moss," I said in a thick voice. I cleared my throat. "Maybe don't break into my house."

"Clearly." He closed the door behind him, shutting himself between the revolving ball of death, and...well, a door. "You are needed."

I pushed myself off the couch, and wine dribbled off my legs and onto the cream rug. Marie, Darius's designer, was going to *kill* me.

"Why?" I tilted my head again, like a dog hearing a dog whistle. What was that *feeling*?

"Vlad has Darius in the lair." The lair was the underground vampire home in the Realm.

I paused in rubbing my chest where that strange feeling had lodged. "What do you mean, Vlad has him?"

Darius's heartbeat was strong and steady, so he wasn't overly concerned about whatever was happening.

"Your bond is illegal."

"Vlad's still pissed about that?" I rolled my eyes and

tore down the Ball o' Death. "What's the problem? Even if they don't know who I am, they know some of what I can do. Besides, I have an elder to back me, and Vlad wants me under vampire control."

"Vlad doesn't want you for our faction—he wants you for himself. He set that war in the Dark Kingdom in motion after he made sure you knew the demons were coming for you." He gave me a look that was more than a little judgmental, but I was too busy gaping in shock to care.

Vlad had given us cover with that war. He'd made completing my goal ten times easier. If not for him, I might not have successfully made it out. That was some serious maneuvering right there. And more, he must've known what it would've meant if the sect had come to the Brink to get me. He must've known that to prevent a war (which he must've not been quite ready for), I had to go to the underworld, and that I'd need help to do it.

All that to get me under his control. He didn't plan to aid Lucifer; he planned to use me as bait to corner him. Or maybe just hang on to me to see what I was really worth to my father. Vlad did all that to get me under his thumb.

Wow.

I had to give the vampire mad respect for all that.

"Anyone who has *met* you would know how you would react to such news of the demons," Moss was saying. "He has orchestrated all of your movements, and everything has been done with an eye toward condemning Darius. He can now claim Darius put you at great risk, illegally. That will allow Vlad to kill him, per our laws, before moving in and claiming you for himself."

I took the last sip of wine, because why waste it, and thought about the events of the Dark Kingdom and immediately before. The battle so near the castle. All the sects prickly and on edge. My father showing up to quell the rage. The areas Vlad occupied in the edges, lurking. Watching for us.

"Oh, that bastard," I said under my breath.

Another thought occurred to me. I was no longer a ripe turnip.

If such a thing existed.

I narrowed my eyes at Moss. "Why should I trust you?"

He stared at me with his flat, dark gaze. "You shouldn't. Ever. You are wild, and fickle, and no one will ever be able to predict which side you'll choose— with us, or against us. But right now, you can save my employer. Only you. For that, I am here, asking your help. Though I do not like it."

"Oh, sure. Throw in that last bit, why don't you." I listened for his thoughts and was immediately reward-ed. Guilt for pursuing his bloodlust instead of accompanying Darius. Fear for what would happen to the kingdom he'd help build if Darius came to harm. Annoyance and anger that he had to ask a ridiculous human creation for help. And beneath all that, a budding bromance for his employer. He simply didn't want anything to happen to Darius.

It was this last bit that convinced me of his truthfulness.

"Right. Let's blow shit up." I set the glass on the coffee table for the minions to clean up and headed for the door.

"Aren't you going to change?" he asked.

"I smell drunk and look crazy. Trust me. My appearance is the first line of defense."

CHAPTER 32

MOSS HAD AN expensive, high-speed car waiting, so he drove dangerously fast to the nearest gate into the Realm. From there he offered to carry me so we could move as quickly as possible.

I put my arm on his shoulder and smugly grinned. I didn't need it. I was the Flash.

Turned out, he was still a little faster than me, which was annoying.

I made up for it when he suggested circumventing the weird rock forest I'd stumbled my way through on my first visit to the lair. Instead, I used my power and shoved all the rocks out of the way. When the rock man wandered in, pissed beyond belief, I used air to punch him while yelling, "Now ask me weird questions that hurt my brain!" We hadn't hit it off last time.

"I don't think you are rational just now," Moss said in a low voice.

Unlike when Darius accused me of that, Moss was totally right. But seriously, Vlad was trying to creep on *my* man? No way.

At the entrance to the lair, I put my hand on Moss's suited chest to hold him back. "Number one, only James Bond wears a suit when going into battle. Number two, I got this. Just follow along and don't get burned."

I kicked the door open. "Lucy, I'm home!"

The darkness engulfed me, but I didn't pay it any attention. I followed the same path as on my first visit. Only a few months had passed since then, but it seemed like so much longer. This time, I had zero fear. Absolutely none. I'd survived the Dark Kingdom. The lair, or what non-vampires called the Dungeon, held no horrors for me.

I stalked down the corridor as the first vampire rushed for me, fangs bared.

"Nope." I flicked my hand, and air-swatted it at the dirt wall. "Follow me and I'll kill you."

It followed me.

Moss jumped out of the way as I jabbed my hand forward like a kung fu master from the old movies. I pierced the vampire's chest with air and clutched its heart.

Its eyes widened.

"Don't fuck with crazy." I tore its heart out of its chest. Which probably would've looked especially cool if I'd taken a bite of it while the vamp died, but ew. No.

I turned, and Moss followed without a word.

Columns rose to the sides, spacious and high. I

glanced up at a ledge strung between them and saw a vampire hiding under one of those sheets that had once made them invisible to me. It looked down at me, watching my progress.

I sent fire to burn away the sheet, hoping to expose him. His body puddled into goo on the ledge.

Oops.

"You shouldn't show your power so frivolously," Moss said.

He was nervous.

I grinned.

"Darius will live, he'll get his bond passed, and I will be one of yours. Don't you protect what's yours?"

"What if there are leaks?"

"Just say I have a demon in me. Easy. Really, Moss, it's like you have no imagination."

Moss's lips tightened. My grin turned into a smile.

Unlike the last time I was here, no new vampires showed up to face off with me. A new boss was in town. One that led by force.

Thanks, demons, for your unwelcome lessons.

The base of the pass widened until it opened to a chamber filled with riches and a dinner table not used for eating.

At the front of the room, Vlad sat in the large throne chair, a smug smile on his face. Two bored-looking vampires sat with him, a man and a woman, on either side of his throne.

The one person standing at this sitting party, Darius flicked his eyes to me, then Moss, then me again. Anger and frustration stole through his previously despondent expression. He was pissed because he thought I was endangering myself.

Or maybe that I had to rescue him.

Again.

He did make a handsome damsel.

"Ms. Somerset," Vlad said in a honeyed voice. I didn't hear any of his thoughts, and had a sneaking suspicion that he'd spent enough time working with demons to figure out that trick they all seemed to know. "So lovely to see you again. Mr. LaRay, put up a wall of privacy just there, please. We had it taken down when we heard you'd dropped in to pay us a visit."

Moss retrieved a spell and did as he was told while I surveyed the elder in front of me.

"Hey, Vlad," I said. "I hear you're discussing Darius's and my bond. Imagine my surprise when I didn't get an invite to this party."

"Your *illegal* bond, Ms. Somerset, and this is a vampire issue."

"Oh. Well, then. Let me barge my way in and make it *my* issue. So what's the problem, and where is the group of vampires that usually decide on bonding matters? I was under the impression there were more than two, and also that you didn't have any part of it." I quirked an eyebrow at him.

"We've decided a smaller group would suffice, given that your magic is such a delicate issue."

"Ah. And it doesn't seem to matter that you have a vested interest in the decision going unfavorably for Darius, hmm?"

Vlad spread his hands like he was helpless. "I am simply trying to uphold our laws. The bond was forged before it was approved. Therefore, we need to review the integrity of the vampire and his bond-mate. In this case, Darius put you, and our faction as a whole, in grave peril because of how he handled the situation. All this so he could gain entrance to the underworld for his own personal gain. Such disregard for the rules simply can't go unpunished." He held up his hand like I was about to argue. "But don't worry, Reagan. We will not permanently harm him. We will simply exile him for a length of time, to be determined shortly, and forbid him from mingling with the politics of our faction."

"And me? You're going to kill me, I take it?"

His musical laugh made me stabby. "Oh my, no. Of course not, no. We realize your value, Reagan. We also realize your unique position of knowing about our greatest secret. The unicorns."

He paused, and I lifted my eyebrows, waiting for the other shoe to drop.

"You must understand that while we do not wish to terminate you, we also can't allow you to drift away, unchecked."

"And, pray tell, what is your grand plan to keep me in check?"

A smile spread across his face. "I think you know."

"Bond me yourself, is that it?"

He clasped his fingers. "As part of Darius's punishment, the bond would have to be stripped from him. Given the magical nature of the bond process, it would then have to be fastened to another, so you don't suffer."

"And that someone else is you, right?"

"One of us, certainly, and we've agreed that I make the most sense." He leaned forward. "We would not have to go through the bonding process, Reagan. That has been done. We would be transferring the bond, not forging it anew. I would simply need a little of your blood—just a taste—and you would take a little of mine. No more than a mouthful. Minimal touching, if that is what you prefer, or intercourse if you desire it. I will yield to your demands."

"Uh huh."

"After that, you will be released to live your life as you ought. I will provide for you in order to keep you safely out of harm's way. You will want for nothing."

He didn't know me at all. Out of harm's way? That

sounded like a death sentence.

His continued smile and cunning gaze said he thought he had me in a corner, and would now hammer the nails into the proverbial coffin. In other words, he thought I was like most people.

Darius's heart sped up. He knew that I was not, at all, like most people. When someone tried to put Baby in the corner, that someone accidentally got killed.

"Well, fantastic," I said joyfully. Vlad's face froze. Darius shifted warily. "And I assume these vampires know about my family ties?"

Vlad bent his head forward in an affirmation. "As I said, it is a very delicate situation, one that will take great strategy and planning down the road to keep you a secret. Your foray into the underworld created quite a stir. I understand that many demons didn't think magic could be so effective. Nor did they think any part-humans could get in through the fog anymore. And while that is still mostly true, it has created a lot of questions."

Vlad's eyes gleamed. Personal questions, I gathered. Of what he, personally, could do if allowed to get past that fog.

"You have privacy spells up all over, right?" I asked. "You know as well as I do that this faction has leaks."

Moss shifted, and that, paired with Vlad's smile turning brittle, told me this was a sore point.

"We do," Vlad said. "This is a closed meeting about a delicate subject. It requires the utmost privacy."

I smiled at him. "I forgot to ask. What if I don't like this plan, and will not stand for Darius being punished or the bond moved? Then what?"

There came that fake helpless look again. "There really is no other way. I apologize about that."

"There are a couple other ways, actually," I said. Darius's eyes tightened. He likely expected me to blow like a volcano. In contrast, Vlad clearly had no clue what was coming. "To start, I could tell my father who started the war in the Dark Kingdom. He would be mighty interested to hear that. Or simply tell him not to work with you on anything. He seems to really want an heir, so I'm sure he'll have an open mind about a grave concern of mine."

Vlad gave me a placating smile.

"But, of course, you know I won't do that," I said. He tilted his head in affirmation and steepled his fingers. "Happily, there is a second way."

"Reagan," Darius said in warning.

Vlad was out of the chair and halfway to me before I registered any movement. Old me would've flinched and tried to grab my sword before being backhanded by a vampire. Old me hadn't gone through demon boot camp.

I snatched him in an air fist and shoved him back

into his seat. "Now, now, Vlad, mind your manners." The other vampires started to get up, and I tied them to their chairs, too. "Now, as I was saying." I lifted all three of them into the air without so much as breaking a sweat. Alarmed thoughts curled up from them, and Vlad's surprise was strong enough to break his thought barrier. It was news to him that I had this much power.

Demon boot camp had been incredibly effective.

I rotated them and encircled each of them in fire so they couldn't see out. Alarm bent to panic. Except for Vlad, who let slip another thought concerning my added worth. The man was as cool as they came. It was strangely annoying.

"A stake of air," Darius said in a low tone, watching the chairs revolve.

"Good call." I did as he said, and set the stakes right at their hearts, making them slowly burrow into their skin. One vampire tried to scrape my air with claws. Magical sparks hit the walls of his fire prison. I repaired the air immediately. "I'm my father's daughter, Vlad," I called up. I didn't know how to do that voice trick my father had used. It was much too complex. I'd have to settle for yelling. "I don't like getting pushed around. I don't like being dominated. It makes me ragey. I'm also my mother's daughter. I *really* don't like you threatening someone I care deeply about. I can kill you easily. All of you. I can walk through this faction with everyone in the place trying to kill me and come out un-scathed. And I'm *nothing* compared to my father, whom I *will* contact if you attempt to kill Darius. I will sacrifice myself for him, just as he keeps trying to sacrifice for me."

The two vampires on the sides were in full-fledged panic mode now. Even Vlad had started to get worried when his claws wouldn't break through my magic.

"You can see that I am an *extremely* valuable asset, can you not?" I yelled, surging more energy into the fire and speeding up the stakes. "Trust me, you want me on your side. You want me to lie low and train. To get stronger, and better. What you *don't* want is to anger me. I get crazy when I'm angry."

I stripped away the fire and stakes and quickly pulled them back to the ground. The chairs settled with bumps. The two vampires on the sides were both in their monster forms, blood running down their chests and torn clothes strewn across their seats. Vlad had a placid, assessing expression at odds with his blood-soaked shirt. Not one hair was out of place.

I had no idea how he did it.

"Darius will not get punished," I said quietly into the sudden silence. "I will not have to deal with any of you. Only him. Our bond will remain intact." I paused, and then figured, why not, I should go for it. "And I can visit the unicorns whenever I want."

The vampire on the right changed back to his human form and glanced down at his chest. "Give her what she wants," he said. "Give her anything she wants."

The other vampire changed back as well and palmed her breast, which really wasn't where the wound was, but whatever. She nodded her assent. "She is valuable. Beyond what you said, Vlad. If she is loyal to Darius, so be it. She is still within our faction. That is enough. We are lucky she agreed to bond at all. Enter her in the books."

Vlad steepled his fingers again and tilted his head to the side, watching me. A slow smile crept up his face. "You make a very compelling argument, Ms. Somerset." His eyes sparkled as his gaze slid to Darius. "The find of the century, Darius. I applaud you. I hope to one day outdo you, though how, I cannot imagine."

"I warned you of her response to all this," Darius said, walking toward me.

"Indeed you did. Though I admit, I thought you were grossly overexaggerating. It seems the jaunt into the Dark Kingdom has done her good."

I snapped. "I almost forgot. Leave my neighbor alone. He was just looking out for me. Don't involve him in any of your plans."

"I wouldn't dream of it." That smile wasn't reassuring. The fear he'd felt in my fire prison was much more so. I was contemplating giving him another scare when Darius slipped his arm around my back and pulled me close. He turned us back the way I'd come before I'd made up my mind. "Reagan," he said in disapproval, and I knew I'd get in trouble for risking the knowledge of my magic for him. "What did you spill on yourself?"

My mouth dropped open. Maybe not.

Moss fell in behind us. "I apologize, Mr. Durant," he said. "I know you said not to involve her, but I didn't see any other way. Vlad had things pretty well wrapped up."

"Though it grieves me, you were right to bring her. I knew Vlad's resolve, but I hoped to talk the others around. Those two elders are firmly in his pocket. They have too much power, all of them. I will need to do something about that."

"Who's hungry?" I raised my hand, answering my own question, as we made our way out. Vampires crowded around the puddles of sticky goo from the two vamps I'd killed. They looked at us solemnly. Darius ignored them entirely. "Who wants to make dinner?" I pointedly looked at Darius.

"How does Louisiana keep enough food to feed her?" Moss grumbled.

"Jealous?" I grinned back at him, and he lowered his brows. He totally was.

We made our way home, Darius and I hand in

hand. I had wanted to stay away from vampires, and when that had proven impossible, I'd wanted to avoid getting intimate with one. When that had gone to hell, I'd forbidden myself to bond. Another strike against me. And now, here I was, utterly, irrevocably, in love with one.

So much for doing the smart thing.

"I love you," I said softly.

He stopped me (and waited for Moss to keep going) before brushing his lips across mine. "You are more precious to me than anything in my eternal life. You are my everything, and I vow to protect you always."

I smiled like a lovesick girl and pulled him down for a deeper kiss. He should have been all wrong for me, but he felt so *right*. He was my family now. My chosen mate. And if life should ever take a turn, and I could ensure we were safe, I wouldn't be totally averse to expanding that family, if he biologically could. We were as close to normal humans as I ever hoped to get, and that was fine by me.

He swooped me up into his arms and carried me the rest of the way.

CHAPTER 33

I KNOCKED ON the door to a pretty swank little spot in upstate New York. Roger had some dough, it seemed. The elves clearly paid well.

Darius waited off to the side, staring out at the lovely trees dotting the landscape, starting to lose their leaves as summer waned. I would've snuck off and done this without him, but he owned the jet that had gotten me there.

After putting Vlad in his place, I'd tracked down my loose-lipped were-dog friend, Red, to get Roger's whereabouts. I needed to call off Roger's efforts to amass an army. I figured he'd need to hear it directly from me. Since Darius owned his own jet, hasty travel plans weren't a big deal. Money was great. It really smoothed out all life's annoying problems. Well, except for the whole "being Lucifer's daughter" thing.

I had raised my hand to knock again when I heard footsteps behind the door. The handle jiggled before the door swung open, revealing a tight-bodied Roger, wearing jeans that hugged his muscular thighs and a white T-shirt that outlined his broad chest. The guy could really work the laid-back look.

Surprise didn't register on his face when he saw me, but his expression did harden when he caught sight of Darius.

"I had to bring him. He insisted." I shrugged. "Can we come in? Or just me, depending on your vampire-tolerance level."

"Red told me you were coming," Roger said, stepping back.

I hooked a thumb behind me. "Is he a yay or nay? We're not here for any trouble."

Roger jerked his head and turned to lead us inside. Darius was behind me a moment later, closing the door after him.

For a man with a casual dress code, Roger really did up his house. Plush furniture and matching decor set off a rustic look that really worked with the surroundings. Time, effort, and money had been poured into the situation, and it had turned out well.

I pointed at a grand piano as we entered a sitting room. "This is going to sound like a dumb question, but do you play?"

"I play some. I prefer the guitar. I have a setup for a band, and the piano rounds it out when someone competent sits at it." His gaze flicked to Darius. He was correctly assuming Darius was someone competent.

Roger put out his hand to indicate we should sit on the leather sofa. "Do you want something to drink?"

"No, I'm good, thanks."

Roger looked at Darius. "Vampire?"

"No, thank you for asking."

Roger lowered into the love seat, and while he leaned back and crossed an ankle over a knee, only an idiot would assume that meant he was relaxed. I didn't know if alphas like him ever relaxed. "What can I do for you?"

"Information share. We've been busy."

"We?" Roger glanced at Darius.

I toggled my thumb back and forth between Darius and I. "We, yeah. I'll start from the beginning, shall I?"

I didn't, at all, start from the beginning. Or tell the whole truth. I told him about calling the demon, about Vlad's efforts to spread news of the coming demon attack, then made up a rambling story about forcing the demons to do our bidding. He couldn't know we'd gone to the Dark Kingdom ourselves—it would give me away, and besides, he didn't need to know. He just needed an assurance the threat was canceled.

At the end of my tall tale, he stared at me quietly with that hard alpha gaze. My magic pounded in my middle, but I kept it at bay. While the new me still did not react well to challenging stares, I could keep from punching people in the face. Mostly. I'd matured a little.

"He helped you with all this?" Roger nodded toward Darius.

"Yes. You probably know, but just like shifters, vampires want to be the king of the hill. Only they go about it differently. By helping me, Darius gained some choice information."

It was true, and also something Roger would understand. There was no way I'd run around saying Darius and I were bonded and in love. I'd have a shifter follower immediately thereafter. They would never trust me again.

"If you're lying..." Roger let the sentence linger, and I couldn't tell if it was a threat, or if he was legitimately asking for me to assure him I wasn't.

I chose the latter. "Look, here's the situation. I created this mess by failing to snuff that demon in Seattle. I'm the one they would be after if they came to the surface. If I'm lying, it's *my* ass that'll be in a sling. I didn't need to tell you any of this at all. I could've just let you wait forever. But you were upfront with me, so now I'm being upfront with you. We're good. I'm safe. Now I'm going to lie low, keep to myself, and let the world turn."

He surveyed me again before nodding. "Okay. Thank you for letting me know." He paused. "I'll forget about the incident in NOLA where you chased a few of mine."

I paused in getting up and grimaced. "Ah. Yes. About that. I was going through something."

"Clearly."

"But they are pretty fast—" I paused, because now I was even faster. I could totally get that were-badger. Probably some of the wolves as well. "Anyway." I let it go. It wasn't a great idea.

Darius and I stood. Roger did so a moment later, playing a gracious host, even to a vampire. Tough but housebroken. The man had many layers.

"No more bounty hunting?" Roger asked as we walked to the door.

"No. No more." I paused on the front porch. "I'm honestly going to lie low. I want people to forget my name."

Roger huffed out a laugh, something that didn't seem natural for him. "What will you do with your time?"

I sighed. I had no idea.

EPILOGUE

I WRUNG MY hands as I waited on the wide porch of Callie and Dizzy's house. It was the night of the big meetup, nearly two weeks since our return from the underworld. A terror-filled, cowardly couple of weeks.

"You need to ring the doorbell, love," Darius said softly. I could hear the humor in his voice. He thought this was hilarious.

"I know, I know. Don't rush me." I had braced my hands on my hips and taken a step toward the doorbell when my phone buzzed in my pocket.

I fished it out and read Callie's text. *You had better get here soon, or I will come and get you myself.*

This was a pre-agreed time and date. I had made myself do it so I wouldn't weasel out and put it off any longer.

I really wanted to weasel out and put it off.

The front door swung open and I jumped back, startled. Dizzy jumped forward with an "*Ah!*" and groped at an invisible satchel.

His eyes focused on me and he sighed. "Oh, Reagan,

it's just you." He chuckled and put his hand on his chest, half covering a burned area. "You scared me. I wasn't expecting you out here."

"I was just about to ring the doorbell." I showed him my pointer finger as though he had asked for proof.

"You don't have to ring the bell, you know that. Just come on in." He gave me a huge smile and stepped out onto the porch to wrap me in a bear hug. "Thank God you're okay. We were worried *sick*! Callie was ranting and trying to figure out how to go in after you. We couldn't, of course. Did the demon find you? Well, wait. Let's get in the house so you only have to tell the story once." He stepped back and jutted out a hand to Darius. "You went with her. You knew she'd go. Boy, am I glad you were the vampire she was hooked up with all those months ago. She got really lucky there."

Darius shook Dizzy's hand and nodded, before stepping back and moving to put his hand on the small of my back. He stopped himself and pushed his hands into his pockets instead.

If Dizzy noticed the slip, he didn't let on.

"Come in, come in." He motioned us in and stood by the door until we complied.

"Were you going outside for something?" I asked Dizzy. His car was in the garage.

"Oh." He paused in closing the door and stared vaguely. His brow furrowed. Then he shrugged. "It'll come to me eventually. My memory isn't what it used to be. Come in!"

With a smile, he led us through the large, spacious house and into the kitchen. That was where we conducted business as well as casual conversations. Or, in this situation, groveling and possible violence.

Callie stood at the island with her hands on her hips, glaring down at her cell phone. She glanced up with an angry scowl when Dizzy entered. "She's going to chicken out. Didn't I tell you? She will. I'm going to go hunt her down."

"Hon."

Callie finally clued in. Her eyes went from angry to *blazing*. In contrast, her face lost all expression.

A shiver of fear worked through me. And I'd thought the underworld was terrifying.

"Reagan," Callie said in an even tone.

"Hi. Look—"

"No, no." She held up a hand to stop me. "Let's get settled first."

"I'm on it." Dizzy brought out the whiskey, and a cognac for Darius. He poured large portions and passed them around the island. Darius and I took a seat. Callie remained standing. And staring. With that horribly flat expression and the raging eyes.

"Now, then. Where were we?" Dizzy said as he sat at the end of the island. Always the good cop, making everyone feel happy and welcome before the battle-axe came down.

"It was the only way," I blurted. "I told you that."

"You told me *something*, yes," Callie said, ignoring her whiskey. "Then did something completely the opposite. I got a letter from a vampire telling me where you'd gone. A stuck-up, stubborn vampire at that. One who wouldn't fill us in on any other information. Who practically ran out of here when I went for my satchel."

"You were planning to torture the information out of him, hon." Dizzy sipped his drink. "You can't really blame him for taking off."

"Oh, I can blame him for a lot of things." She braced her hands on the island and leaned toward me. "Then you ran off into a world you were unprepared for without so much as a hasty plan."

"I did have a hasty plan. Of sorts." I grimaced when sparks went off in her peepers. It wasn't a good sign.

"There is no way any of that should have worked. It was a fool's errand, Reagan." She took a deep breath and her eyes misted. "I thought I'd lose you, after only just meeting you again."

"I know," I said softly. "That's why I didn't tell you. I knew you wouldn't want me to go. That you wouldn't understand. But they were planning to come for me, and it would've been a slaughter if an army of them had come for me. Those demons were incredibly powerful. I would've been taken, and a lot of innocent people would've died."

She took another breath, this one decidedly more ragged. "I know why you did it. And I knew you would, if I'm honest with myself. You're just like your mother in that way. Purely bullheaded." Her gaze shifted to Darius, and the anger rekindled. "You took the vampire in with you."

"He said he'd help me," I said meekly.

"You know what I mean."

Yes, I did. She knew about the bond.

"It was the only way," I rushed to say. "He had to share my power to get in, and I needed him. I knew I couldn't do it alone, and he was my best, and only, bet."

"Reagan, you are bonded to an elder. For life." She sagged and pulled over a stool. "I don't have the energy for all this."

"Okay, but in my defense, he does actually love me. And he has put his life on the line for me more than once. He's genuine. I know that's hard to believe, and it's not how this usually works. I also know he'll try to keep things from me, because that's his MO, but he is a good guy. Despite the fact that he is not actually a guy."

"Vampires can't love," Callie said accusingly.

"Not usually, no," Darius said in his eloquent voice. "And I do not know why it is possible now. Many things might be possible now. But it has happened. I do love Reagan, and one day, I will make her my wife."

"Whoa, whoa, whoa." I held up my hand. "No one said anything about marriage. That's a hard no. Hard *no*."

"Oh, lovely! I love weddings." Dizzy beamed. He was going out of his way to be the nice guy. Callie must've been a terror these last weeks.

Callie ran her hand over her face. "I am now glad I never had children. You want the best for them, and then they go and make the worst possible decisions regarding their lives."

"I'm sorry," I said simply. A drip made me jerk and look up. It took a moment to realize it had been from the faucet in the sink. The drips from the edges of the underworld might just haunt me forever.

Callie wiggled her nose and looked away, not reacting to my strange antics. She blinked rapidly. With tight lips and a clenched jaw, she nodded, and I could tell she was trying her damnedest not to break down in front of everyone.

So maybe *that* was why Dizzy had been trying to stay so upbeat. Callie clearly didn't like crying in front of people.

"I'm also eternally grateful you sent that demon to help us." I took a gulp of whiskey. "We got lucky on the way to Agnon's sect and found a demon that was all about my old pouch. But the way back would've been a shit show if not for that demon you forced into helping us."

"That was a stroke of genius, that was." Dizzy pointed at Callie. "All her, too. She came up with that on her own. I told you. My wife is not to be messed with when she is up against tough odds."

"Bah." Callie waved away the compliment. "That was logic, is all. Good. I'm glad I at least helped. I had to do something, after all."

"So…do you want to hear about it, or…" I let my voice trail away.

"Of *course* we want to hear about it!" Callie made a gesture indicating I was insane.

"Start from the beginning and tell us everything," Dizzy said. "I've been able to think of nothing else. Well, ever since we found out you'd come back in one piece." He leaned forward in anticipation.

"First, did you know that dragons are real?" I grinned.

Their eyes rounded and smiles slid up their faces like children on Christmas morning.

I talked through the night, describing all the beautiful places and ugly creatures we had seen. The goats bewildered them as much as they did me, and they wanted more information about the dragons and the strange boatmen on the river. When I was done, silence filled the kitchen.

"Wow," Dizzy said, leaning back and scratching a place on his stomach that looked like it had a coffee stain. "That must've been some adventure."

"And you killed everyone who knew about you?" Callie asked.

"Except that demon you branded. They were being tight-lipped about it."

Callie nodded, and given Darius's thoughts on the subject, and Vlad's only telling two elders under his thumb, that made sense.

"So you're clear," Callie said.

"I'm clear." I sighed through my relieved smile.

"Except for him." Callie pointed at Darius.

I laughed. "Right. Clear except for having bonded an arrogant yet romantic vampire."

"So now what?" Dizzy asked.

I shrugged and leaned against the counter. "I disappear for a while. Darius has to 'manage his estate,' which means he'll be checking on properties or toying with nations or something, so I might travel with him for a while and see the sights. I want to lie low and let all this die down. I want people to forget my name."

"That's probably wise. You've been too much in the limelight. You need to settle down." Callie lightly tapped her fingers on her glass. "Things will go back to being boring."

Dizzy reached over and patted her arm. "I'm sure

something will come up, hon. Oh. You didn't give him the scroll."

Callie glowered at Darius. "I'm not sure he deserves it."

Dizzy patted her hand again.

Callie rose and left the room. When she came back, she had a scroll in her hand, like the map we'd taken into the underworld. She put it on the counter in front of Darius. "The demon came back with more information on Vlad's activities in the underworld. Most of it is probably hearsay, but maybe you can get something from it."

Darius touched it lightly, smiling. "Thank you. This will be invaluable, I have no doubt."

"How'd you get it from the demon?" I asked.

"Told it to leave the scroll behind when it left. Pretty simple, really. At that point, I think it figured you were on the way to meet it. Stupid creature. They must think humans are all idiots or something." Callie shook her head.

Darius put his hand on my thigh and squeezed, his way of thanking me for asking in the first place.

We continued talking until it was nearing dawn and Darius needed to get to safety. As we stepped out onto the porch, with Callie and Dizzy waving goodbye, Darius put his hand on the small of my back. The secret was out. We were an item.

I leaned into him as we made our way to his car.

"That went better than I expected," he said as he opened my car door for me.

I waited until he closed it and climbed in the other side before I commented. "Much less violence than I expected." I sagged into the chair. "So that's it. Like, really it. I'm free. Or, at least, back to where I was before, keeping secrets and trying to lie low so my dad doesn't find out about me. If we don't say anything about that little underworld break-in issue, I'm pretty sure we'll be good." I shrugged, because in my life, that was all I could do. Since birth, I'd lived in danger. This was just a return to normal. I sighed. "What will I do with myself?"

"You'll travel with me, as you said. And you'll take a much-needed break. Eternity starts now."

I smiled and took his hand. That sounded good.

The End

Printed by Amazon Italia Logistica S.r.l.
Torrazza Piemonte (TO), Italy

17068223R00228